HOW TO CLAIM AN UNDEAD SOUL

HAILEY EDWARDS

D1737207

How to Claim an Undead Soul
Copyright © 2017 by Hailey Edwards
All rights reserved.

Edited by Sasha Knight
Proofread by Lillie's Literary Services
Cover by Gene Mollica
Tree of Life medallion drawn by Leah Farrow

ONE

A scream got hung in my throat, and I choked awake with it lodged halfway to my lips. I registered the unyielding press of the hardwood floor under my butt and the comforting wedge of the corner where I invariably spent my days huddled in a nest of sheets. I cracked open my eyes, which were damp with tears, and then I screamed again, louder and longer, until my uvula swung like a clacker against the sides of a cowbell.

A wraith billowed in front of me, its emaciated arm extended, its skeletal fingers outstretched.

Alerted by my frantic shrieks, Woolly flipped on every light in my bedroom and cranked them to blinding levels like halogen alone might banish the creature.

"What do you want?" I touched my stinging cheek, the skin beneath my probing fingers icy where it had caressed me. "What are you doing in here?"

The creature didn't voice an answer—I wasn't certain it could do more than wail—but it did swing its withered arm toward the window.

I flicked my wrists, shooing it away before shoving to my feet.

Keeping a wary eye on it, I crossed the bedroom, but it just hovered there. Through the glass, I spotted my new neighbor standing in the grass, gazing up at me. Through me, really. His main focus centered on controlling the wraith.

Linus Andreas Lawson III wore a pair of green-and-white-striped cotton pajama bottoms and a white T-shirt. His dark-auburn hair, mussed from sleep, hung around his face. His full lips mashed into an unforgiving line, and his jaw flexed with his concentration. His eyes, so blue they appeared black from this distance, brimmed with power.

Hands trembling, I fumbled open the latch, nudged up the sash, and leaned out the window. "What is that thing doing in my room?"

Thirty seconds lapsed, tracked by the alarm clock on my desk, before he blinked clear of the darkness swirling through his eyes.

"I heard you." He cleared his raw throat, as though he had been the one screaming. "Woolly wouldn't let me in, so I sent the wraith to check on you."

The last time Linus unleashed his wraith, it stole my undead parakeet right out of its cage and left behind an invitation I couldn't refuse.

"You broke into my house?" I snarled up my lip, grateful my heart pounded now for reasons other than terror. "*Again?*"

"Woolly granted me permission." He had the nerve to act offended I would suggest otherwise. "She was worried about you too."

"Is that true?" I jerked my head back in the window. "You let it in here?"

A guilty moan escaped the floorboards under my desk.

"You haven't left your house in a week. The only person you're allowing in or out is Amelie." An undercurrent of annoyance rippled through him. "We're wasting time."

Ah. Message received. What he meant was *I* was wasting *his* time.

And maybe I was. Just a little. Mostly to mess with him since I was still irked he had been foisted on me. But I had also been digging through boxes in the attic, thumbing through tomes in the library, exploring all the old girl's nooks and crannies, in search of clues that might help solve the mystery of what had happened to Maud, and to me. Only the basement, sealed behind its spelled door, escaped my grasping hands.

The floor register hummed an inquiring noise, and the latch on the window flicked open and then shut.

While I appreciated the sentiment, I waved away her offer. "There's no use locking him out now."

A quick scan of the room proved the wraith had vanished along with Linus's concentration, so there was that. I turned back to the man standing in my garden.

"Join me for breakfast." He made it an order. "We need to establish a schedule."

Facts were facts. I couldn't avoid him forever. And he had offered to feed me. "Okay."

The window squeaked an apology when I lowered it, and the latch snicked back into place.

"I'm not mad." I trailed a finger down the cool glass. "I was just startled, that's all."

I shot Amelie a brief text to let her know I was venturing out into the world—or, you know, across the yard—so she wouldn't worry if she popped by and found the house empty for a change.

"I'll be back in a bit," I told Woolly as I pulled on clothes. "Unless the breakfast is lame. Say a bowl of those high fiber cereals served with almond, soy, or cashew milk. In which case, I will scurry home for my usual bowl of strawberry oatmeal with real dehydrated apple bits—" masquerading as strawberries, "—and full-fat milk."

Let Boaz keep his frozen blueberry waffles and imitation maple syrup. I had standards.

On my way through the living room, I stopped to check on Keet, who hung upside down from his swing like a bat from a cave ceiling. I reached through the bars and scratched his cheek. "Stay weird, my friend."

Barefoot, I padded through the kitchen and out onto the back porch where I checked the wards. Weak, a faint melody that tickled my ears, but steady. Pleased our meager protections were holding, I hit the stone path that wound through the rose garden and led to the carriage house.

The mingled scents of coffee and frying meat hit my nose when I walked through the door Linus had left propped open, and my stomach rumbled in appreciation for the spread decorating the kitchen counter.

"You've been making yourself at home." The living room and eating areas had been tidied, all surfaces dusted, and a few of them polished. "Did you do all this, or did you bring in someone?"

The idea of a stranger on the grounds without my permission set my molars grinding.

"I violated your hospitality once." He caught the drift of my thoughts. "I won't do it again by inviting someone onto your property without asking."

"Time will tell," I muttered, unwilling to forgive him just yet. An acknowledgment of wrongdoing wasn't an apology, after all.

"I had time on my hands, so I got organized." He returned to his station at the stove. "I clean when I need to think."

This sleeker Linus bore only a passing resemblance to the solemn boy he had once been, with red cheeks and pudgy fingers, but the lightning flash of intelligence in his eyes remained unchanged.

"In that case, you're welcome to visit me anytime you've got something on your mind." I approached the table and spotted a newspaper folded neatly into quarters. The word *ghost* leapt from the headlines. "Do you mind?"

"Help yourself." He palmed a set of tongs and sizzling commenced. "I've digested all the news I can stomach for one evening."

His choice of reading material was the local paper, not the weekly Society-issued bulletin, and the heft of the newsprint was peculiar in the digital age. The story that caught my eye was an interview from a bed-and-breakfast owner who claimed her resident spook had vanished.

"Now that's something you don't read every day." I glanced up from the article. "Most humans want their homes and businesses to be ghost-free. She wants hers back."

"Her business is dependent upon thrill seekers and ghost hunters."

"Hard to bill your B&B as the most haunted in Savannah if you're down a ghost, that's for sure." I refolded the paper and tucked it beside his place setting. Humans might not know the difference, but everyone else would note the lack. "An interview in the local paper wasn't her brightest idea. Anyone searching for haunted lodgings will see this and be warned away."

"Perhaps that's part of her plan," he mused. "What's better than an active haunting? Proof the soul continues on in some form?"

"A banished ghost," I reasoned, following his line of thought. "Proof that the soul can be made to discontinue?" I used the word *proof* here lightly. "And if exorcists are real, then so too must be what they exorcise."

Basically, a backwards way of proving the existence of ghosts by proving the sudden absence of one.

Nodding, he focused on the hissing pan before him. "Meaning she can lure in a fresh crowd."

"People who want answers as to how it was done or if it was done at all."

"Some of those will be return visits from ghost hunters or would-be exorcists, but it opens the door to religious elements and other opportunities her previous business model was unable to capitalize on."

The haunting was a well-documented case that had drawn national attention, meaning any number of the TV shows, ghost hunting crews, fanatics or casual enthusiasts might come back to compare their original findings against their current ones. The publicity might not save her business in the long run, but it would buoy her for a good while if she milked it properly, and she was squeezing the teats of public interest with both hands.

"Are your dreams always that intense?" He selected pale sausage links from the fryer and placed them onto a paper towel-lined plate. The package near the sink claimed they were made from chicken and apples. I had my doubts. "Is it all right to ask?"

"I might as well be honest with you." I stole one of them, burning my fingertips, and started nibbling before it cooled. Hmm. My doubts appeared to be unfounded. The sausage was delicious. "You're going to hear me on occasion if tonight is any indication. You have my permission to use noise-dampening sigils if you want."

"It happens every night?"

Every. Single. One. "Pretty much."

"There are sigils to help you sleep—"

"*No.*" I choked on the bite I'd sucked down my windpipe. "I don't want to risk being stuck in the dream."

"*The* dream." He moved on to stirring a double boiler filled with creamy grits, and I wondered if he realized avoiding eye contact made talking to him easier. "As in it's the only one you're having? A recurring nightmare?"

"Yes." I helped myself to a glass of orange juice from the fridge. "And before you ask—I don't remember what happens. I wake up terrified with a vague sense of déjà vu, but that's it."

"Do you mind?" He palmed a bag of sliced artisan bread on the counter and passed it to me. "The toaster smoked the first time, but I cleaned out the dust. Maybe open the window just in case?"

The toaster had been cocooned inside a knitted cozy. Dust shouldn't have been an issue. But if he was paying me a kindness by offering a breath of fresh air to clear my head, I wasn't about to complain.

The window required a hard jiggle before it raised, but that first gasp of night air paid off my sweat equity in full. As my lungs expanded, the tightness in my chest from talking about the dream lessened. But it refused to budge all the way now that I was paying it attention, so I shifted my focus elsewhere.

The same breeze tangling my hair rustled the lush ivy climbing wild over the eastern wall. I ought to thin it. I needed to trim back the roses too. The peonies wilted on their stems, their heads in need of cutting. So much had gone undone during my absence, and I'd done nothing to rectify the situation. As much as it pained me to admit, the garden was looking shabby.

Maud would have a conniption fit if she was here to see this.

A pinching sensation in my chest warned me away from those thoughts. They hurt too much to examine this early, so I asked Linus for a distraction. "Who taught you how to cook?"

"Books. Food Network. YouTube." He checked a saucepan full of simmering water and bobbing eggs. "Our old cook, Louie, used to let me help him prepare breakfast on the weekends. I figured it was a skill I should learn for when I moved out on my own."

"You have a driver. You didn't want a cook too?" He could certainly afford both.

With reluctance, I abandoned my view and the nascent dream of hiring a gardener to whip the property back into shape while I started on the toast.

One of my duties as Dame Woolworth would be rebuilding my household from the ground up, but that could wait until I decided what staff I wanted on the grounds with me and how often. Until I figured that out, I was fine being on my own.

"I don't have a driver. I borrowed Mother's." He passed me a glass butter dish and a dull knife. "I don't need a cook. I can fend for myself or order takeout. Atlanta has everything I could want."

The knife clattered from my hand onto the counter. "You live in Atlanta?"

He must have heard the shock in my voice that his mother let him that far out from under her thumb.

"Yes." He cocked an eyebrow at me. "I teach at Strophalos University, among other things."

Knock me over with a feather.

Linus was actually qualified for this job? I'd assumed his mother had palmed her most loyal pawn off on me to act as her spy while training me in advanced resuscitation theory. She couldn't very well auction my services to the highest bidder then sit back and hope for the best. Not when clients would expect a one hundred percent success rate as a return on their investment. But this? He was a bona fide teacher from a prestigious university who could offer me the education Maud had denied me. That didn't make his apron strings any shorter, but it did make him crashing in my carriage house that much more appealing.

"What about your classes?" Selfishly, I had only considered how the Grande Dame's proclamation affected me. I had dismissed Linus as a throwaway heir, one of his mother's yes-men, and that had been shallow of me. At least this was all to my benefit. He had nothing to gain by helping me except his mother's favor. As her only son, he must be drowning in that. "How long will you stay?"

"I'm on sabbatical." He plated the sausage, grits, and soft-boiled eggs. After I added a few pieces of buttered toast to his burden, he carried it all to the table. "I can stay for a year before I have to file more paperwork. I won't know if that will be necessary until after we start your training."

"What about your home?" I rinsed out my glass then poured milk for each of us since that had been his breakfast beverage of choice for as long as I could remember. "What about your friends?"

"The loft will still be there when I return." He carried two pressed napkins to the table and placed them at our settings. We both stood there, looking at one another. "Thanks to modern technology, my colleagues are never more than a call, text, video chat, or DM away."

I startled when he crossed to me, but all he did was pull out a chair and wait for me to sit. I did, and then I returned the favor. The table was small, meant for two even though it had four places, and I stretched out my leg to push his seat back with my toes.

"Thank you." He let me take a few bites before starting on his own meal, but he didn't have much of an appetite. "There are seconds if you'd like more."

A flush I blamed on the steam rising from my plate pinked my cheeks. "Are my table manners that bad?"

One too many frozen dinners had left me ravenous for a home-cooked meal, and this one was excellent.

"No." He bit the edge off his toast, chewed methodically, and had trouble swallowing even that one small bite. "I just don't want the food to go to waste."

The first helping vanished before I registered its taste, and I heaped a second plate high with leftovers. He watched me eat, his fascination making me slow the fork-to-mouth action. I demolished the sausage before the awkward scrape of my silverware drove me to conversation.

"The night I helped unbreak your nose—" after Woolly had slammed her front door in his face to bar his entrance, "—you told me we would address my magic, but I skipped class the next day." And the six days that followed. "Can we do a makeup lesson?"

"Of course." He sipped his milk, but the level remained unchanged. "What would you like to know?"

The desperate edge in my voice shamed me. "Will I ever get it back?"

"You still have your magic, Grier." He set down his glass then watched until the ripples stilled. "The drugs and disuse have stunted it, but it's like a muscle. The more you practice, the more you learn, the stronger you'll grow."

Torn between disappointment that it wasn't a quick fix and relief it was repairable at all, I nodded.

"Now." He wiped his mouth with a napkin. "Time for a pop quiz."

The milk in my mouth soured. "I heard you should wait thirty minutes after eating before taking a test."

The look he shot me confirmed his professorial status. It said he'd heard every excuse in the book at least three times, and hearing them a fourth wouldn't do me any good. I sat up straighter while he cleared the table and hoped I didn't make a total fool of myself.

"We'll start off easy with a review of material you should have covered with Maud and go from there." He placed a thin stack of graph paper in front of me then passed me a pen, the plain, black-ink kind. Not one of his modified ones. "Draw me four basic defense sigils for a home."

For a home. Those three words cemented his promise to help me restore the wards around Woolworth House, and I sat a little straighter in my chair.

Despite the wording of his request, sigils didn't fall into animate and inanimate categories. They were singular, and it was up to the practitioner to modify them based on their application.

"Here goes nothing." Summoning the designs from my rusty memory, I worked to get the fine details correct as I blocked each one out in its own grid. The pen was slippery in my hand when I finished. "There you go."

He slid on a pair of black-frame glasses that made the blue of his eyes that much darker then lifted the paper.

The silence while he graded my work left me bouncing my leg under the table.

"Explain each of these." He placed the paper back in front of me and tapped the largest one. "Start here."

"This one protects against attacks both physical and magical." I pointed out the next with the pen cap. "This one is for strength. It's a combination that boosts the power of any other sigil." The next was a nifty modification to the one I had used during my escape from Volkov. "This is an obfuscation sigil. It doesn't disguise a home as much as it makes the residence so uninteresting no one notices it. Or, if they do, they don't remember it for long." The last was a staple in my arsenal. "This one is for healing. It can't fix a cracked foundation or physical damage, but it can bolster failing wards until repairs can be done."

Poor Woolly was covered in them.

"Interesting."

I set the pen down before my sweaty grip sent it flying. "What does that mean?"

"Your technique is superb. You were trained with a brush, and some students can't divorce the sensation from one medium to the next, but I don't see any reason why we can't proceed with an altered pen like the one you used to heal my nose. Unless you have a personal preference?"

"Having a pen like yours might come in handy." For homework, it would mean less drying time for my notes too. "You once mentioned using a brush for resuscitations and other ritualistic work. I think that would be my choice too." He hadn't stopped staring at that paper. "What did I do wrong?"

"The sigils you're using, the way you're drawing them, is nonstandard. I don't recognize the style at all, even though I can read it well enough to tell what it does." He braced his palm on the table, tracing the curves with his fingertip. "It's not wrong. It's personalized in a way you don't typically see in fledgling necromancers. It's like a signature. Are all your sigils drawn this way?"

"I...guess?" I rubbed my thumb over the tabletop. "I copied them down the way Maud taught me."

"Maud didn't teach you this." He canted his head toward me. "Has anyone else seen your work?"

"Amelie and Boaz." I had no other necromancer friends, no High Society friends at all.

"They would have no reason to recognize the symbols, correct?"

A few Low Society necromancers were self-taught to maximize what little power they had inherited. Even rarer was the prodigy whose natural power propelled them to High Society status. But, as much as it pained Amelie to have any limits imposed upon her, that was not the case for either of my friends.

"No." I propped my elbow on the table and my chin in my palm. "Why would that matter?"

"Let's try an experiment before I answer." He sketched out an unfamiliar design on a fresh sheet of paper. "This sigil muffles sound." I winced at the reminder of how I woke him. "The most common usage is insulating the walls of homes in predominantly human neighborhoods. I want you to draw it for me."

I shook out my hand and gave it a go. The lines were simple, and it only took a minute to complete and then check against the original. "Ta-da?"

Linus claimed each paper then held them in opposite hands while he compared the finished products. His brow creased as his gaze flicked back and forth. "Do these sigils look identical to you?"

"I'm out of practice," I groused, "but it's not that bad. You're acting like you can't tell they're meant to be the same thing."

"No, I'm trying to understand." He held them up, side by side, facing me. "These are not identical. They're the same at their core, but yours incorporates a flourish. Mine are standard, unembellished. It's a habit picked up from teaching that makes it easier on my students." He flipped the pages over, facing him, and studied them again. "Fascinating."

"Is fascinating a good thing?" Right now, it sounded like a polite way of saying Maud had been right to condemn me to a life as an assistant rather than as a practitioner.

"Mother was wrong about your blood," he said distractedly. "It's not just that, it's this too. Your mind..." He shook his head then tucked the papers away, no doubt saving them for later deliberation. "I'm starting to understand why Maud kept us separate even when we studied the same lessons."

"She didn't want anyone else to see what I see." A frown sank into place. "Do you think this is the reason she enrolled me in human school?"

As much as I longed to hear him say yes, that her decision was a protection and not a condemnation, I couldn't shake those engrained insecurities that came from being told by one of the world's most gifted practitioners that I wasn't enough.

"No one can know for sure, but it seems likely given what we've learned." He crossed the room, and I lost track of him behind the trunks. "I wish we had access to her library. She must have made notes about your condition. She could never leave a good puzzle unsolved. Reading those would help us understand how your brain functions, how your blood works. We could save time building on her knowledge."

"The basement won't open for me." I hammered my heel against the nearest chair leg, but it did nothing to dispel the frisson of unease shivering through me. "It's the one room Woolly can't manually unlock."

Going down there hadn't ranked high on my priority list until the Grande Dame explained what it meant that I was goddess-touched. That's when it hit me that whatever Maud had known, I had to know too. I hadn't tried breaking the wards. Yet. Assuming they could be jimmied. Given how determined Maud had been to hide my nature from me while she was alive, I was willing to bet the extra layers of security activated after her death wouldn't crumple under a lock-breaker sigil and a few swipes of my brush.

Odds were good Linus could batter his way into her inner sanctum. He was an apt pupil, after all. But once the wards came down, I had nothing to replace them, and I couldn't afford to leave the library vulnerable.

"That's too bad." Wood scraped over metal in the direction Linus had gone. "We can add that to our to-do list."

Mentally, I scratched that right out. There would be no witnesses when I descended those stairs for the first time post-Maud, and that meant I had to figure it out on my own.

"I hope you don't mind." Linus reappeared with a rectangular bundle wrapped in butcher paper. A wide burlap ribbon banded around its middle, and a white wax seal had been pressed to its seam. "I brought you a gift."

"What is it?" I accepted the parcel and weighed it in my hands. "It's heavy."

"Open it." He leaned a hip against the table. "I commissioned it for you a few months ago."

Startled by his casual mention of the timeline for my release, I forgot what I had been about to do.

"Mother lobbied for over a year to have you exonerated," he explained. "I had time to prepare."

Too bad I hadn't been given the same forewarning. A spark of hope goes a long way in the dark.

"You can always save it for later." His hands sank deep in his pockets. "You don't have to open it now."

But he had put time and effort, and likely a good bit of money, into buying this for me. The way he kept pushing his glasses up his nose before they got a chance to slip told me he was excited to see my reaction. He had done the same thing as a boy each time he picked up a new mystery novel from the library.

"I'm curious what's put that look on your face," I admitted as I tore into the package then froze with numb fingers. A shudder of revulsion rocked me, and I had to fight my instinct to drop the thing onto the table. "This is, um, wow. You shouldn't have."

I stared at the grimoire, and the grimoire stared right back.

Exposure to light caused its nine eyes to squint after so long in its wrapping. The cover was a patchwork blend of black and brown leather in varying shades that had been stitched together with broad thread. The hide was smooth in places and rough in others. I peeked at the underside and found it sewn from similar scraps, these covered in lumpy warts. Cracking open the cover, I flipped through the hundreds of pages of crisp, white paper awaiting my mark then set it back on the counter.

"What's it made of?" I rubbed my finger between two yellow eyeballs with slitted, vertical pupils, and its lids fluttered with pleasure. "It's...livelier than the ones Maud used."

Crimson leather with gold inlay was more her style. Even in that regard, she had been a traditionalist.

"A number of things I imagine." He tapped the corner. "A goblin who consults for Strophalos makes them from creatures who have been condemned to death by Faerie."

"You know an actual goblin from actual Faerie?" The fae were ruled by the Earthen Conclave in this world. That was the governing body the Society brushed against when fae caused issues for necromancers. But the location of their home realm, and how they accessed this one, was a secret fae immigrants guarded with their lives. "Have you ever seen him without glamour?"

"Yes, and no." Linus straightened. "Contact with the fae is forbidden outside contracts negotiated between our solicitors, so I'm not allowed to speak to him directly. I've never actually met him."

About what I'd expected to hear but still comforting to learn that even the vaunted Lawson reach was limited.

"Well, thank you." The thing was so ugly, it was almost cute. "It was kind of you to think of me."

"Ah." He held up a finger. "You haven't asked what it does."

I examined it for clues. "Other than blink creepily?"

"Write a combination sigil, something basic, but leave a quarter of it unfinished."

I did as he instructed then waited for the magic to happen.

"Close the book." He gave it about thirty seconds. "Open the cover."

"The book completed the sigil," I marveled. "How?"

"More eyes on a problem make for less work."

I laughed under my breath. "That is such teacher logic."

He shuffled my quiz papers into a neat stack then turned to carry them back to the office. I captured him by the wrist, and his pulse jumped under my fingertips. Wisps of black clouded his eyes when he glanced back until he blinked them clear, and I loosened my grip.

"Thank you," I said again, meaning it this time. "You didn't have to do this."

"I wanted to," he countered, holding so still he seemed to enjoy being caught. "I want to help you, Grier."

Him and everyone else with something to gain, but all this help was five years too late in coming.

"I should go." I released him and stood in a rush, snagging the grimoire at the last moment. I couldn't afford to forget why he was here or who had sent him. "This—" I gestured around the mess we'd made in the kitchen, "—was nice."

His gaze dipped to the chair I had vacated. "What are you doing for breakfast tomorrow?"

Boxes of oatmeal, all bought on clearance, awaited me in the pantry. "Reconstituting dried fruit?"

"Would you consider joining me?" Linus still hadn't glanced up from my seat. "I have bacon."

How could I say no to that? "Are nightly pop quizzes going to be a thing with us?"

A smile flirted with his lips. "It's not a pop quiz if I warn you ahead of time."

Flushing because he was right, and I wanted to impress him despite the nagging voice warning me not to care what he thought of me, I darted through the door into the cool garden before I stuck my foot in my mouth again. I might eat a lot of PB&J, but toe jam was not my favorite flavor.

TWO

I was kneeling on the grass, pinching the drowsy heads off a row of peonies, when a curvy Indian woman about my height cranked open the side gate leading into the garden. She strode through the four connected archways dripping with fragrant jasmine and clusters of lavender wisteria to stand before me. Her outfit of tight black tee and fatigues clued me in to her identity seconds before her boot swung at my head.

I dodged—okay, I fell flat on my back like a turtle—and shrilled, "Are you insane?"

The flash of her teeth was dazzling. "Maybe."

"You must be Taslima." I accepted the hand she offered like an idiot. "I'm Grier."

"Anyone who's known Boaz more than thirty seconds knows who you are down to what size panties you wear." She used her grip to yank me to my feet. "Either you've lost weight recently, or he hasn't gotten in your pants yet. He's off two sizes by my estimate."

While oddly flattered he had spoken of me to his friends, I was still going to murder him for what he had told them. "The answer is both."

Using her iron grip, she reeled me stumbling into her, putting us chest to chest, and latched her arms around me. A manic grin split her cheeks while I gasped for breath. "You can call me Taz."

"Taz," I wheezed. "I can't breathe."

She yielded not one inch. "Do something about it."

Dots flickered in my vision before my brain got the message she wasn't kidding. With my arms trapped at my sides and her body plastered against mine, all I could do was slam my forehead into her nose with as much power as I could leverage.

A sickening crunch made me regret the hearty breakfast I'd eaten, but her arms loosened enough for me to wriggle out of her hold.

Backing toward the porch, I couldn't swallow down my reflexive manners. "Are you okay?"

"Did Volkov ask if you were okay when he kidnapped you?" The promise of swelling muffled her voice. "And if he did, tell me you weren't dumb enough to stand around cataloging your boo-boos."

My heel banged against the bottom step, and I turned to climb onto the porch.

A hard kick took out the back of my left knee, and I crumpled. Taz followed that up with a boot to my spine that made me cry out before she clocked me across the mouth. I face-planted in the grass and regretted ever asking Boaz for help. Clearly his choice of tutor was deranged. Had she misunderstood this was basic self-defense and not an assassination attempt?

"Get up," Taz snapped. "You're wasting my time if you don't even try."

Blood dribbled down my chin from a split in my bottom lip. I wiped my mouth with the back of my hand and focused on the vermilion bindi dotted between her eyebrows until the two Tazes floating in my vision merged into one. And then I blinked again.

Black mist whispered around her ankles, murmuring up her legs, until the wraith coalesced behind her with a threatening groan. Its skeletal hand palmed her throat, and the edges of its black hood brushed the spot below her ear, making me wonder if wraith had teeth.

Linus strolled from the carriage house, drying his hands on a dish towel. "What's all this about?"

"I asked Boaz for self-defense classes." I used the railing to haul myself onto my feet. "He sent me Taslima." The wraith hissed, a death rattle in its chest, and its fingers tightened. Ignoring the whimper of my hindbrain, I wobbled over to her and pried at the wraith's skeletal hand with my bloodied fingers, but it refused to obey me with its master present. "Let her go."

A flash of respect glinted in Taz's eyes, but then she glared at Linus. "You heard the lady."

Linus studied me, evaluating the damage Taz had done, his lips mashed together to keep his opinions to himself until they whitened. Still I expected him to invoke his mother's name to get his way or threaten to tattle on me if I didn't stop damaging the Grande Dame's investment.

"Come see me when you're finished." His tone had gone so cold I imagined his lips bluing along their edges as the wraith bled into the shadows gathered under the porch. "I'll do what I can to patch you up."

"That's it?" I asked dumbly. "No threats? No ultimatums? No locking me in the attic until I see reason?"

"Grier, you're a grown woman. I can't stop you from doing anything you want to do."

I squinted at him, certain this must be some kind of trick. No man was this reasonable.

"Taslima?" Eternity, bleak and endless, swirled in his eyes. "Teach her. Don't use her as a punching bag." Linus tossed me the damp rag to wipe my face. "You can't beat lessons into your students' heads, or I would carry a mallet instead of a tablet to class with me."

With his chastisement ringing in my ears, Linus retreated and left Taslima and me staring at one another.

Sensing Taz was waiting on me to decide if I'd suffered enough abuse for one day, I balled up the cloth and flung it on the back steps. "Again?"

Cackling merrily, Taz sank into a fighting stance and waited for me to mimic her. "Again," she agreed. "This time, I won't pull my punches."

Maybe her earlier hits had given me brain damage. I don't know why else that would have made me smile.

LINUS HELD his tongue while playing nurse after Taz finished tenderizing my face, and I was grateful he was willing to let me pursue my independence how I saw fit. I took a selfie before he broke out his pen, tempted to send it to Boaz as a thank you for today, but a lifetime of knowing him counseled it was better he didn't see this caterpillar until she emerged from her cocoon. Still, I owed him some thanks for keeping his word and settled for a quick call as I wandered the garden.

"Go out with me."

"Hello, Boaz. How are you? Me? I'm fine. Thanks for asking."

"Hello, Grier. How are you? I'm fine. Thanks for asking." A smile warmed his voice. "Go out with me."

I plucked a few dead leaves from a thorny stem. "What if I say no?"

"I'll give you time to see the error of your ways then ask again."

"Mmm-hmm." The man was energy caged in skin. He couldn't sit or stand still. He wouldn't last a full day if I turned him down before he was asking again, and each time would be harder to deny than the last. "What if I say yes?"

"Then I promise to be a gentleman and treat you with the care and respect you deserve."

I laughed until I realized he wasn't chuckling with me. "You're serious."

"As a heart attack."

Talk about hitting a nail on the head. The idea of a date with Boaz gave me arrhythmia. "I'll think about it."

"You do that." Satisfaction deepened his voice. "All day long, while you're sleeping in my shirt, you think about how much fun we're going to have."

I lost focus and pricked my finger. "I haven't said yes yet."

"You will." He sounded so sure, so cocky, I almost turned him down on principle. But then his tone softened, and a shy hint of the boy who'd helped me get into trouble most of my life peeked through. "I hope you will."

There might be a girl somewhere in the world able to resist Boaz Pritchard when he shucked his charm and became earnest, but that girl was not I. Each glimpse of his big heart made me hungrier for the next. And yet... Though I had already made up my mind—as if there had ever been any doubt—I relished holding the upper hand for once.

"I'll think about it," I said again, breathless.

He must be fluent in the language of my exhales, because I heard his relief. "You do that, Squirt."

"I have to go." I climbed onto the back porch. "I'll see you soon, right?"

"Only if you're a very good girl," he teased. "Or a very bad one."

I bit the inside of my cheek to keep from laughing then said my goodbyes before he distracted me again. Not until after I hung up did it hit me. All his talk of dating had derailed my reason for calling, and I forgot to thank him for sending Taz, which I did in a text rather than tempting fate by hitting redial.

A plan had taken shape while I was trying to keep my head attached to my body with moderate success, and I was eager to set it in motion. But first, I had one more call to make.

"Odette?"

Odette Lecomte was a seer. The desperate, the hungry, and the curious traveled from all over the world to beg for an audience with her. Clients paid in favors and promises, gold and jewels, and other more precious things to sift their futures through her gnarled fingers.

Those glimpses into other lives, other minds, made her a veritable encyclopedia of knowledge both common and forbidden. And she had been one of Maud's best friends. That made her as good as an honorary aunt to me.

"*Ma coccinelle.*" *My ladybug.* The endearment, shouted over the crash of waves, was better than a hug. "You called for an update, yes?"

"Yes." I crossed my fingers tight. "Have you found anything?"

"Nothing good, *bébé*, nothing good. Let me get in the house, and I will tell you what I've found." The steady roar quit like a pulled cord on a noise machine. "There. That's better." Her breath caught before she groaned, a long exhalation, and I imagined her sinking into her plush couch. "I spoke with Dame Marchand."

Dame Severine Marchand, my maternal grandmother, whose name Maud had forbidden spoken in her presence, whose existence had been all but scrubbed from my memories, until it occurred to me she might have answers about my absent father and Odette a way to get them. "And?"

"The Marchands have disowned Evangeline and wiped her from the family histories. Her own mother attempted to pretend she had no idea who Evie was until I reminded her with whom she was speaking."

Evangeline Marchand, my mother, died when I was five. I don't recall much about her. The way she smelled when she peppered my face with kisses, the melodious current of her voice when she sang to me in her native tongue, those things were lost to time. Thanks to Maud's photo albums, I know I'm the spitting image of her. We share the same thin lips, high cheekbones, and sharp chin. Whoever my father was, his only contributions had been the wave in my dark hair and the color of my eyes.

"Oh." Mom hadn't been close to her people, but disownment within the Society was an irrevocable severance of the bloodline. There was no going back even if a reconciliation was reached. I tried to laugh it off, but the words got hung in my throat. "That would explain why they skipped her funeral."

This also shed light on why my grandparents had never come to claim me. Maud would have fought them tooth and nail to keep me, but she had never had to sharpen her claws. I had no memory of them, I wasn't sure I had ever met them, but none of that mattered now. As far as they were concerned, I was no one and nothing to them.

"Evie's relationship with her mother and stepfather was always strained, she never explained why, but I had no idea such extreme measures had been taken. Though this explains why she sought asylum with Maud. Without her family name, no other Society family would have acknowledged her, let alone aided her."

I sank into one of the rockers bracketing the back door before my legs gave out on me. "Do you think Maud knew?"

"Maud wouldn't have cared if she had known. She loved your mother fiercely. She wouldn't have allowed the Society—or anyone else—to dictate the rules of hospitality in her own home."

Hearing that allowed me to relax enough to push off the planks with my toes. Maud was to Mom what Amelie was to me. "Do you have any idea when they disowned her?"

She hesitated long enough I could tell the answer pained her, and that it would hurt me too. "The day you were born."

I shut my eyes and focused on my breathing until I was certain I could hold myself together for Odette. "Do they know who...?"

"Dame Marchand swore Evie kept his identity a secret." Odette paused for a moment. "For what it's worth, I believe her. The risk of scandal would have been too high for her mother to ignore. I imagine they would have given her the choice of her family or you."

So much for holding myself together. Fat tears rolled down my cheeks. "And she chose me."

"She was your *maman*." Her voice wavered. "Of course she did. Every time. Always."

"I appreciate your help," I said weakly, eager to sever our connection and lick my wounds in private. "I'll drive out to see you soon."

"You know where to find me. *Je t'adore.*"

"Love you too."

I ended the call and sat there for a while, listening to the night birds and the buzz of insects.

"Things can never be simple," I complained to the old house. "A phone call to clear up my paternity was asking for too much." I ground the heels of my palms in my eyes. "Someone must know or at least suspect his identity. We just have to find them."

The porch light flared in encouragement.

Hinges groaned as Woolly opened the back door, urging me in away from the mosquitoes, and I heeded her advice. After a hot shower to loosen my twinging muscles, I set the plan Taz helped shake loose into motion by dressing in my nicest jeans and least holey top.

I was going to beg Cricket to give me my job back.

I might fail just as hard on this front as I had on all the others, but I needed an outlet, and being a Haint meant something to me. Plus, knocking around the house alone for a week had me bored out of my gourd.

Since Linus hadn't fitted me with an ankle monitor, and Boaz hadn't tied me to a chair before he left, I assumed whatever security measures they had put in place after Volkov's attack comforted them enough not to bother me with the fine print.

The odds were better than good that the Grande Dame had bankrolled a protective detail to skulk after me whenever I left the house. All things considered, I ought to be more grateful, but it took so little to feel cold stone beneath my cheek, to hear my cellmates sobbing, that any restrictions placed on my movements sent spasms through my chest.

Hopping on Jolene was, as always, a revelation. Her steady rumble between my thighs, her roar in my ears, the night stretching long and dark before us, unclenched the spot between my shoulders that kept hitching tighter and tighter the farther I strayed from home.

The sensation of being watched, I chalked up to paranoia that vampires were out to get me.

Except vampires *were* out to get me. And it was only a matter of time before others joined in the hunt.

The last seven days might have passed in blissful quiet, but only a fool would expect that trend to last.

Reaching HQ unmolested left me shaking with relief. Going out alone for the first time since I had been kidnapped had me jitterier than if I'd tossed back six shots of expresso.

A few of the girls waved or called out to me, but they were on their way to lead tours and couldn't stop to chat. Depending on how things shook out in the next few minutes, there would be gossip aplenty waiting on them when they got back.

I spotted Cricket Meacham sitting at her desk, victory rolls pinned neatly on top of her blonde head, unlit cigarette pinched between her lips, and marched into her office. Head held high, I listed my demands. Well, demand. "I want my old job back."

She didn't glance up from her schedule. "Not happening, honey."

This nut was going to be harder to crack than I'd thought. "I know I messed up—"

"You're flakier than fish food, Grier." She penned in a few more names. "I need guides I can rely on, and that's not you." After matching groups to guides, she capped her pen. "Don't get me wrong, you're one of the best I've got. When you're here. But you tend to ghost on me, and I only pay for spooks when they're part of the tour."

"I was—" *imprisoned for five years the first time I bailed and kidnapped by a vampire the second,* "—very inconsiderate. I understand that. But I need this job. Please."

Boredom was a handy excuse, but the truth was all the upheaval in my life had made me desperate for an anchor. Haint Misbehavin' could be that for me. I loved the work, it kept a portion of my nights occupied, and it allowed me to hang with my friends. The Haints gave me a safe place where I could feel like the old Grier, the one who had a dawn curfew before Maud started making phone calls.

"I can't help you." She went back to her paperwork. "Though I will admit I was impressed you bothered to return your costume and accoutrements. Guess you learned that lesson at least."

Her one requirement for taking me on a second time had been that I pay her back every cent of my previous costume's worth since there had been no opportunity to return mine after my sentencing. I had been a tad too busy never seeing the light of day again to fret over a few hundred dollars' worth of skirt and corset. But, as a result, I'd lived on ketchup and crackers at one point to stretch my budget to fit her repayment schedule. For her to say I had returned my things meant Amelie had covered for me.

"I don't have to be a guide," I blurted. "Let me help Neely or Dom. There must be something I can do."

"Dom called in sick." Her sigh rustled the papers on her desk. "You can scrub toilets for minimum wage if you want. That's it. That's all I got."

"I'll take it."

Cricket squinted up at me, noticing my face for the first time. "Damn girl. Good thing you're not working the beat tonight. Your face is as purple as an eggplant."

I touched my cheek. "I fell."

Her humorless snort caught me off-guard. "Honey, that's what they all say."

Ducking my head, I figured it was better she thought I was a domestic-abuse victim than if she knew the truth of how I'd spent my evening picking grass out of my teeth. Or maybe the other way around was more accurate. "I'll go get started."

"The to-do list is tacked on the wall in the downstairs bathroom." Her attention settled back on her work. "Use the dry eraser to wipe the board clean, then mark off each task as you finish." She pointed her pen at me. "And for the love of God, stay out of sight. I don't want you spooking the victims prior to departure."

I backed out into the hallway, pulling her door shut behind me, and sagged as relief swept over me.

"*Grier.*"

I had no time to brace for impact. One minute I was standing there, counting my blessings, and the next a blur of buttery yellow satin torpedoed into my side, knocking me against the wall. "*Oomph.*"

With her golden-brown hair pinned in a corona around her head and her brown eyes blazing with fury, Amelie embodied a wrathful sun goddess. The matching parasol clutched in her gloved hand might as well have been a scepter given the imperious way she waved it under my nose.

"What happened to your face?" She covered her mouth with her empty hand. "Who did this to you?"

"I had my first self-defense lesson." I smiled, and it pulled on my healing lip. "Taslima is fierce."

"Taz did this?" Amelia growled through her fingers. "I'm going to kill my brother."

Given her reaction to my appearance, I left out the part where Linus had worked his mojo on me. She didn't need to know how much worse I had looked before I loaned myself out as a guinea pig to test one of his new healing sigils.

"I asked Boaz for help." I clutched her arms to hold her steady. "It's fine. Really."

"This is all my fault," she groaned. "I never should have told him you left the house. He must have called her."

"You told him—?" The little sneak had used my text against me. "That explains Taz's miraculous timing. I figured she must have been hiding out in the garden, stalking her prey before going in for the kill."

Amelie flushed, but she didn't apologize. "What are you doing here?"

"I came to ask for my old job back."

"Are you insane?" She hooked her arm through mine and dragged me into the parlor where the female Haints changed. "You could buy this place if you wanted. Why would you work here again?"

"Things are changing so fast. I'm having trouble coping." I sank onto the spindly Victorian couch parked in the corner. "Nothing changed in Atramentous. You lived the same day over and over and over. I'm trying to catch my balance. I did for a while there, but then—"

"Volkov happened," she supplied. "Vampy bastard."

Tempting as it was to blame it all on him, he'd had help overloading my circuits.

"The pardon happened. The release happened. The return home happened. The scraping together of a life happened." And then it was all blown out of the water. "I was getting a handle on things until the inauguration." When the Grande Dame had reinstated my title as the Woolworth heir, Dame Woolworth, and shared with me the true reason for my release. I was goddess-touched. I could make true immortals. And she got dollar signs in her eyes every time she looked at me. "And then, yeah. Volkov happened."

"When you put it like that..." Amelie perched beside me. "I get it."

I grunted what passed for a gloomy acknowledgment.

"Get this through your thick skull." She rapped me hard on the knee with her parasol. "You've got this. You made it out. You're not going to stop until you own your power." She fluttered her lashes. "Besides, this means more girl time for us. Pretty sure if we hit Mallow after work together it halves the calories."

"Not exactly." I winced. "Cricket wouldn't let me have my old job back. She offered me Dom's spot for the night, and I accepted. I need to keep my hands busy while my brain works out what I want to do next."

"Far be it from me to come between a woman and her coping mechanism." Amelie wrinkled her nose. "Also? The janitor gig might not be as long term as Cricket let you believe."

"We're not losing someone, are we?" A few Haints were seasonal hires, but the core group had remained the same for years. "As much as I want to move up in the world, I don't want it to be at someone else's expense."

"No, it's nothing like that." She stood and searched each dressing room stall to make sure we were alone. "Cricket bought shares in River Street Steam. She's cooked up a scheme with the owner to start running nightly haunted dinner cruises aboard the *Cora Ann* in addition to the standard packages offered now. She'll have to bring on at least a dozen more girls, and putting you to work as a guide means no learning curve."

"I haven't been on one of those cruises since high school." Talk about a walk down memory lane. "Remember how those used to be the height of romance?"

"Hey, don't knock it. I got my first kiss onboard the Peachy Queen from Kevin Rood."

"Kevin Rood." I couldn't even remember his face. "Military brat, right?"

"Yep." She toyed with her fan. "He went to school with us for six months to the day before his mom got reassigned, and off he went." She swooned against me. "Taking my heart with him."

I patted her arm. "Suuure."

She harrumphed. "Are you doubting that he broke my heart or that I have one to break?"

I thought about it. "Both?"

"Fine. So I've never been in love." She sat upright and straightened her skirts. "That doesn't mean I'm not open to the possibility, with the right person, at the right time."

"Does love ever happen at the right time, with the right person?"

"No idea." She twirled her parasol. "Maybe we should ask Neely. He's the only friend we've got in a functional romantic relationship, let alone a marriage."

Good point. "Do you think it's easier for humans?"

"Maybe," she mused. "Relationships are hard enough without adding magic into the mix."

For me, Boaz had been a classic case of unrequited love. Wealth, status, power—none of it had mattered when all he could see when he looked at me was his kid sister's best friend. I wasn't sure what he saw in me these days, but he did see me. That was progress, right?

This whole happily-ever-after thing would be so much easier if fated mates were a thing, but the closest necromancers got were arranged marriages with ironclad prenups. "Have your parents ever mentioned picking a husband for you?"

"No." Her slight hesitation made the room smaller, the air thinner.

"*Ame.*" I grabbed her arm and shook her. "Spill."

"Okay, fine, so they sent out inquiries for Boaz. He's the firstborn, and that means he gets stuck honoring familial duties. He must marry, and he must produce the next Pritchard heir." She had to have noticed the blood draining from my face. "It was years ago, Grier. Before..." *Atramentous.* "Three families sent their eldest daughters to visit us for a week. He was maybe thirteen."

I found breathing a smidgen easier considering his age and the fact he wasn't engaged. "And?"

"This is Boaz we're talking about here. What do you think he did?"

"I would say he charmed his way into their panties, but at thirteen, they were probably safe from all but visual molestation."

Allowing it was a fair point, Amelie shrugged. "There was light fondling. He was a teenage boy, and they were gorgeous girls offering themselves up to him. Until he realized there was a catch, he was in hog heaven."

Snorting, I had to shake my head. "This does not surprise me."

"What pissed Mom off most was how he used his etiquette training against her. He told the girls they were beautiful, that a man would be lucky to have any of them for a wife, but that man wasn't going to be him." Her lips pulled to one side. "I haven't seen Mom turn that shade of red since. He humiliated her in front of prominent

Low Society heads of families by refusing those suits, and no one has offered for him since."

"You make it sound like Boaz is still on the market," I joked.

Amelie didn't laugh. "He's the eldest son of a Low Society matron, Grier. Think about it."

"You mean anyone could come along and barter for his hand in marriage?" I tried wrapping my head around the idea and failed. "Would he have to accept?"

"He's made it plain he won't have his bride chosen for him, and most girls are smart enough not to want their hearts broken." She fingered a stringy piece of lace on her skirt. "He's got a few more years to select his own wife before our parents start applying pressure."

That might explain Mr. Pritchard's concern over our friendship. A match between a Woolworth and a Low Society sentinel, even a member of the Elite, was as likely as snow in Georgia in August. But he had to know his son had been the biggest obstacle. Given half a chance, five years earlier, I would have put a ring on it without a backward glance.

"What about you?" The Pritchards had three kids, after all. "Does that mean you're off the hook? What about Macon?"

Macon was the youngest Pritchard sibling and still in his *all girls have cooties* phase.

"As long as Boaz produces an heir, yes." A soft laugh shook her shoulders. "You'd think he'd have sired fifty by now, but he's been careful."

Boaz in all his promiscuous glory was never going to be my favorite topic of conversation. I could laugh about some of the highlights, sure. But the reality of his past was often a tough pill for me to swallow. I choked down my jealousy, I always did, but reliving his escapades still hurt.

"I should get to work." I stood and hauled Amelie to stand. "Toilets don't scrub themselves."

She groaned as she settled back on her swollen feet. "Hey, you want to hear something weird?"

"Hit me."

She cocked her arm and punched me in the shoulder then shrugged. "What? You had to see that coming."

"Fine, Little Miss Literal." Rubbing the tender spot, I scowled. "*Tell* me."

"You know that flickering lamppost on Whitaker Street we always hint is a ghost trying to communicate with us from the great beyond?"

"Yeah." There was a benign disturbance in the area, but it was too weak to do more than interfere with that lone bulb. "Victims love whipping out their EMF meters for readings there."

The small devices measured electromagnetic fields, and ghost hunters used them to determine hotspots.

"No longer." Her sigh carried. "I walked past there twice tonight, and there was nary a wink in sight."

"That really is weird." The city had rewired that lamppost, replaced the bulbs, killed the power to it on more than one occasion, all to no avail. Or so we told the tourists. The truth was probably that the neighbors complained about the light and nothing was ever done about it, allowing us to embellish how we liked. It was a dependable stop while on that route, and it had the bonus of being authentic. "Did you see that story in the paper about the B&B?"

"I overheard Mom and Dad talking about it. In loud voices. She's not thrilled with the newspaper coverage, but he doesn't seem to think anything will come of it." She swished her way toward the door. "So, are we on for Mallow after work?"

"Yes, please." A hot chocolate would rinse the bleach taste from my mouth quite nicely. "Go forth and scintillate."

"Oh, I shall." She bobbed in a practiced curtsey that had nothing to do with her job and everything to do with being Society born and bred. "Don't have too much fun without me."

"I make you no promises."

Once Amelie left, I set about tidying the chaotic parlor. I had an armful of accessories bound for the closet when a knock on the doorframe made me turn. A gaunt woman dressed in a navy pantsuit appraised me from across the threshold. Her slate-gray eyes narrowed on my face, and I got a bad feeling about the nature of this visit.

"Hello." I scanned the hall behind her, but she was alone. "Can I help you?"

"Are you Grier Woolworth?" The question came out flat. She already knew the answer.

"Yes."

"I'm Detective Caitlin Russo with the Savannah Police Department." She stepped into the room. "I hear you disappeared for a few weeks then came back to work sporting a shiner." Her gaze slid over me. "Ms. Meacham says it's not the first time this has happened. You vanishing without a trace."

Involving human law enforcement in Society business was a huge no-no. Cricket, despite her good intentions, could have done me less harm if she'd pulled the pin on a grenade then lobbed it at me.

THREE

"I'm not an abuse case if that's what has you worried." The smile I turned on her pulled the scab on my lip taut, and she caught my wince. "I live alone. I don't have a boyfriend—"

"Ms. Meacham seems to believe otherwise." Detective Russo consulted a small notepad on her palm. "She says you're dating the brother of one of her other employees, one Amelie Pritchard. The brother's name is..." she skimmed her information, "...Boaz."

"Boaz is my friend, not my boyfriend." I kept tidying the room to hide the tremble in my hands. "He and Amelie are my neighbors. We all grew up together."

"Is there any tension between you two?" She held a pen poised above the paper. "Has he made any unwanted advances?"

I snorted out a laugh. "Um, no."

Her expression remained severe. "Why is that funny?"

"He's always been like an older brother to me." Minus the whole platonic-love thing siblings had going on. The love I'd had for him had not been so innocent. "He wouldn't hurt a hair on my head, and he would take exception with anyone who tried."

Except for, you know, the woman he recruited to use me as a

grappling dummy.

Maybe I ought to leave out that part.

"All right." She removed a card from her back pocket. "If you say you're okay, I have no recourse at this time but to accept your word."

Meaning she didn't believe me for a hot minute.

"I'm fine." I palmed her card and tucked it away while she watched. "Really."

"If you say so." She turned to leave, pausing to glance over her shoulder. "Keep that. You might need it one day."

Giving up on convincing her otherwise, I patted my pocket. "I'll do that."

No sooner had I gotten her out of my hair and slumped on the couch than Neely barreled through the door. He gasped at the sight of me and clutched his chest with both manicured hands. I brushed my fingertips over my lips. "It's not *that* bad."

"You vanish for a month and come back looking like *this*?" He crossed the room and sank down beside me. "Amelie mentioned a family emergency, but I saw those men lurking outside the building the night I covered your shift. They were looking for someone. Dare I say someone Grier-shaped? That's why Boaz got involved, wasn't it?" He gathered my hands in his. "You were dating Danill Volkov, and you edited out that tidbit of information with the detective." He hushed me when I protested the part where he'd been eavesdropping on official police business. "What happened?"

Turns out Danill was just as crazy as you thought. He kidnapped me and held me prisoner for a month on a country estate. The men you noticed were his vampire lackeys, and Boaz was holding them off to give me a chance to run home to my haunted house to safety.

"I did have a family emergency." Keet had been kidnapped, so that lie had some meat on its bones. "My face is a separate matter altogether." I debated how much to tell him then stuck as close to the truth as possible. "You called it. Volkov was *way* too possessive. He didn't take me leaving town well, so we broke up, and I enrolled in self-defense classes in case he ever comes around again."

"Oh, Grier." Neely squeezed my hands. "I'm so sorry." He noticed me in street clothes well past tour departure time and frowned. "Why aren't you dressed?"

"I lost my job. Again." And Cricket was well within her rights to fire an employee who tended to vanish like fog on the river without so much as a note. "I came in to beg for it back, but she axed that idea. She's letting me fill in for Dom tonight, but I don't know about tomorrow."

"All is not lost." His eyes sparkled in a wicked flash of inspiration. "Have you heard about the *Cora Ann*?"

"Amelie was just telling me I might get my spot back when Cricket starts hiring girls to fill her roster."

"That's a possibility, but the launch is weeks away. We need work for you *now*." He whipped out his phone and fired off a text. "The owner is a client of mine. I'm going to put in a good word for you with him, see if you can get hired on there. You'll still be paid by Cricket, and the familiarity with the boat might help you land one of those hostess spots."

Grateful tears made my vision swim, but I blinked them back on the sobering reminder he was sticking his neck out for me because he thought I would starve without a paycheck. But if I explained I had an insta-fortune, he would ask questions. He already knew too much as it was thanks to his run-in with Volkov and his goons. I wouldn't endanger him further.

"Thanks, Neely."

"Don't thank me yet." He tucked away his phone. "Did Amelie explain the sudden interest in boats?"

"Nope." I had been out of the loop for too many weeks to know the latest buzz.

"There have been ghost sightings during the dinner cruises. Word is the apparition started out benign. People seeing a little boy dressed in a dark-blue sailor suit with ankle socks and canvas shoes. Some reports mention a white cap, others mention his blond curls. For a while, bookings increased. That's where Cricket got the idea to buy in." His expression shifted. "But the last cruise ended with three people getting treated for injuries sustained while onboard. They claimed a ghost was hurling cutlery at them during their meal. A few claim a boy's voice was yelling, 'I'm hungry. I'm hungry. I'm hungry.'"

Foreboding slithered up my spine. "This was in the news?"

"Yep." He slanted me a pitying look. "I forgot you're one of those weirdos who doesn't watch TV."

I wanted to laugh at his disdain for my preference in viewing streaming movies and television shows online, but I couldn't shake the chills. First a B&B owner was down a spook and handing out interviews, and now there was a riverboat with an active haunting on the local news. What did it mean? Spurts of paranormal activity weren't uncommon in cities like Savannah. That wasn't the problem. The problem was humans were aware of it, capitalizing on it, this time.

"The news coverage means Cricket is champing at the bit to get the *Cora Ann* rebranded before the commotion dies down," he said. "She's trying to book one of those ghost hunter shows for the maiden voyage."

The longer he chattered about Cricket's plans, the more I wondered what stance the Society would take. Ghosts weren't a priority for them. There was no money in exorcisms, except when a third party hired them to cleanse a space. But, at the same time, there was a difference between an orb of light caught on film and a specter capable of damaging property and harming people. From the sound of things, the B&B ghost leaned more toward a low-level entity while the *Cora Ann* harbored a burgeoning poltergeist.

"Does this mean you're going to work a split shift?" I noticed the quiet, wondered when he had stopped talking, and made a valiant effort to fill the lull. "Or will Cricket be hiring another stylist?"

"There will be two haunted cruises nightly until the buzz dies down. One coincides with our first tour at dusk and the other with the late-late tour. Since passengers will board early, the River Haints, and yes, that's what I overheard Cricket calling them, will need to be primped in advance. I've got time to style them then rush back to the office before the first walking tour leaves. I'll handle touch-ups here until it's time for the late-late tour, and then I'll head back to the boat to refresh the girls there."

"That sounds like a lot of work."

"Cricket is paying for the gas, so I can't complain." He lifted a wrinkled copy of *Vanity Fair* and pressed it to his chest. "I'm going to miss the downtime, though. That's when I get caught up on my reading."

"Um, Neely." I cocked my head at him. "When do you sleep?"

"I work from home during the week, and I'm very good at what I do." The upscale accounting firm responsible for half the pens in the office, whether they knew it or not, was a testament to that fact. "There are no clauses in my contract prohibiting me from holding a second job. As long as I'm available for conference calls and questions, my boss doesn't care what I do with the rest of my time." He traced the dark circles under my eyes. "Besides, I could ask you the same thing. Do you ever sleep?"

"Oh, I sleep." Sometimes for whole minutes strung together. "The problem is how I wake."

"Nightmares?"

"Yeah."

He nodded as if he understood. "Talking helps."

"I have someone," I assured him before he made the offer I sensed coming. "She's helping me work through my issues."

"Let me know if you need another ear." He cupped his and leaned closer. "I'm always *hear*."

"Ha ha." I shoved him rocking back on his heels. "I'll keep that in mind."

"I have to get back to work." He rolled up the magazine and tapped me on the shoulder with it. "I'm glad you're back. I'm relieved you're safe. Just do me a favor and call me next time? Amelie kept me in the loop, but I worry about you. I would have rested easier hearing updates direct from the source."

"I'm sorry." I touched his wrist. "I didn't mean to worry you."

With any luck, he didn't notice I hadn't promised to call. When I vanished, the only cells I had access to tended to be the barred kind.

"I hid your dress. Just in case." He jutted out his chin. "I refuse to acknowledge a Blue Belle who isn't you."

"You're the best," I told him with absolute conviction. "Cruz has no idea how lucky he is."

"Oh, I remind him every now and then." He winked. "I hope this thing with Volkov doesn't put you off dating. It was nice seeing you all dolled up and hitting the town with a hot guy on your arm instead of riding your death machine home and crawling in bed alone."

Alone meant no one saw, really grasped, how deep the cracks extended in my façade. No matter what Woolly thought, it wasn't always a bad place to be. "Guys are a lot of work."

"Amen, sister." A dreamy expression blanketed his features. "The right one is worth it, though."

Between studying with Linus, self-defense with Taz, figuring out what it meant to be the Woolworth heir *and* goddess-touched, my dance card was full. And then there was Boaz. I had no idea where to pencil him in.

A prickling rush of heat tingled in my cheeks when I thought of the press of his lips on mine the night before he left to rejoin his unit, but I had seen him smooch enough girls that his technique had never been in doubt. It was all the rest of it—the mechanics of a relationship with him—that made me question his skills. And mine.

"I'll hold you to that." I checked the time on my phone as I stood. "I have some thrones to polish before I head your way, but I'll see you in about thirty."

"There's a chance of rain in the forecast. Maybe you'll get lucky and the girls will track in mud for you to mop." He unfolded to his lanky height. "Failing that, I'll sprinkle bobby pins like confetti so you can hang out with me longer."

"Thanks." I snorted. "You're a prince."

He smoothed back his hair. "If the crown fits."

After swatting him on the butt to get him out the door, I got down to business. By the time I marked off the last item on my to do list, a victim had blown chunks on the sidewalk leading up to the front door. I blasted the concrete clean with a hose and reevaluated my life choices. When the late-late tour returned and Amelie flounced up to me with my spare helmet dangling from her fingertips, I was miles past being ready for sweet chocolate oblivion.

AMELIE WAS the first brave soul to hop on the back of Jolene and let me take her for a spin after Boaz taught me how to drive his one true love. That same trust had her crowding behind me so I could zip us over to Mallow. Plus, I think the bike reminded her of the brother she missed something fierce.

The best thing about Mallow, besides the fact everything on the menu was mouth-wateringly delicious, was the fact it stayed open until dawn. Most folks in town thought it was a gimmicky tourist lure, but the truth was the owner was a necromancer, and she kept Society hours.

After I parked, we crossed the lot together, our shoulders bumping, and got into a shoving match to see who could squeeze through the door first. She won by tickling me until I almost wet my pants, then she slid through the opening like a greased pig at a county fair.

"You play dirty," I grumbled with admiration. The only person who could tickle her was Boaz. Try as I might, I couldn't get so much as a giggle out of her. "You should buy me a drink to apologize."

"Crybaby." Rolling her eyes, she approached the counter. "I'll take two hot chocolates with extra marshmallows and a side order of Kleenex."

The cashier blinked at her owlishly then passed over a handful of napkins.

Amelie thanked the woman then stuffed them down the front of my shirt, giving me a lumpy third boob, cackling all the while. I ducked out of her reach before she could tweak my nonexistent third nipple and caught movement outside the shop from the corner of my eye.

"Be right back." I left her waiting on our order while I stepped up to the large display window. Jolene was the only vehicle in the lot, and I saw no pedestrians. I lingered a moment longer, scanning the area, but I came up empty.

"Grier?" Amelie walked up behind me. "Is everything okay?"

"Yeah." I rubbed my hands down my arms. "I thought I saw something."

The light went out of Amelie's eyes, and she took a look around as well. "Do you think we were followed?"

It had happened before, and it likely would again. "I'm not sure."

"I'm texting Boaz." She whipped out her phone. "He'll skin me alive if I don't keep him in the loop."

"It's probably nothing." I closed my hand over her screen. "Besides, he's not my keeper."

"No, but he is my brother, and he is your wannabe friend with benefits." She pried her phone out of my grip. "He's earned the right to worry." When she spotted the face I made, she laughed. "He's four states away. He can't drop everything and run home to shine a flashlight at shadows for you."

"So you say." Her brother was more resourceful than she gave him credit for, and more commanding too.

"He was right there. He saw the car pulling away, you inside it, and he couldn't save you." The playfulness in her swirled away like water down a drain. "Neither could I."

"Ame," I breathed, yanking her into a hug. "You did the best you could. You both did. I don't blame either of you, and neither of you should blame yourselves."

"We just got you back," she said, echoing the sentiment I had shared with Boaz not that long ago. "I don't want to lose you again."

"I'm not going anywhere." I hauled her to the counter in time to pick up our order while it was steaming delicious curls. "I'm working on getting stronger, and I'm going to fortify Woolly too." We took our drinks and settled at our usual table. "Plus, Linus lives shouting distance away. I've got 'round-the-clock backup."

Amelie blew across her mug. "How weird is it having him as a neighbor?"

"Pretty weird." Impatient as always, I sipped too soon and burned my tongue. "It's odd having a guest, let alone one staying in the carriage house. No one's ever lived there. It's strange to think I can walk across the yard and talk to someone if I want."

"I hate to break it to you, Grier, but you've been able to do that basically all your life." She snorted into her cup. "I'm right across the yard in the opposite direction, in case you've forgotten."

Linus was different, though. He had answers for so many of the questions I was just thinking to ask. Amelie was a friend, a shoulder to cry on, a sister of the heart, but Linus was a resource as valuable as any book in Maud's library.

"You know what I mean." I played it off like it had been a slip of the tongue instead of me realizing how much I liked the idea of having a living encyclopedia on the grounds. "He's *right there*. There's no buffer. It's almost like having a roommate."

"Has he changed much?" Her eyes fluttered closed on her first sip, and she licked the melted marshmallow off her upper lip. "I haven't seen him in years."

"He's taller, thinner. He grew out his hair." I pictured the wraith in his gaze and shivered. "His eyes are darker." I didn't tell her why, and I couldn't explain keeping his secret, except conversations on magic between Amelie and me always dead-ended with each of us put out with the other. "Otherwise, he's pretty much the same. Still prefers books to people. Still dresses like a little professor." Except now he was one. Maybe there was something to the old adage of dressing for the job you wanted after all. "You should pop in and say hi sometime. He might enjoy having another social outlet."

"Nah. I'll pass. He never liked me much." She wiped her mouth with a napkin. "He hated Boaz when we were kids, no idea why, the

possibilities are limitless. He snubbed me since I was tainted by association."

"I always thought..." Rolling in my lips, I wished I hadn't opened
my mouth.

"That it was a class thing?" Of course, Amelie knew exactly what
I'd meant. "Linus was a little snob. How could he not be with Dame
Lawson for a mother? But he was polite to other Low Society girls.
He did have some manners. He just never used them on me. He
wasn't mean when you weren't around, nothing like that, more like I
ceased to exist."

"Well, we're all grown up now." I poked the bloated marshmallows with my finger to watch them bob in their chocolatey bath.
"Maybe things have changed."

"Maybe." Her attention drifted to the door behind me and stuck.
"I still don't like this. I wish we'd taken my car. Jolene leaves us too
exposed."

"I can check in with Linus if it makes you feel better." With Boaz
gone, we didn't have a whole lot of other options.

"*Linus?*" She laughed so hard she swatted her mug on its side and
spilled the last few swallows of chocolate. "Are you sure he's qualified
to act as a bodyguard?" She wiped up her mess. "Or were you hoping
he'd borrow a few of his mother's henchmen?"

Again I found myself biting my tongue about his wraith. "He's
got some tricks up his sleeves."

"Call him." She spun her now-empty mug in her hands. "We've
got no one else unless we want to involve my parents."

The Low Society tried to stay as far away from High Society politics as possible. Involving them would be a last-ditch effort since any
assistance from the Pritchards would put them in the Grande Dame's
crosshairs.

There was only one small problem with my plan. I didn't have
Linus's cellphone number. All I could do was dial the landline and
hope there was still a working phone plugged in at the carriage house
and that he would pick up.

"Woolworth residence," an amused voice answered on the seventh ring. "How may I be of assistance?"

"I can't believe you're playing receptionist." I laughed at the mental picture. "Are you that bored?"

"Not at all," he assured me. "I was working on a syllabus when Woolly started flashing her lights in Morse code. I put down my notebook to play cypher, and that's when I heard a faint ringing coming from the kitchen in the carriage house. I assumed that's what Woolly meant, so I answered."

Amelie cleared her throat and rolled her hand in a *get to it* gesture.

"The reason I called is I'm at Mallow with Amelie, and I maybe saw something outside." I stuck out my tongue at her. "I checked, but I didn't see anything. Do you think it's safe to go home, or do I need to wait on backup to arrive? And when I say backup, I mean *you*."

A sigh gusted over the line. "Step outside."

"Oookay." I pointed toward the door so Amelie knew where I was headed, waved off her protest, then stepped out onto the sidewalk. Still alone as far as I could tell. "What am I supposed to be—?" Movement above my head had me slapping the air like a bee might land on me. "Oh, my goddess."

"Grier, it's all right."

Tipping my head back put me face-to-faceless with his pet wraith. "You're spying on me?"

He scoffed at me. Actually scoffed. "You really believed I let you leave without protection?"

"No?" I backed toward the door, unnerved when the wraith followed like a lost puppy. "I expected Elite sentinels dressed in catsuits prowling through the bushes, tracking my every move. Not this."

The mental picture of Boaz crammed into a spandex jumpsuit made me snort, until I was tugging at my collar when my imagination supplied an image of all that muscle wrapped in one stretchy package. Oh, geez. I was not going to think about packages. Nope. Nah-uh. No way. My brain was a delivery-free zone.

"You already felt caged by the agreement you made with Mother," he murmured. "I didn't feel inclined to point out the bars."

Learning he could monitor me so easily didn't come as a shock, exactly. Wraiths made perfect spies and assassins. Stealthy and silent, they blended with the night. But he should have warned me that the bodyguard he had selected for me lacked, well, a body.

"I prefer to know where the bars are." I miscalculated my retreat and bumped into the display window. "Comes in handy for figuring out how to squeeze through them."

"You need protection. You're not safe on the streets alone."

As much as I wanted to fling it in his face that Amelie was with me, that I wasn't alone, we both knew she and I had failed to save my skin the last time. Necromancers weren't built to combat vampires. Magic was our only hope, and that defense required tools, preparation, and time assailants didn't allow before attacking.

"I understand you have to take precautions." I was proud of how even I kept my tone when what I really wanted to do was track him down and thump him soundly on the head. "But next time you take preventative measures, give me a heads-up, okay?"

"Do you object to the wraith?" he asked without answering me.

"No." Better the shadow than the man himself. "I'm getting used to it hanging around." The creature inclined its head as though appraising me. "How sentient is it?"

"When fully bonded, they possess limited faculties. They follow orders. That's all. They remain in a type of stasis when they're not deployed."

"Is it male or female?" I studied the billowing hood, the gnarled fingers, and had no clue.

"They're spirit and bone. That's it. That's all."

How sad to be reduced to an *it* when you once were a person. "I'm going to call him Cletus. He looks like a Cletus."

A choking noise filled my ear. "You're going to *what?*"

"Cletus," I enunciated clearly. "You can thank me for naming him later."

"If it makes you more comfortable to humanize it, fine." He sighed. "You can call it Cletus."

"I'm going to give Amelie a ride back to her car, then I'll head home." Realizing he would be there, even if it was across the way, struck me as oddly comforting. "See you at dusk for our first lesson."

"Sleep well." He hesitated. "Let me know if there's anything I can do to help."

"Thanks." Nothing short of magical or pharmaceutical intervention would suppress the dream, and I'd had enough of being suppressed to last a lifetime. "I can manage."

After warning me he couldn't promise to always be at the carriage house when I needed him, we exchanged cell numbers and ended the call. I paused a moment to wonder where he might be going at night but reminded myself it was none of my business. He was born in Savannah and raised here too. He had family in town, and friends. He probably had work too. His mother wasn't the type to let a valuable resource go to waste, and I would only take up a few hours of his nights.

I strolled back into Mallow to find Amelie ordering us to-go chocolates, proving why she was the best friend a girl could have, and I sidled up to her. "We're good to go."

"Is Linus coming?" She kicked up an eyebrow. "Or dispatching someone?"

"He already has." I picked up the tab before she could dip into her wallet. "We're safe to go as soon as our order is filled."

"He's having you followed," she said, thinking it over. "Good idea."

"I wish he would have told me," I grumbled.

"Would you have thanked him or fought him?"

I cut her a smile. "What do you think?"

"I get the feeling Linus is going to have his hands full with you."

Poor guy. I got the feeling she was right.

FOUR

After spending a week cooped up at home, my night out drained me. I parked Jolene and started toward the front porch, ready to grab a shower and update Woolly on all the gossip we'd missed over the past few weeks. Rustling in the bushes pulled me up short, and I sent up a prayer to Hecate that Taz hadn't come back for seconds. Creeping around the side of the house, I went to investigate and spotted a flash of red hair. "Linus?"

Dressed in a crisp navy button-down, the sleeves rolled up to reveal corded forearms dusted with freckles, Linus made for an elegant gardener. Dark-wash jeans hung low on his hips, the knees damp, and he wore a pair of scuffed, black boots coated in mud. He'd pulled his long hair into a neat topknot, and the same pair of black-framed glasses he'd worn at breakfast perched on the end of his nose. His elegant hands were covered in a mixture of crimson ink and clumps of... Was that concrete?

Skipping my gaze from him to Woolly, I sucked in a sharp breath at the smooth expanse of foundation running along this side of the house.

"I got to thinking about the wards." He dropped into a crouch in front of a small trough filled with a wet mixture. A trowel handle stuck out of the center like a bulbous candle on a birthday cake. "The only way to repair the damage to the foundation is to first repair the foundation."

Hardly breaking news, but the blank canvas he'd created made her look so naked, so vulnerable.

"Woolly can't function with a quarter of her wards down." I rested my hand against the siding like that might help me feel her heartbeat. "I promised her you wouldn't do this again. I gave her my word I would protect her. You should have asked me before you started. I could have talked to her, warned her what was happening so she wouldn't be afraid."

Linus let me rant at him until I ran out of steam then cocked an eyebrow at me. "Are you finished?"

"No." I sucked in air for part two then promptly deflated. "Wait. Are you laughing at me?"

He plucked a blade of grass and let it drop. "You don't trust me much, do you?"

"You broke into my house and kidnapped my bird."

A grimace twisted up his face. "There is that."

Whatever excuse I expected him to recite never made it past his lips. He owned the blame for his actions, though he must have known I suspected his mother of issuing the orders. Had he thrown her under the bus, I would have gladly switched it into reverse then taken my own turn behind the wheel.

"I transcribed the existing wards before I mixed the concrete." He indicated the lowest board on Woolly's siding. What I had assumed was dirt was actually tiny rows of interlaced sigils. They had been drawn on with a permanent marker with a crimson undertone. Another of his inventions? "Woolly is fine. I talked to her myself, and I asked her permission before I put a hand on her."

The window above our heads swung open then clicked shut in agreement.

"Oh." I knelt beside him, thankful I had done all the prep work of scrubbing the foundation clean weeks ago. "Are you sure it will hold?" I tipped back my head and examined the sky. "Neely said it's going to rain."

Linus got busy stirring his mixture. "Who's Neely?"

"Neely Torres. He's a friend from work." I patted my hair, not remembering until I touched frizz that he hadn't painted me into my character tonight. "He does hair and makeup for all the Haints. He's also a kickass accountant."

"Oh." Comprehension dawned across his face. "He's married to Cruz Torres."

I blinked at him. "You know Cruz?"

"We do some business with his firm. He manages the Society's human interests."

I wet my lips. "How long has he worked for the Society?"

"Three years." He studied me. "Are you two close?"

The clenching knot in my gut uncoiled a fraction upon learning the Grande Dame hadn't scooped up Cruz the second the cell door clanged shut behind me. I didn't like him working for her, but there was no way to convince him to drop what must be lucrative contracts without a thorough explanation. And what would I say when I had no idea why, out of countless attorneys, she had selected him?

"That's not the word I would use, no." Cruz didn't do close. Neely was the sole exception to my knowledge. "More like he's tolerant of me because Neely values our friendship." And that was stretching things. "He still gives me stink eye because he found me alone and half-naked in the men's changing room with Neely once."

Goop dribbled from his trowel. "Any particular reason why?"

"Why he gives me stink eye, or why I was alone with Neely?"

"I understand why Cruz might find it odd to discover a naked woman with his husband." Linus didn't stumble over acknowledging their union, smoothing hackles I hadn't sensed rising in anticipation of a defense I was grateful to avoid. "What were you doing?"

"Amelie covered the first part of my shift the night Keet died, again, and I had to sneak in to work late in order to avoid getting written up." Hard to believe there was once a time where that was the worst thing that could happen to me. "He figured the last place she'd look was upstairs, where the guys change, so that's where he stashed me."

A soft laugh escaped him. "Sometimes I forget how human you can be."

The same hackles I'd thought soothed snapped to bristling attention. How *common*. That's what he meant. Low Society necromancers had little to no magic. They earned human degrees, worked human jobs, lived human lives, albeit much longer ones, and the two people I loved most hailed from that caste. Factor in Neely, and I had an actual human friend. Compare that against my whopping zero High Society pals, and yeah, I wasn't the caliber of girl Linus was acclimated to by a long shot. In hindsight, maybe his mother had only sent him over for playdates with me as a social experiment.

"Maud raised me to be integrated into their world." Now I had to wonder why, and I hated questioning her ghost. Not in the literal sense. Thank goodness for small mercies. "The previous Grande Dame stripped me of almost everything I had and tossed me in a hole to rot. The High Society, including your mother, did nothing to protect me. Humans, and my Low Society friends, offered me a hand up when I had nothing." I stood and dusted off my knees. "Forgive me if I can't find the insult in being human. It beats being inhumane by a mile."

"That's not what I meant." He reached for me, and his fingertips trailed down the seam of my jeans. "Grier, please."

"I'm going to bed." I stepped out of his reach. "Keep your wraith out of my room from now on."

Picking my way over his supplies, I shoved through the gate. From the corner of my eye, I saw him sigh as if I frustrated him before he returned to his work. And the hell of it was, I felt guilty for giving him a hard time when *he* had insulted *me*.

Oh, yes. The Grande Dame had chosen my tutor well. Her spies would have told her I was clinging to my childhood friends. While

Linus wasn't exactly that, given his antisocial tendencies, she must have figured I would still prefer someone I shared history with over a stranger. She was right about that. But she was wrong if she thought tossing us together like salad fixings would make us mix any better than last time.

LINUS HAD the good sense not to send Cletus to wake me from my nightmare the following dusk. He let me come aware on my own, screaming bloody murder as usual. Woolly made inquiring noises, but she let me off the hook when I assured her the dream was the same as always.

I had ideas about what it meant, what repressed memories skittered through my brain at night like cockroaches while my consciousness thinned enough for them to press into the forefront of my mind. But grasping for the fading tendrils was like raking a hand through a wraith. You came away empty-handed and disturbed by the experience.

Determined to be a model student, I showered and dressed casually before tucking the grimoire, who I decided to name Eileen in honor of its plentitude of eyeballs, under my arm. The flutter of its paper-thin lids against my skin made me grateful for the absence of ticklish eyelashes. That would have been too weird, too humanizing.

The carriage house smelled as delicious when I arrived as it had last night, and my stomach gurgled a greeting when Linus met me at the door. Pretty sure when your intestinal tract starts holding conversations with people it's cause for alarm. But bacon.

"I'm sorry I blew up at you." I had a right to be angry about a lot of things, but not even half of them were his fault, and when had stomping away ever solved a problem? "You know how Maud raised me. You know who my friends are, what they are, and you know what I think of the High Society." *And your mother.* "Can we agree to avoid hot-button topics?"

"I apologize for intimating there was anything wrong with being who you are, and I didn't mean the comment on your humanity as an insult against you or your friends." He lowered his chin, his attention catching on the grimoire. "You won't believe me, but I meant it as a compliment."

He was right. I couldn't fathom him using *human* in a positive context. But breakfast smelled good, progress was happening on Woolly, and I wasn't in a mood to argue this early. "What's my lesson for today?"

"First, we eat." He stepped back then escorted me to the table. "I got distracted with a book I'm reading, so I went simple. I hope you like omelets. And bacon, of course."

"I like anything I don't have to cook," I answered honestly as he passed me a plate that looked picture perfect, the browned crescent of fluffy egg overflowing with ham, bacon, and cheddar. "This looks incredible." A thought hit me as I took my first bite. "Are you feeding me because you were told the way to my heart was through my stomach? I mean, it's true. Obviously. I'm just curious."

"I'm feeding you because I don't like dining alone. Usually I eat in the cafeteria with the other faculty members." He kept his eyes on his plate, moving food around with his fork. "You've lost a lot of weight. You need the calories." He took a bite and puckered his brow like the flavor wasn't quite what he'd aimed for, though I had no complaints. I wolfed mine down in record time. "Consider it a trade. You keep me company, and I'll help you replace all the calories Taz burns."

The reminder I had a session with her in a few hours made me groan. "It's a deal, but I'm pitching in on the groceries. It's not fair for you to foot the bill *and* cook. Actually, make me a list, and I'll supply all the food since you're providing me with a personal chef."

"There's one small problem with your generous offer. I usually don't know what I'm going to cook until I'm doing it."

"Oh." I nibbled on my bottom lip. "Then I'll load up on the usual suspects and let you do with them what you will."

A spark of amusement glinted in his eyes. He must think it ridiculous that I cared about pulling my own weight or paying him back when neither of us was hurting for money, but it mattered to me. A few weeks ago, I had been living off ramen and oatmeal without a penny to my name. As fast as I had been named an heiress, it could all vanish. It had once already. There was nothing stopping it from happening again. Solving all my problems with plastic in the meantime would only make things worse if it did.

"That sounds fair," he agreed with a tiny smile, and he opened a notebook with the word *syllabus* scrawled in cursive across the front. "As for your assignment, I hope you don't mind the clothes you're wearing getting dirty. We're working outside today. We need to focus on the physical foundation repairs before we start on the magical ones. Woolly is our priority."

Heartened by the sentiment—one I wholeheartedly shared—I forgot my earlier annoyance. "I couldn't agree more."

"We're going to apply a second layer of concrete to the foundation. I primed all four sides last night to ensure I had perfected the mixture. The next is your responsibility."

"I can handle that."

"Your homework tonight will be practicing the sigils for hardening and waterproofing."

"Hear that, Eileen?" I petted the grimoire. "I'll be defiling your pages tonight."

Linus hesitated, lips parted, and I wasn't certain which part of what I'd said had stalled him out. Was my pun that terrible? Or was he worried what I meant by *defiling*? Either way, he shook his head and kept reading from the paper.

"We'll also be using ink from Maud's supplies." Before I could argue over the waste, he raised a hand. "We don't know what mixing in your blood would do to Woolly, and using mine would fundamentally link me to her. You don't want that, so we don't have many options. Any blood used in the repairs will give that person a back door into the wards."

As much as I hated parting with even a drop of such a precious resource, I understood his concerns. "I appreciate you explaining this to me. You could have used your blood, and I wouldn't have known the difference." Until it jumped up and bit me on the butt, at least. I felt like a heel, but I put it out there anyway. "Why did you tell me? A back door would save you the headache the next time you need an in."

"The fact you've realized there will be a next time should be answer enough."

"You're protecting me from yourself." Again, I had to ask, "Why?"

"Do you need to change?" He carried his plate to the sink and fed his omelet to the disposal. "You might want to tie your hair back so it doesn't get in your face once we start."

Tempted as I was to press him for an answer, I decided his reasons didn't matter as much as the outcome. Though I was starting to get curious about his dietary needs. The man loved to cook, that much was obvious, but he pecked at his food like a bird.

"I'm good." I had dressed nice for him, but even my nice was thrift store-caliber nice. I carried my plate and our cups to the sink while he filled one side with sudsy water. I almost suggested the dish-washer, but then I remembered what he'd said about cleaning when he needed to think, and I claimed the spot beside him. "I wanted to thank you."

The rag in his hand stilled. "You shouldn't thank me for doing what any decent person would do."

It took a beat for me to realize he must think I was still hung up on using Maud's blood. "No, I mean dropping your life to race down here and play tutor for me. I appreciate it. There's so much I don't know, and it's nice having someone around I can ask."

His hand resumed its scrubbing circles. "I'm happy to help, but you understand this isn't an act of altruism on my part?"

Yes, I had known that. Too bad he brought it up right when I was feeling charitable toward him. "Your mother—"

"No." He leaned his hip against the counter, angling his body toward me. "My field of study is necromantic evolution. I catalog the growth and change of our powers over time in an effort to predict what they might become during the next generations as well as how to maximize the current magics we possess."

"I'm a research project for you."

"Yes." He examined my face. "The promise of working with you is how Mother lured me down here."

"Okay." I gusted out an exhale and felt ten pounds lighter. "I can deal with that."

More than dealing with his admission, I embraced it with both hands. It was oddly reassuring to know he was here, at least in part, to sate his own curiosity. While I didn't love the idea of being the topic of future research papers, I did need his help figuring out how my magic worked, and he would be more driven if he was quenching his own thirst for knowledge at the same time. And, to be honest, it was easier trusting a man who experimented on himself too. It made the whole thing feel less...clinical.

"You're not upset?" The plate he had almost scrubbed a hole in slipped from his hand into the dingy water. "You don't mind me chronicling your journey?"

"No." I rescued the dish and rinsed it clean. "This is more honest than any reason I had assigned you."

"Ah." His laughter was brittle. "I see."

The sound made me flinch. "It's hard for me to trust anyone these days."

"I understand." His sudsy hand covered mine, chilly despite the warm water. "Come on. We don't have long before Taz arrives." He retrieved a fresh dish towel for me while he dried off. "Are you working tonight?"

"I'm not sure. I lost my job at Haint Misbchavin'. Cricket, the owner, has agreed to let me fill in as needed." Sort of. "She bought a haunted riverboat that's apparently been in the news recently.

There's a chance I'll get picked as a hostess after the launch, but until then I'm in limbo, really."

"You'll have to drop down to part-time hours once our studies become more intensive," he warned. "We'll be taking field trips in the weeks to come, some of them overnight, and there will be assignments you can't perform indoors without access to a basement. Meaning we may have to rent an underground space."

"That sounds fair." It's not like I planned on being a Haint forever. I only wanted that tiny dose of normal each night for as long as it lasted. "Just give me a heads-up so I can let Cricket know in advance."

Maybe the third time would be the charm and I could manage a two-week notice.

Together we finished cleaning up our mess and gathered our supplies. I left Eileen on the table, uncovered, so she could entertain herself while we were outside. I figured the worst thing to do to a multi-eyed book was blind it with darkness. Actually, that was the worst thing you could do to anyone.

Mixing the concrete was easy-peasy thanks to the machine Linus had the foresight to rent for the job. The resulting goop held a faint pink tint, courtesy of Maud's blood, but it cleared up after we blended in some powdered hawthorn berries and calendula.

The process of slathering it on the foundation like icing on a cake required a technique Linus had, of course, mastered. Me? Not so much. Mostly I slopped trowels full of the stuff over his tidy work from the previous night while he followed behind me scraping off the excess and finessing the remainder to a smooth finish.

We completed two sides before Taz announced herself with a playful yank on my ponytail that made my eyes water and might have dislocated a few vertebrae.

"What are you two doing?" She peered over our shoulders. "Why does it smell like that? Coppery?"

I wasn't sure what worried me more—that she had been playing with me and almost broken my neck in the process, or that she could smell blood through the herbs and wet concrete scents.

"Just some home improvements." I skirted the truth. "Linus was kind enough to lend me a hand."

"This couldn't keep until tomorrow?" Her thin eyebrows winged higher. "Boaz will be here by then."

Beside me, Linus curled his fingers around the handle of his trowel until his knuckles pushed against his skin.

"Boaz is coming home?" A glob of concrete plopped onto my knee. I couldn't stop the smile stretching my cheeks. "That dirty sneak. He didn't say a word."

"You didn't know?" Her face screwed up into a scowl. "He should have told me it was a surprise."

"It's fine." I scraped my tools clean. "Linus, do you need help tidying before Taz and I get started?"

"I'll keep going if you don't mind." He wasn't looking at me now. "I want to smooth these edges before they set."

I leaned into his field of vision. "I can stay and help if—"

"You should practice." The wraith moved behind his eyes, his lips almost blue in the shadows. "You don't have much time before work."

Shrinking back, I got to my feet and rolled my shoulders. I didn't bother dusting off my pants. I would be rolling in the dirt again soon enough.

CRICKET MET me in the parking lot at HQ with a scowl pinned on her puckered mouth. Dressed in a black satin swing dress, this one with spiderweb lace overlaying the fabric, she looked like she'd stepped out of a funeral photo from the fifties. Her personal style clashed with the Southern belle shtick she pedaled, but she made it work. Skirts rustling in agitation, she crossed to me in neck-breaker stilettos. "You went to Sean Voorhees behind my back."

"Sean Voorhees?" I echoed. "I'm not familiar with—"

"He owns River Street Steam. He's my new partner for the haunted history cruises."

"*Oh.*" So that was the name of Neely's contact. "Since janitorial work is too light at the main office for both Dom and me, I thought I would check and see if he needed extra hands."

The unlit cigarette stuck to her bottom lip gave a perilous wiggle. "You called a man up and asked for a job without first learning his name?"

Put that way, it did sound bad. "Yes?"

"You've got more balls than brains, hon." She pursed her lips. "I could use a girl on the inside. I'm not saying Voorhees is swindling me, he quoted me a fair price for my share of the business, but the restorations we agreed on shouldn't take half as long as he's estimating. We need to get that boat back paddling water as soon as possible so we can cash in on the summer rush."

Savannah was lousy with tourists during the summer, so the timing could be ideal. The guides would have a few months to tweak their presentations in front of small, captive audiences before peak season arrived. Not to mention being able to capitalize on the local buzz.

I linked my hands in front of me. "Are you saying I've got the job?"

"He called me to check your references." Her blonde curls bounced as she shook her head. "I can't believe I'm saying this, but yeah. You got the job. Report to the dock. You can't miss the *Cora Ann*. Introduce yourself to Voorhees, and he'll tell you what needs doing." She stabbed a black nail in my direction. "I expect weekly progress reports. You've got a cellphone. I've caught you and Amelie texting each other from across the room enough times to know that much. Use it to take pictures. Let me see what I'm paying for, all right?"

"I can do that." I would have to run it past Neely first, though. I didn't want to get him in trouble if I caught Voorhees mid-shenanigans. "Thanks for the opportunity."

"Don't thank me." She rolled her unlit cigarette to the other side of her mouth. "Assigning you there won't cause a staff shortage here if you vanish. That's the only reason I'm giving you one last chance. Blow this, and you're done. You'll never work for me again."

I reined in the impulse to keep from asking if I might climb the rungs back up to tour-guide status. She had agreed to let me work on the *Cora Ann*, and that was the closest to full-time employment as I was likely to find with my available hours. Plus, I had to admit, I was more than a little curious about the ghost boy.

The haunting must be an old one, or the papers would have splashed the story of recent tragedy across the pages complete with stomach-churning pics of his parents attempting to cope with his loss and sudden fame. What had riled a stable entity up to poltergeist levels? And could it also be to blame for the disappearance of the B&B ghost? Something hinky was afoot downtown. I might as well investigate while I was there, right?

"I won't let you down," I promised, backing toward Jolene.

"Don't make promises you can't keep." She spun on her spiky heel and clip-clopped into the building.

"I deserve that," I mumbled as I mounted my bike and sped toward River Street. Jostling over the cobblestones while my teeth chattered was never my favorite thing, but it was worth it for the prime parking spots usually vacant this time of night.

I found the *Cora Ann* in the same spot as always, right off Rousakis Riverfront Plaza, her berth easy to spot from the street while shopping the vendors crowding the market. Two other steamboats docked behind her, the rest of Voorhees's fleet, but the bustle surrounding the *Cora Ann* told me I was in the right spot.

A long metal walkway—a gangway?—stretched over the water and up through a gateway in the railing where several men and women hurried about on their own errands. Two older men stood apart from the chaos, carrying on a conversation while gesturing toward the wrought-iron railing circling the upper deck. I walked right up to them and smiled in the face of their bewilderment. "Hi. I'm Grier Woolworth."

"Cricket send you?" the taller one, whose handlebar mustache tickled his jawline, asked. "You've the look of one of her girls."

"Yes, she did."

"Told you the old bat wouldn't settle until she had eyes and ears onboard." He belted out a hearty laugh the other man shared. "I'm Sean Voorhees." He indicated the man standing beside him, who sported a rather impressive beard that frothed around his mouth in tight curls. "This is Captain Dale Murray."

"It's nice to meet you both." I craned my neck to see what I was walking into, but Mr. Voorhees cleared the deck with an imperious sweep of his hand. "I'll take you up to the dining room. You can help pull out the old carpet and padding."

The dining room. Straight into the heart of the haunting. They must really want to spook me away.

"Wear a mask," Captain Murray called as I was led away. "Water breeds mold."

"We'll provide you with a mask and gloves tonight," Mr. Voorhees said, "but tomorrow I expect you to show with your own supplies. You might also want to invest in a chisel, a hammer, a Phillips screwdriver and a straight edge too. The work will go faster if you're not waiting on someone to finish up with the tool you need, and I don't have to tell you Cricket wants this done yesterday."

"I can do that." Though my unused debit card winced away from the cost of such supplies, minor as they were to me these days, I convinced myself I would be able to use them during Woolly's renovations as well. And that was assuming I couldn't find all I needed in the tool chest out in the garage. Gus, Maud's driver, had kept all sorts of supplies out there. "I'll get a list from one of my coworkers on the way out."

"Good idea." He sounded amused, like he never expected to see me again, as he led me into what must usually be an elegant dining room but now resembled a haunted house ride at a theme park. Wallpaper peeled in curling strips, sections of the floor revealed battered hardwood and steel beneath their carpet coverings, and one square of the ceiling exposed dangling wires. He put two fingers in his mouth and whistled. "*Klein vogeltje,* I've got a new girl for you."

A brunette about my age popped up from under one of the few remaining tables. Dirt smudged her cheek, and sweat glued her bangs to her forehead. A vibrant red birthmark covered her chin and lower jaw, spreading down her throat where it disappeared below the neck of her tee. "Why must you insist on embarrassing me in front of the new hires?"

"I do it to remind you you'll always be my little bird." A fond grin creased his cheeks as his eyes cut to me. "And to warn them who they're working for, what the consequences will be for ruffling your feathers." He shoved me forward as he stepped back. "Marit will set you to rights."

"Thank you." I drifted over to her as he strolled away. "Hi. I'm Grier."

"Marit." She held up her gloved hands in apology then jerked her chin in the direction her dad had gone. "Don't let the old man get under your skin. He's harmless, really."

Uncertain I believed that, I surveyed the wreckage, surprised when it appeared she was solely responsible for the entire mess. "Where do you want me?"

"Give me a hand with the carpet. I need it gone so I can prime the floor." She abandoned whatever task she'd been attending under the table to walk me across the room. "It's called a salmon patch."

Puzzled, I glanced around, expecting to see fish-patterned wallpaper or themed kitsch. Neither of which belonged on a steamboat on the Savannah River. "What is?"

"My birthmark," she said without breaking stride. "People call the ones on your face angel kisses, or the ones on your neck stork bites. Cute names, right? Mine looks like I dribbled a mouthful of wine down my chin."

"Oh." Articulate as always. "Do you have gloves I can borrow?"

"You really don't care, do you?" Marit sorted through a toolbox until she found a pair of scarred leather gloves then tossed them to me. "Most folks gawk and wonder, so I tend to get it out of the way." She met my stare, unflinching. "Sorry if I came down hard on you."

"It's a birthmark. Most of us have one somewhere." I yanked on the gloves and flexed my fingers. "I have one shaped like a cowboy boot under my left butt cheek if you'd like to make us even."

"I'll pass, for now." Marit chuckled under her breath. "Maybe we can get drinks after work sometime. Get enough liquor in me, and I might change my mind."

The chorus from the country song "Bad Boys Get Me Good" started playing, and I wrangled my phone from my pocket. "Do you mind if I take this?" I yanked off one glove. "I'll make it quick."

"Take twenty-five, but it counts as your first break. Just so you know."

"That's fair." I flicked the green circle on the screen. "Hey."

"Hey back." A smile warmed Boaz's voice. "I've been thinking about you."

Uh-oh. "Really? That's nice." I smothered a grin. "I've been thinking about you too."

About how Taz claimed he was coming to town, and he hadn't said a word to me.

"Missing me already, Squirt?"

"I always miss you when you're gone," I said truthfully. "It's when you're around that you annoy me so much I look forward to you leaving again."

"Brrr." He chattered his teeth for effect. "That's cold."

"I'm at work, Boaz." I bit back a laugh. "Did you need something in particular, or were you just calling to harass me?"

"As much as I enjoy harassing you, I do need something in particular." He hesitated. "You."

"Um." Heat flooded my cheeks, and I turned my back on Marit. "Can you be more specific?"

His husky chuckle warned me I'd made a fatal error. "How

specific? Are we talking pics or drawings or...?"

"Boaz," I groaned. "Please behave."

"Never."

"Then please stop wasting my first break terrorizing me. What's the favor?"

A pause lapsed during which I counted five beats of my heart.

"Go out with me," he repeated his earlier plea. "Just me and you. No sister to hide behind."

Always so quick to accuse me of hiding from him. How it must annoy him that I no longer ran headfirst into his arms every time he opened them. And that thought was exactly why I worried about the attention he paid me. I worried what he wanted was what he couldn't have and not, well, me.

"Earlier you said you'd give me time to see the error of my ways before you asked again. I figured I had a solid twenty-four hours at least." I gazed through one of the windows out at the darkened river. "Why the rush?"

"I'll be in town tomorrow," he admitted at last. "I thought about surprising you, but I didn't want to drop in and assume you'd have time for me."

"See me as in put eyeballs on me or see me as in go out on a date? Dates end with kissing." I ground the toe of my shoe into the plaster-covered carpet. "You've never been satisfied stopping there."

"No one said anything about a date." He wisely refrained from pointing out that since he hadn't asked me out until now, I had no idea what satisfying him entailed. "I'm asking my best girl to keep me company while we eat good food and maybe go dancing."

"What happens if I ask for more time?" Teasing him might not be the wisest idea I'd ever had, but I had never been smart where Boaz was concerned, and the idea of whirling the night away in his arms appealed to the starry-eyed teenager in me who would always idolize him just a little.

"Then I'll ask you again tomorrow night, and the next, and the next, until you cave."

I hid behind closed eyelids. Asking questions was safer in the dark, especially where my heart was concerned. "Why do you want this so much?" He had given me the easy answer, but I didn't want easy. "Telling a girl she's a convenient pit stop on your way through town is *not* the way to get her to say yes."

"I shouldn't have kissed you goodbye that night in your front yard. Or stolen your first kiss without asking." Gravel churned in his voice. "I can still taste you, Grier, and I want more. I can't stop thinking about you. Have mercy on me. Say yes."

Stolen kisses, no tongues involved, had brought Boaz to heel? I couldn't believe it. In fact, I *didn't* believe it. But goddess, how I wanted to. "Okay, Boaz Pritchard, I'll give you one date to prove yourself."

"Grier Woolworth, you won't regret it," he vowed. "And, since you called it a date, expect me to cash in on the kissing you mentioned."

"No tongue," I said, just to be contrary. "And no touching below the shoulders."

His pained groan lifted gooseflesh down my arms. "Cold, cold woman."

"You must like it." I couldn't stop my grin. "You're still talking to me."

"The thing about ice…" He lowered his voice to a growl. "When you hold it in your hands long enough, it burns."

Delicious shivers coasted down my arms. "You're assuming you're going to hold me at all."

The chuckle he gusted across the receiver spoke of bad intentions and melted my kneecaps.

"I have to go." I cleared my throat when I noticed Marit eaves-dropping. "I'll see you tomorrow."

Satisfaction rang through his voice. "Is that a yes?"

"Yes." I sighed, defeated. "That's a yes."

"Good girl," he murmured.

Coming from a bad boy, the praise wasn't all that comforting.

FIVE

"You've got a boyfriend? Bummer. I should have taken you up on the offer to moon me when I had the chance," Marit grumbled. "Do you know how hard it is to find girlfriends who aren't attached to their man at the hip?"

"Don't worry." Boyfriend was a loaded word, and I wasn't ready to pull the trigger. "We can still get that drink sometime, and I can't promise you a full moon won't be in the forecast. I haven't hit a bar since I turned legal, and I've never really drank much of anything, so I'll be trusting you to protect my virtue."

A rakish glint sparkled in her eyes. "I can do that."

"Mmm-hmm," I teased. "I recognize that look. Maybe I'll bring a friend along just in case."

"As long as it's not your boyfriend, you've got yourself a deal."

Explaining all the ways Boaz wasn't my boyfriend would take longer than it was worth, so I let it slide and ignored the illicit thrill that came with imagining he was mine, even for a moment, even if it wasn't true.

"Unless he's got a single, morally ambiguous friend." A calculating gleam lit her eyes. "Then I might be convinced to make an exception."

Pretty sure anyone who hung out with Boaz checked the morally ambiguous box, but still.

"I was thinking about my bestie, Amelie. We're starting a new tradition. Girls' night once a week. No boys allowed." I grasped the edge of the carpet where Marit indicated, and we started tugging. "Amelie is Boaz's little sister, so that has more to do with the *no boys allowed* ruling than anything."

"You're dating your friend's big brother?" She whistled. "I hope for your sake that you guys stick."

I winced but hid it behind a fierce yank on the carpet. The fallout of a breakup would get ugly. Amelie and I would survive it, that much I had no doubt. But my friendship with Boaz? It would crash and burn if I didn't guide us through this exploration carefully.

The sound of our voices echoed throughout the room as we exposed more of the steel underfloor, and it drove home the absurdity of one girl demoing this entire deck. "Are we the only two working this level?"

"It's The Haunted Dining Room, and yes. You heard that in all caps." She bent to tuck the frayed ends of the carpet so we made a tight roll. "No one wants to be in here. I've done most of this myself."

"That's right." I acted like my interest was casual instead of sparking hot in my chest. "A friend of mine was telling me about the ghost boy scaring people away."

"How did you miss the news coverage? Do you live under a rock?"

"I was out of town for a few weeks." Locked in an ocean-themed room and drugged out of my mind. Ah, just like the good old days. "I'm not current on all the local happenings."

"I bet you were kicking yourself for that, huh? Papa mentioned you work for Ms. Meacham. That makes you a Haint, right? Tips must have been amazing with everyone all revved up for ghosts."

Another time, yeah. I would have bemoaned the missing of an oppor-tunity, but I was too grateful to be here at all to regret I'd missed the surge. It helped, too, that I was no longer dependent on tips to feed myself.

"Well, I'm back now." I grunted when the carpet snagged on a bolt that would have to be ground smooth before the new flooring was laid. "And I'm on the boat in the heart of the action, right?" We finished crossing the room then sat on the roll to catch our breaths. "Have you seen him?"

"The guys are calling him Timmy." She scrubbed her forearm across her cheek, scratching an itch. "Have you ever noticed all the bad things happen to guys named Timmy?"

"I can't say that I have." Bad luck seemed pretty equal opportu-nity in my experience. There was no person too high to be brought low, and no person too low to sink farther. We crossed back to the starting point and picked at the next seam. "So, have you seen Timmy?"

"No." She paused for a quick breather. "He doesn't bother me, and I'm in here most nights. Alone. Maybe he likes girls. His victims were mostly guys."

Or maybe an audience of one wasn't large enough to make mani-festing worthwhile. Poltergeists were known for moving objects, touching people, causing mischief. All that required energy, and when you were a ghost who didn't eat, drink, or sleep, you had finite amounts of it before your tank emptied for good.

The nature of poltergeists was yet another reason why the Society couldn't be bothered with banishing any but the most violent souls. Left to their own devices, except in the rarest of cases, they burned their rage or grief or whatever remnant of emotion fueled them, and the problem took care of itself without intervention. Even-tually, all poltergeists became lamppost flickers like the one on Whitaker Street.

Cricket wasn't going to be thrilled with the reason why it was taking so long to update her new toy. Then again, if rumors spread that not even workmen could finish their jobs thanks to the ghost, that might boost the spook factor right there.

"What's next?" I surveyed our efforts and grimaced at the tacky clumps of foam padding left behind. "Let me guess. It involves a lot of kneeling and scraping."

"You catch on quick." Marit presented me with a chisel that had seen better days, a match to her battered tool, and we knelt on carpet scraps she'd had the foresight to save, which protected our knees from the hard floor. "You're not a bad worker. Will you stick around if Timmy pops in to say hello?"

"Not much choice if I want a paycheck at the end of this week."

"For pretty girls like you in a tourist town, there are always opportunities." She burst out laughing at the expression on my face. A High Society dame working a street corner? Maud's heart would roll over in its box. "You should see your face. I wasn't suggesting prostitution. Though, I mean, that *is* an option."

The virgin prostitute. Boaz would bust a gut laughing if he could hear us. And then he would bust anyone else in the gut who hinted they might be interested in taking me up on the offer.

"I meant there are other ghost tour companies. I can think of two more off the top of my head, and one of those buses its victims around in air-conditioned comfort. The other doesn't require its girls to wear costumes. There are a billion shops on River Street or in City Market who would love to hire a local. You could check with the thrift shops on Broughton Street or the boutiques on Whitaker."

"I'm a history geek," I confessed. "I love haunted history, the grimmer and grislier the better. Spending five nights a week talking to people eager to hear my version of a story is addictive."

"I'll take your word for it. Public speaking falls in the same category as waterboarding with me." Her scraping slowed. "Why are you here instead of working your beat if you love it so much?"

"That trip out of town I mentioned? I didn't clear it with my boss first." I gave one greenish clump of musty foam my particular attention. "I had a family emergency, and there was no time to do anything but go." To be fair to Cricket, I added, "It's not the first time I've vanished on her, so I get why she's leery of penning me on the schedule again. It's next to impossible to find people willing to fill in last minute, and tours that get cancelled mean refunds and bad reviews. Those are her top two pet peeves."

"I get that." An earnest quality entered her tone. "Papa's the same. He's always..."

The overhead lights dimmed to a soft glow, flickering in eerie pulses that reminded me of a beating heart.

Knowing better, I still played clueless human. "Electrical problem?"

"Maybe." She didn't sound convinced, but she didn't act worried either. "It's still bright enough to see. We should keep at it and let the guys handle the wiring."

The hesitant scritching of our chisels grew heartier the longer the twilight lingered and nothing else happened. Marit exhaled a small laugh, perhaps surprised our conversation about Timmy had gotten under her skin. She didn't bother hiding her relief, since she had no way of knowing about my acute night vision.

The chill that exhaled through the room could have been blamed on the air conditioning switching on, except that the dimness made it hard to believe the vents could pump out more than an anemic gust at this point.

"This kind of thing never happens to me," she marveled. "Timmy must have sensed what you do for a living."

Seeing as how that was a distinct possibility, though not for the reasons she supposed, I worked on looking sheepish. "Guess so."

The clatter of metal against metal wasn't alarming at first. There were rooms below this one where others worked, and someone, likely Mr. Voorhees, would be coming up to check on his daughter if the electrical issue wasn't addressed soon. Assuming it affected the rest of the boat and wasn't a contained phenomenon.

"Ouch," Marit cried out, slapping a hand over her thigh. "I think..." Her hand came away bloody. "Grier?"

A crimson stain crept down her leg to soak the scraps where we knelt, oozing around a steak knife that quivered where it protruded from dense muscle. The subtle flex of the handle called to mind someone sawing back and forth to slice a difficult cut of meat.

A whistling noise had me reaching up to touch my stinging earlobe. "What in the...?" Blood smeared my fingertips, perilously close to my carotid, but I had gotten lucky. A new piercing wouldn't kill me. "I've got you." I leapt to my feet and plunged through a cold spot. *Hello, Timmy.* I swiped my sticky hand through the air, hoping the disturbance would sent him skittering, but his icy presence twined higher up my leg the longer I stood there. "Give me your arm. I'm going to help you stand, and we're getting out of here."

Eyes wide, she clasped forearms with me, and I hauled her to her feet. A sharp gasp told me she had put weight on her wounded leg, but she didn't complain. I hooked an arm around her waist while she clutched at my shoulders, and together we hobbled toward the exit.

This time the tinkle of metal brought sweat beading on my forehead. This was a dining room. A defunct one, but a dining room all the same. There was no telling where the ghost had hidden his stash of cutlery, but I had to assume he was well-armed.

Halfway to the exit, Marit tensed in my hold and cried out, tears clinging to her lashes. I didn't slow down to find out what had happened but kept her shuffling toward the open door. Once across the threshold, I called for help.

Mr. Voorhees barreled up the stairs, followed by the captain whose name I no longer remembered. His gaze touched on Marit leaning all her weight against me, slid to the blood covering our hands, and then dipped to her thigh.

"What happened?" He bellowed inches from my face. "What's wrong with my daughter?"

"The ghost," I panted. "We were scraping up foam when the lights dimmed. We could see okay, so we kept working. The next thing I knew, a knife was sticking out of her thigh."

Unwilling to let his daughter brave the steps, Mr. Voorhees swept her up in his arms, hollering orders down the stairwell to the others. The captain had his phone out, and he was talking to someone in a commanding voice. He grabbed my elbow, hauling me down after him, and asked, "Are you injured?"

"No," I lied, unwilling to be examined. "The blood is Marit's."

The urge to backtrack and confront the ghost thrummed in my veins, but I had no kit with me. I would be as defenseless against it as Marit had been, and I had no reason to believe my luck would hold if I presented him with a singular target for his wrath.

The crew gathered around Marit as her father lowered her onto a makeshift pallet, taking care to arrange her on her left side, facing away from me. The fluffy pink cushion beneath her resembled insulation, and I was glad someone had the forethought to cover it with one of the thick vinyl signs advertising *New Cruises Coming Soon!*

One of the crew members who looked an awful lot like the captain stripped a hoodie over his head and passed it to Mr. Voorhees to use as a pillow. While he held Marit's hand and murmured reassurances to her, he glared at me, like this was somehow my fault.

Apparently he had been counting on the fact the ghost never bothered Marit when he assigned her the dining room as her pet project. Just as obvious was his fury over his foiled plan. No doubt he'd hoped a night of hard labor in spook central would send me scurrying to Cricket to beg for my toilet wand back, but his daughter had been the one who limped from the room and not me.

"Grier," Marit panted over her shoulder. "Thanks for getting me out of there." Her fingers tightened around her father's much larger hand. "I wouldn't have made it without her."

I started to brush off her comment, but then I noticed the wound that had caused her to cry out as we made our escape. Four steak knives protruded from the back of her left thigh, each one a fraction closer to the inside of her leg, as though each toss had been aimed mid-stride, and the topmost blade had come within inches of piercing her femoral artery.

"Thank you," Mr. Voorhees rasped to me, his attention finally locking on his daughter's face.

"I'm glad I could help," I mumbled, wondering how I was going to get back upstairs to confront the ghost. Tonight it would be impossible. Tomorrow would have to be soon enough.

With all eyes on Marit, I decided to make myself scarce before the cops arrived. I crossed the gangplank at a lope to beat the EMTs then power walked for Jolene. I straddled her then pulled on my leather jacket, muttering a curse at the sticky zipper.

"Ms. Woolworth," Detective Russo called. "A moment of your time."

This night just kept getting better and better.

I kept my seat and let her see me get comfortable. "How can I help you?"

Much to my annoyance, her notepad made another appearance. "You witnessed the attack on Ms. Voorhees?"

A sliver of paranoia wedged beneath my skin. Russo must have been stalking her radio for action. The alternative, that she had been stalking me, had me searching the black sky for signs of Cletus.

"Yes." I ran down a highly edited version of events leading up to Marit's injury. "And that's it."

"What's wrong with your ear?" She peered at me over her notepad. "Were you hurt too?"

"No," I repeated my lie. "It's Marit's blood."

"You were sitting right beside her." Russo stared at my ear like she was waiting on fresh crimson drips to prove me a liar. "You didn't see who attacked her?"

"It was dark." How dark, by human standards, I wasn't sure.

"There must have been some light." She checked her notes. "You told Mr. Voorhees you two kept working. It was only *after* the attack that you left the dining room."

Fiddlesticks.

"I told you what happened." I unhooked my helmet from its lock and held it in my lap. "I can't help what you believe."

"There's a lot more to this, and to you, than the eyes can see."

"Why are you here?" Now that I was paying attention, she wasn't standing with the other cops, and she wasn't consulting with them either. Maybe I hadn't been too far off the mark with my stalker comment. "Why the interest in me?"

"Ms. Meacham filed a missing person report two days after you disappeared five years ago."

Shock rearranged my features before I could smooth them. "I didn't know."

"You were a nice kid from a good family, never missed work, never gave her any trouble, and your best friend was employed by her too. You were solid and dependable, not the type to blow off work or quit and not bother to tell anyone." She kept glancing between the page and me like her notes stretched back that far. For all I knew, maybe they did. "She drove out to your house the second night you were a no-show. A crew wearing white biohazard suits was working in the living room. They were cleaning what looked like blood out of the carpets, the curtains, everything."

The muscles in my abdomen clenched tighter and tighter until I imagined my navel touching my spine. Details. She had details. Details I needed if I ever wanted to piece together what really happened to Maud. But the cost was too high. Paying her would emotionally bankrupt me. I had to cut my losses and figure out a way to get my hands on her case notes. "She must have misunderstood what she saw."

Russo wasn't buying what I was selling. "Your guardian was Maud Woolworth, correct?"

"Yes," I whispered, tasting bile.

Woolworth House was iconic. She might not be part of any walking tours, but I couldn't stop buses from passing the house or guides from sharing her history. She was a landmark in Savannah, both mundane and extraordinary, the bronze plaque rooted in the front lawn said so. Factor in my last name, and there was zero hope of a mistaken address pulling my buns out of the fire.

"She passed away around the same time you stopped coming to work." Russo tried on a smile, but its edges were sharp. "What happened to her?"

Bright spots flickered in my vision, stars filling my eyes, blinding me with their proximity. "Heart attack."

"Heart attacks are clean, quiet affairs. My grandfather died from one after eating Thanksgiving dinner four years ago. Everyone thought he was asleep until he didn't get out of his chair for pie."

A hazy swirl of memory clouded my thoughts.

He has a new girlfriend. His third one this week. Just as mundane as all the rest.

Why not me? Why won't he ask me? I would say yes. He knows I would say yes. Maybe that's the problem. Maybe I should play hard to get. Maybe then he would see we were meant to...

The carpet squishes under my feet, and cold slime seeps between my toes. I shiver, confused, my anger at Boaz forgotten. The smell hits me then, copper and rose water and thyme.

Maud.

"Ms. Woolworth?" Russo palmed my left shoulder with enough crushing force to keep me from sliding off Jolene onto the pavement. "You're in no shape to drive." She turned all solicitous. "You can sit in my car until you get your head on straight."

"No." I tried wetting my lips, but my tongue was too thick and too dry. "I'm fine."

"You're not fine." Her right hand locked around my forearm. "You're white as a sheet."

The panicked bird trapped in my chest smashed its skull against the bars of its cage. "Let me go."

"I only want to talk," she soothed, but that hunger for truth lingered around her mouth.

Made claustrophobic by the pinch of her steely fingers, I flowed into a move Taz had shown me. Turning my palm over so it faced me, I made a fist as I brought my arm up, almost like I wanted to tap myself on the shoulder, then struck high with my elbow. Her hold broke, and she stepped back. "Am I under arrest?"

Her eyes narrowed, reassessing me. "No."

"Then I'm going home."

I didn't wait for permission. I cranked Jolene and blazed a path for Woolly.

JITTERY after my confrontation with Russo, I stashed Jolene in the garage and locked it for the day. I was too exhausted to search for tools, and I wasn't convinced I'd need them after tonight. As I trudged across the yard, I questioned the bright idea to join a demo team. The whole reason I had wanted to stay employed in the human world was to keep my feet on the ground, and they were certainly dragging now. But working for Cricket had set me in Russo's path, and that wasn't a place I wanted to be.

The more aches presented themselves, the less motivated I became to return to the *Cora Ann*.

At least until I recalled the pain etching Marit's face. The poltergeist had to be handled. Cricket might think haunted cruises were a great idea, and I had to agree there, but people wouldn't pay to get maimed. She would fail in this venture unless someone knocked Timmy down a few notches before some unlucky human lost their life.

With that cheerful thought in mind, I shoved through the garden gate, walked up to the carriage house and knocked on the door. Linus answered after a small pause wearing a gray dress shirt held closed by a single button at his navel. Hints of dark ink and pale skin drew my eye before he gathered the halves of his shirt in a tight fist. A mechanical buzzing filled my ears, and an antiseptic scent made the air taste stringent.

"Am I interrupting?" I kept my eyes glued to his face.

"No." He stepped back and gestured me in. "I was just thinking about you, actually."

More like he had been pondering new tortures to inflict upon me. "Oh?"

Papers scattered across the kitchen table, each covered in ornate sigils. A few of the designs niggled at forgotten memories, but all of them were lovely. Linus claimed his work was standardized. From where I stood, it looked like I wasn't the only one who had trouble recognizing their own talent for flourish.

"Tell me you weren't holed up designing pop quizzes," I pleaded. "Is one on the agenda for tomorrow?"

"Again," he said on a soft laugh, "they wouldn't be pop quizzes if I warned you about them."

"Right." I shook my head. "It's been a long night."

"You're not dressed for work." He noted my clothes, my mussed hair. "Where did you go?" The final detail, the dried blood on my hands, earned me an arched eyebrow. "What happened?"

I weighed his reaction and determined it to be genuine. "You mean Cletus didn't tell you?"

"I had plans tonight." His gaze dipped to his ink-stained fingers. "I set the wraith to follow you but gave explicit instructions not to interfere unless you were in danger."

Between one blink and the next, the wraith clouded his eyes, an alien sentience that made him appear timeless, ageless, immortal. His forehead wrinkled into neat rows, and he nodded to himself a few times as though listening to a conversation beyond my hearing. All the while, his midnight gaze never left mine.

Funny how my hands hadn't itched until he mentioned them. Now the skin pulled beneath the dried blood, and I wanted nothing more than to scrub away the reminder of what happened to Marit. About the time I decided I had overstayed my welcome, his vision cleared, and he was simply Linus once more.

"You boarded a riverboat," he said, confirming my theory he'd been communing with Cletus. "The wraith couldn't follow."

"The river." Water disrupted magic, and moving water negated its power entirely. Not all supernatural creatures could cross even stagnant water. Others shied from currents and still more avoided oceans and their salt. I hadn't, until this moment, realized wraiths were averse, but the current was strong, and the Atlantic Ocean was eighteen miles away. "I didn't give it a second thought."

He scratched his thumbnail on his shirt button. "What were you doing on the *Cora Ann*?"

"First things first." I presented my hands. "Blood doesn't bother me, obviously, but this belongs to a friend." Or someone who had, until the lights dimmed, the potential of becoming one. "Do you mind if I use your sink?"

The absence of potential in human blood was unsettling. Marit's coated my hands, about as magic as red paint.

"Help yourself." He gestured toward the kitchen and followed me in there. "Will you tell me what happened?"

"Have you heard about the *Cora Ann* haunting?" I cranked the water up hot and poured soap, some fancy brand he'd bought that might as well have been named *Cha-Ching*, in my palm and started scrubbing. "Apparently it's been all over the news."

"I don't watch television." He took out his phone and performed a quick search. "Ah. I see. This Cricket person you work for purchased shares in the company?"

"More like she's bought the right to use the *Cora Ann* at night for haunted cruises. She doesn't care about the other boats. If things go well, she might mix it up to include some of the daytime history tours we do too."

"The injured woman was human?"

"Yes." I did a double take before thinking through how much the wraith must have seen from its spot on the docks. "The owner's daughter. I was assigned to help her in the dining room, where the most activity has been logged. Marit told me the ghost boy never bothered her, so my presence must have agitated the spirit."

"Poltergeist," he murmured. "It's escalated to causing physical harm."

Ever the teacher, he made the correction automatically. It had been a slip of the tongue on my part, but I didn't want him thinking I was making excuses. Plus, poltergeist was a mouthful. Odds were good I would keep calling him ghost boy regardless of his actual state of existence.

"Will the Society get involved?" He would know better than I. "Their policy is usually to sit back and let these things resolve themselves, but it's an aggressive haunting. People are getting hurt."

"I'm not sure." His lips pulled to one side in the beginnings of a sly grin. "I can call Mother if you'd like."

I failed to conceal my grimace before it registered, and it amused him all the more. "Sorry."

"Don't apologize." He offered me a dish towel to dry my hands. No paper towels for Linus. "I didn't mean to make you feel uncomfortable."

"You didn't," I lied, searching for a new topic that wasn't how much I distrusted his mother, and by extension, him. "So...do you know anything about a Detective Caitlin Russo with the Savannah Police Department?"

"The name sounds familiar." He mulled it over then shrugged. "Who is she?"

"A problem." I sucked in a breath and outlined her escalation from concerned officer with a soft spot for domestic abuse cases to a hard-ass with a hard-on for proving Maud did not go into that good night, gently or otherwise. "I'm not sure how tight she is with Cricket, but a friendship between the two would explain how Russo knew I was back in Savannah."

"I'll look into her." A frown gathered in neat rows across his forehead. "Let me know if she approaches you again."

"Count on it." As much as I hated outing her to the Society, I couldn't risk being the reason she outed the Society itself. "I told you about my night. What's with all the drawings?"

"I've been working on a project." He shrugged like it was a small thing and passed over an ornate sigil I had never seen before, the combination unknown though I recognized the individual parts hidden within the art. The drawing was a yew tree, one of Hecate's emblems, and its black limbs stretched through a crescent moon. Its tangled roots grew to form a circle, a symbol of power, that encompassed the topmost portion of the design. "It's not perfect yet, but I'm making progress."

I traced the emblem with my fingertip. "What does it do?"

Linus decided the papers were in need of shuffling. "It's a talisman against Last Seeds."

"What?" I caught him by the arm. "Why?"

He studied where my hand touched him and made no move to escape. "Do you really have to ask?"

We were no closer to discovering the identity of the master vampire who had kidnapped me. Though it made sense he would be a Last Seed since they topped the vampire hierarchy. Not to mention other clans had volunteered their heritors, at least two Last Seeds themselves, to the cause. That required the kind of power you couldn't amass in a made vampire's lifetime. Or several of them.

And then there was Volkov. He hadn't died in the massacre when I made my escape. Boaz had made certain of that. The idea he might escape one day... That he might serve out his sentence and be released...

Forever was an interminably long time to imagine until it came with an expiration date.

I noticed I was still clutching him and willed my fingers to let go. "You did this for me."

"It's a useful protective sigil no one has fully explored since Last Seeds are so rare most necromancers will never meet one, let alone interact with one." More papers in a different pile also required extensive straightening. "I can patent its composition if I can perfect it. Patents can be quite lucrative. This one in particular, now that the Undead Coalition is hemorrhaging members."

"True," I allowed. "But thank you anyway."

He shook his head, just once. "Don't thank me."

"Too late. I already did." Even if the design was inspired *by* me rather than designed *for* me, the result would be the same. I could wear it on my skin as a protection, as a comfort that I would never be helpless against their compulsion again. Volkov would no longer be the monster under my bed. This was as good as plugging in a night-light. "Can you teach me how to paint it?"

"Once it's marketable, yes."

The dream of wearing his sigil as a shield evaporated, and I deflated on the spot. If he was seeking to patent a new design, he wouldn't want to share it until the paperwork was finalized. That could take months. Years.

"I didn't design it for application in the field," he explained. "I had a more proactive approach in mind."

The impermanent nature of our ink meant all sigils were intended to be drawn the moment before their use. Otherwise, the blood dried and the ink flaked, nulling its power. "What do you mean?"

"Let me show you." He unfastened the single button he'd been twiddling and parted the halves of his shirt, exposing the hard planes of his stomach. The yew tree tattoo covered his left hipbone in one of the few blank spaces left on his torso. The rest of his chest and abs were a masterpiece in progress, a canvas filled with loops and whorls, with magic. "I've been testing it on myself."

I traced the design, mesmerized, and his abs clenched under my touch. Gooseflesh rose on his skin beneath my fingertips, and a hot wash of embarrassment singed my cheeks.

"You did that?" I crossed my arms over my chest and tucked my hands under my armpits where they couldn't get into more trouble. "You tattooed yourself?"

That might explain the whine I still heard pumping from the other room. I'd sat with Boaz while he got inked often enough to be familiar with the process. Though his tattoos were nothing like this.

These pulsed with magic that invited fingertips to investigate their purpose. They glittered, blood red and liquid, almost alive beneath his skin.

"I apprenticed with a local artist for four years while I attended Strophalos. I still drop by on weekends or fill in when they're over-booked. It's a good skill to have."

And the ability to tattoo himself meant no one else saw what he was dabbling in. Win/win.

"You are full of surprises." Of all the paths I might have predicted for Linus when we were kids, tattoo artist was not one of them. Then again, neither was mad scientist willing to experiment on his own, very valuable, person. "You're nothing like how I remember."

He studied me, weighing my words. "I take it that's a good thing."

"There are worse things in life than to be predictable," I allowed, uncomfortable beneath his direct stare when his intense focus raised the black in his eyes. "Can I get one too?"

"Once the design has been registered, yes. Right now, it's imper-fect. A Last Seed was able to compromise me after prolonged contact."

The towel dropped from my hands to fall in the sink. "You visited Volkov."

We had just established how rare Last Seeds were, how beloved by their clans. None of them would volunteer an LS for experimenta-tion, not in these troubled times when vampire politics were shifting. But Volkov was a prisoner, and that meant he got no say in how he spent his time or what was done to him.

Pity welled up in me, from one captive to another, but I stomped it down hard. He had lost the right to burden my conscience the moment he imprisoned me on his master's estate. Whatever he got, whatever the Elite did with him, was no less than he deserved.

Volkov had forever to do as he pleased. His sentence, whatever it was, wouldn't cost him any time at all, really. Perhaps learning his lessons young would help him spend the rest of his eternity wiser.

Or maybe this would hone him into a blade that cut down any who threatened to cage him again.

I hated having even that much in common with him.

"I did." Linus pulled his shirt closed, his elegant fingers doing up the buttons. "Last week. I told no one."

Clearly, my observation skills were negative zero since I hadn't noticed him leaving or returning.

"Does that mean...?" I homed in on his face, wishing I could read this new Linus better. "Does your mother know?"

He huffed out a laugh. "No."

One did not show one's experimental magic to one's all-powerful mother and then explain how you knew it worked because you'd tried it on yourself, her heir and only child, first.

"I might be able to help with your experiment." And his mother would end me if she had any idea I was encouraging his self-destructive tendencies. "Volkov gave me an avowal when we first met." The blood-filled glass bangle had protected me against the power of his lure so long as I wore it. "I still have it up in my room."

Linus paused while tucking in his shirt. "He courted you?"

"He proposed an alliance, yes. The avowal was his way of leveling the playing field."

"Why did you—?" He cut himself off before he could compound my list of *what ifs*.

What if I had said yes? Would I have still ended up under lock and key? *What if* I had kept wearing the bangle? Would it have done me any good against his brute strength? The night he came for me under the guise of returning my things, I had reached outside the wards to claim them. I had made the mistake, no bangle required. Even if I had worn it, Volkov could have removed it the second we got in the car.

The avowal contained his blood, his gift, and its magic obeyed him. I was no good to him as a thinking, feeling woman. He'd wanted a piece of arm candy with strange magic in her veins. I might have been worshipped as a queen, but eventually I would have been bled as a prized cow headed to slaughter.

Not that the Society was winning any awards on that front either. Both wanted the same thing—for me to bleed. But at least the Grande Dame was willing to educate me. She saw the value in honing her weapons. No matter my personal opinion of her, I would be a fool to turn away what she was offering.

"I wanted a clean break from him," I managed. "After the Lyceum..." I shook my head. "He knew what I was, what was about to happen, and he told me nothing. He made it so I would have to accept his suit to receive his help standing up to your mother."

Linus pressed his lips into a flat line.

"He convinced me to keep it until I was certain I wanted to formally refuse him." Returning it would have meant a hard no that could never be taken back. It would have meant that if the Grande Dame had come after me instead of welcoming me back with open arms, I would have had nowhere to run. "I wonder if that's why Volkov took me when he did?"

Linus attempted to follow my logic. "Your rejection would have been a blow to his pride."

"That's not what I meant." I forced my theory into words. "He was raised cloistered with older vampires, right? Our conversations were his first with a necromancer, or so he claimed. He was a stickler for tradition." I worked out the rest before saying, "I believe he felt he had to act fast, while the bangle was still in my possession for his claim on me to be legitimate."

"You hadn't said yes," Linus agreed, "but you hadn't said no either."

"He mentioned in the car, on the way to the estate, that he wanted a willing partner." Not a wife, but an equal in the profitable venture that would be our marriage. "He wanted to earn my trust."

How he'd expected that to happen when he had all but tied a steak around my neck before shoving me into the lion's den, I had no idea.

"I can ask," he offered quietly. "If it truly matters, I can find out for you."

I snapped my head toward him. "You're going back to see him?"

"I'll have to if I want to test the sigil again." He wasn't looking at me when he said it, and a flash of insight warned me off asking him what other reasons might entice him to return for Volkov. "It won't cost anything to ask while I'm there."

For unfathomable reasons, I got the impression that yes, he did pay for what he got. But what?

"No," I decided. "The reason doesn't matter. His master wanted me, and Volkov would have taken me eventually. The timing isn't important. The outcome would have been the same."

A slight loosening in his shoulders told me I'd made the right call to let the matter drop. "Let me know if you change your mind."

"I won't," I reassured him and was rewarded with his stance easing even more. "I appreciate the offer, though."

A few sharp knocks on the door brought my head around, and I raised my eyebrows at Linus. "Expecting company?"

"No." He smoothed a hand down his shirt. "You?"

"I saw Amelie and Neely earlier, and Boaz won't be home until tomorrow. That's the extent of my social circle."

Linus strolled over to answer. "Hello." His eyes swirled with yawning darkness as they raked over an awestruck Amelie. Judging by her calm demeanor, I assumed this meant she lacked the magic to see him for what he truly was, what lived within him. "Can I help you?"

"Oh. Uh. Hi," Amelie rambled. "Is, um, Grier here?"

"Yes," I called as I loped to the door and nudged him out of the way with my hip. "What's up?"

The sight of me knocked the stars from her eyes, and she forgot about Linus standing behind me.

"I heard about what happened on the *Cora Ann*." She palmed my shoulders and shook me until I got whiplash. "Why didn't you call?"

"I was going to, promise." I pried her off me. "I came to consult Linus first—"

"Linus." Her gaze slid past my shoulder. "*Linus?*"

"Hello again," he said from near my elbow, his voice a low threat I didn't understand.

"I'm sorry." Large blotches of color splashed across her cheeks. "I didn't recognize you, and I didn't introduce myself, but I'm Amelie. I live next door, which you probably remember from, you know, your whole life."

"You were worried for Grier." He dismissed her slight with crisp acceptance. "I understand."

"I..." Her mouth worked over what she wanted to say. "Yes. That."

"We'll get out of your hair," I told him as I shuffled her into the garden. "Night!"

The door shut behind us, and I had to strong-arm Amelie, who was digging in her heels and craning her neck, onto the front porch. Maybe she was right about Linus branding her guilty by association with Boaz. He wielded politeness like a scalpel when he chose.

"You said he was taller. Thinner. That he grew out his hair. You didn't say he was *gorgeous*."

"Is he?" I bit my lip. "I didn't notice."

"You are a dirty, rotten liar. You have two eyeballs. You have a pulse. You noticed."

"You remember the part where his mother is Clarice Lawson?" Speaking her name gave me the heebie-jeebies, like if I chanted it three times fast in a mirror she might appear behind me with an old-fashioned straight razor poised in her hand. "He probably peeks through my windows at night to gather intel for her."

"Let's do some spying of our own." She rubbed her hands together. "Let's peek through his windows. During the day. When he's in his pajamas." She sucked in a sharp breath. "Or *out* of them."

"You're terrible." I hauled her away, the two of us giggling like the schoolgirls we once had been, and we collapsed on the front porch swing. "I'm not going to spy on my teacher."

Except, a few hours later, we sort of did. Blame it on the night being filled with the echo of childhood horseplay. Blame it on the color in Linus's cheeks before he unbuttoned his shirt. Or blame neither of those. Both of them? Whatever the reason, I followed Amelie out into the dawn with the avowal in hand as an excuse in case we got caught.

We checked each window in the carriage house as we passed them, clamping hands over our mouths to stop laughter from spilling out. There was no sign of him, not that I had expected him to be lounging in plain sight at this hour.

Amelie palmed the doorknob and gave it an experimental twist.

"What are you doing?" I whisper-screamed. "We can't go inside."

"Of course not." Her mouth formed a smile a beat too late. "I was just pulling your leg."

"You got me." I laughed, the sound as forced as her expression. "This was a dumb idea. Let's go."

"Yeah," she murmured, lingering in the doorway, her hand still tight on the knob. "You're right." Her eyes flashed at me. "We'll go as soon as we scout his bedroom like the pervs we are."

"Fine." I rolled my eyes. "Let's just be quick pervs."

A snort escaped her. "Aren't they all?"

But when we circled around back to the bedroom windows, there was a crack in the blackout curtains I had been counting on to protect him from our shenanigans.

His bed was empty.

SIX

I woke in the usual manner, which is to say sweaty, trembling, and miserable, to find a clipped message on my phone from Mr. Voorhees.

"Marit is stable, but they're keeping her for observation." A growl sounding a lot like blame rumbled through his words. *"The police want to interview all the employees present last night."*

Seeing as how I had already been put through the wringer by Russo, I had no choice but to believe if she hadn't reported my accounting, it was because she was cowboying. A quick call to her supervisor might scrape her off my bumper, but following my case for so many years smacked of obsession.

"There's no work tonight," he continued. *"Go to the station and do your duty to Marit."* Silence reigned, a call waiting to end, until a girlish voice murmured a protest, and he sighed. *"Work starts tomorrow night at eight."*

All my noodlelike upper-body muscles protested as I pulled on ratty jeans and a battered tee. I was more out of shape than I'd realized if one night of rolling carpet had me ready to cry uncle. Not bothering with shoes, I padded out onto the back porch and tested the wards. Their music was subdued but melodious.

Woolly's happiness to find herself at the center of a project was infecting her magical signature.

The notion made me smile as I strolled for the carriage house. The front door was open wide in welcome, which always caused me to hesitate. Certainly, it had never seemed welcoming before Linus moved in. I found the man himself at the kitchen table with his head bent over a stack of drawings he tweaked with sharp scratches of his pen.

Since he didn't jump up and yell *aha* at me, I assumed Amelie and my snooping had gone unnoticed.

"Bagels and cream cheese are on the counter," he murmured. "There's fresh fruit and cream in the fridge. Help yourself."

"Self-serve." I set about daubing strawberry cream cheese over a blueberry bagel. "I see how it is. Lure me in with home-cooked meals and then switch to processed once you've got me hooked."

"Are you?"

I paused with a clean butter knife dipped in the herb spread I was planning on slathering over an onion bagel guaranteed to taste like regret. "Am I what?"

"Hooked."

The knife wobbled in my fingers as I angled my head toward him. Dressed in a French blue button-down, he didn't give the shirt a chance to make the color of his eyes pop. He kept doing what he was doing, giving no indication he had asked what he'd asked in the tone he'd used. Maybe I was imagining things. "Free food is hard to resist."

He spared a glance for me, his mind so obviously elsewhere that I relaxed. "You're buying the groceries, remember?"

"Hmm." I hadn't bought anything yet. There hadn't been time. Grocery delivery should be a thing. Was it a thing? I would have to ask Amelie. "You'll have to give me a list of things you like to eat."

When he didn't answer, I wondered if that was because he had no favorites or because he didn't eat.

But he had to, right? No one could live on air and crumbs. Tonight he wasn't even pretending hunger.

"I'm enjoying our lessons," I said, changing subjects. "Though mostly it's been more like shop class."

"That changes tonight. I've outlined a rough ward that takes into consideration Woolly's special needs. Your task is to break the design apart and analyze each component." When he glanced up, a smudge of ink streaked his cheek. "Once you've finished, assuming you pass, we'll do it again. And again. Until you grasp the intricacies of the ward enough you can duplicate the framing to create your own."

"Come on." I dropped into the chair across from him with a put-upon sigh. "Can't we go outside and play in the cement some more?"

"No." His lips twitched as I kicked my feet for emphasis. Maybe that's what sustained him. His students' tears. "I have a field trip planned for the end of the week if you're a good girl and finish all your homework on time."

Delighted he was playing with me when I'd doubted he knew how, I slumped forward in a sprawl across the table. "Homework is dumb."

Linus swept a handful of hair off my face to better see me. "Would you rather leave Woolly dependent on the ink on her siding?"

I popped out my bottom lip. "No."

"Then you better get started. The concrete requires forty-eight hours to set. We need to be ready to move in half that time so it will be soft enough to take the sigils more easily."

That sobered me. "I've got twenty-four hours to figure this out?"

"More like twenty-three if you count breakfast and all the wallowing you just did."

"That was hardly wallowing. I didn't roll across the floor or anything." I held out my hand and accepted the stack of papers from him. The sigils were complex, some overlapping in ways that made my brain throb. "What if...?"

What if Maud had been right all along? *What if* my magic was wonky and not miraculous? *What if* he was better off bleeding me and inking the sigils himself? *What if* I really was only ever meant to be an assistant?

I definitely needed a new game to play. *What if* was getting a mite repetitive.

"You can do this." He rested his hand on my forearm, the weight of his cold fingers snapping me out of my spiral. "If you get stuck, ask for help. That's why I'm here."

"Helping a student with a test is cheating." I tried to recapture our earlier playfulness. "Well? What do you have to say for yourself?"

"I hereby forfeit all future apples as penance for my crimes." He bowed his head, and it was all I could do to keep from tugging the dark-auburn tips as they swung forward. We might be working toward an understanding, but I wasn't certain it could ever be friendship without trust. "Will that suffice?"

"That suffices."

"You have one hour." He set a timer on his phone. "I'll be in the office if you need me."

After that, he left me to my bumbling attempts at deciphering the intricacies of his masterpiece. His mother's brags hadn't been empty on that front. I recognized the configurations, the way his mind attacked problems. Maud's had worked the same. Her guiding hand was present in each line of every sigil on the page. Having that link to her anchored me in a way that told me I hadn't realized just how far I'd drifted from the kid she'd adopted.

The hour lapsed in a blink, and I jumped when a hand landed on my shoulder.

"Time's up." Linus leaned over me, his lips parted, and his exhale raised chills up my throat. "Let's see how you've done."

"Linus?" Glancing up put us almost cheek to cheek. "Why is your skin so cold?" I covered the hand he'd left braced on my shoulder with mine, and he allowed me to trace the length of his graceful fingers. "Lots of people have cold hands, but touching you is always like plunging into an ice bath."

"It's a side effect of bonding with a wraith."

There seemed to be a lot of those.

He straightened, taking my pages with him, and the frown I'd caused smoothed as he studied my work. The edge of his mouth kept hitching higher, until he was smiling at the paper. Marveling at it, really.

I ducked my head to hide how much his silent praise meant. I would never be the practitioner Maud had been, that Linus was, but I would be more than I'd ever dreamed thanks to the anomaly of my blood that made me worth educating. Linus wasn't Maud, but his approval was the next best thing.

"You've gotten a few of these additions wrong." He pulled a mundane red marker from his pocket and corrected the lines until they flowed one into another. "All in all, I would say this is a solid C plus."

"I'll take it." I beamed up at him. "How does a girl get extra credit around here? I want Woolly to have A-plus wards."

"There are no shortcuts, Grier. Practice is how we strengthen your magic, how we hone your craft. Study is how you learn to protect yourself, how you secure Woolly and Maud's legacy. You'll pay for your education with blood and with pain, and you'll hate me when we're done. All my best students do." He gave me the marked-up paper to study. "But when I finish with you, you'll be able to decorate her foundation with gold stars."

A HAND CRAMP forced me to put down my pen. Linus still wasn't satisfied, and that made me dissatisfied too. None of the previous incarnations of this ward had earned his seal of approval, and I doubted this latest one would either, but I was beat. A bronze medal would have to be good enough for tonight.

I tucked away the cheat sheet I'd made to help me decipher the more complex sigils. Those doodles would live to fight another day.

Not that they had done me much good since I'd yet to earn higher than a B minus. Linus was not pleased when I used my notes as a crutch, but I didn't see the difference in what I was doing and in memorizing formulae for math class.

"Here." I thunked my head onto the table and lifted the paper in the air for him to fetch. "Be kind."

"Kindness won't protect Woolly," he reminded me, all prim and proper. "Grier..."

"Flunk me quick." I rolled my head to one side, pressing my cheek to the smooth wood. "I can take it."

"Your C plus wasn't a flunking grade," he said, amusement clear in his tone, "and neither is this."

"B plus?" I ventured. "That would be an all-new record for me."

"Maud schooled you well in protective wards, particularly those designed with Woolly in mind. She always meant for you to continue caring for her." A sweep of his arm encompassed the stacks of papers, the notes, the quizzes, all of it. "You knew this. You were proficient in this. You were just out of practice."

"What I'm hearing is this was all remedial, and the hard work hasn't yet begun."

Thinking back on those weekends cooped up in Maud's study, he was right. Warding had been my best subject. One of the few Maud had taught me. Assistants could become proficient in this area. Even a few Low Society folks with talent could use them. I had been allowed this one thing, and Linus was right. It was only because the task of maintaining Woolly was always meant to be mine.

"Baby steps." He wrote on the paper and pushed it across the table with his fingertips. "This is your final grade."

Braced for the worst, I sat upright and pulled the grade closer. "An A minus?"

Linus studied me as he capped his marker, like he couldn't read me. "Are you disappointed?"

"Are you freaking kidding me?" I leapt to my feet with a whoop and tackled him with a hug. "This is the best grade I've ever made."

"Oomph."

"I'm not squeezing that hard." I tipped my head back and laughed at his frozen expression. "You'll live."

Faint color blossomed under his skin, pinking his neck all the way to his hairline. "You startled me."

"The whooping wasn't your first clue? It's like an early-warning system." Neither I nor my excitement were subtle. "Next time you hear it, run if you don't want to get tackled."

"I'll remember that."

A few curt raps on the window nearest us startled me into squishing the breath out of Linus for real.

Boaz stood in the garden, a frown tugging on his lips, and raised his voice to be heard through the glass. "Am I interrupting?"

Linus tensed beneath my hands, the muscles in his back pulling taunt. Through the fabric of his shirt, cold bled into my cheek where it mashed against his chest until one half of my face went numb. He rested ice-block hands on my shoulders and set me back, away from him.

"Refine your design." Mist poured over his lips. "We'll start etching the foundation tomorrow."

"Yeah." I tried not to look like a barnacle chipped off the side of a ship and wondering where to cling next. "Okay."

Without a backward glance, he vanished behind the stacked trunks he had yet to relocate.

"How can you stand being cooped up in here for hours with him?" Boaz had invited himself in and now leaned in the front doorway, his arms folded over his chest and his ankles crossed. "He's as dull as dishwater."

An instinctive defense for Linus rose in me, but I didn't want to start a fight when we had plans. I could always pry open that can of worms after I'd been wined and dined. And probably dump them over his head.

"You're early." I linked my fingers and reached toward the ceiling, stretching out my sore back. "What about my session with Taz?"

"I hate to break it to you, Squirt, but Taz left an hour ago. She saw you two working and figured it was more important." He watched the show like he was wishing for popcorn. "Besides, she knew we had plans tonight."

"Fiddlesticks."

A scowl cut his mouth that he aimed in the direction Linus had gone, like it was his fault I'd let the hour get away from me. "That is not what a guy wants to hear when he comes to pick his girl up for a night out."

"You pout almost as much as I do, and you've got a fuller mouth, so you look better doing it."

"You've noticed that, huh?"

The way a scar bisected his bottom lip, giving it an almost heart-shaped appearance? Or how that same pinkish line curved through his upper one, twisting the edge? Both injuries from a stunt gone wrong, one that had stopped my heart until he flashed a bloody smile at me and flipped up both his thumbs. Imperfections that made him uniquely Boaz. Had I noticed his lips? I would go to my grave with that answer. I had obsessed over them, what noises he might make if I bit down on that scar, what sounds I might make if he let me. But he didn't need to know any of that. Ever.

"As much as you love to run your mouth?" I mimed him jabbering away with my hands. "It's hard to look away once your gums start bumping."

"Hmph."

"I'm sorry I'm not ready." I tidied my stack of papers, stuffed what I needed in my grimoire, and joined him in the garden, pulling the door closed behind me. "I wanted to look nice for you, but now I'm tired, and you're stuck with me as is. I hope that's okay."

"He's working you that hard?" Boaz threw a companionable arm around my shoulders and guided me toward the house. "I'm surprised he doesn't keep a ruler handy for rapping you on the knuckles when you answer wrong."

"Thanks for the vote of confidence." I wedged my elbow between his ribs and dug in. "I like how you assume I answer wrong often enough he needs to keep it on him."

"Do you always celebrate the end of class with a round of hugs?" He clamped me tighter against him, trapping my arm to avoid another jab. "Isn't that a little kumbaya for you?"

"I'll have you know," I said haughtily, "I made an A minus on a warding test."

"And that merited a hug?"

Jealousy was usually my thing, not his. I doubted he had envied anyone in his life. Until now. Until Linus. The green-eyed-monster look was new on Boaz. I wasn't certain if I liked it reflected back at me.

"You have no idea how hard this is." In a move that would have made Taz proud, I hooked my leg through his and sent him stumbling. "I have brain cramps from what I did today."

"Goddess, Grier." He managed to correct his balance before he ate dirt. "That's not what I meant."

"Well, it's what I meant." I refused to apologize. "I was excited. I don't see the crime."

"You're playing with fire letting him get on your good side. He's ingratiating himself to you."

"Are you robbing me of my achievement by mansplaining that all the work I did today was a ploy? Are you insinuating that his plan was to undercut my confidence all evening then give me high marks to provoke a physical response?" I planted my feet and anchored my hands on my hips. "Do you think I'm being conditioned to equate higher marks with affection? That I would ever drop my panties for a passing grade?"

"He has a lot of power over you at the moment, whether you see it or not."

"I see him clearly, Boaz." I didn't own a single pair of rose-colored glasses. "Stop acting like a jealous boyfriend. You don't have that right."

"You've been through enough," he growled. "If I can protect you from one more thing, I will. No matter how pissed off you get, as your friend, as someone who loves you, that *is* my right, and I have earned it."

The argument I intended to make spluttered in the face of his righteous fury.

"The Grande Dame locked you away, tossed you in a black hole, and I couldn't do a damn thing about it except clang on the front gate and get beat to shit by the guards." His face reddened as he stalked toward me. "I watched Volkov take you, saw you curled in his fucking lap like a drowsy kitten, and I couldn't save you." He jabbed a finger in the direction of the carriage house. "Now I see that viper's son coiling around you when he's the last person on the face of the planet you ought to trust, and you expect me to sit on my hands for a third time? Hell no."

My cell in Atramentous was so small, so dark, I forgot sometimes that others had been in there with me. Not really there, not trapped like me. But Amelie and Boaz had been in my thoughts every single night, and I had been in theirs. We had all suffered together, though we had been apart, and those years had marked us in different ways. None of us would ever be the same again. We had each been broken into different patterns, the cracks deeper and sharper in some areas than in others, and expecting our jagged edges to fit the way they used to was the ultimate folly.

One thing remained true, though. Boaz coped through violence, sarcasm and suffocating affection. As much as I wanted to kick him in the shin and stomp away, I had to remember he was trying. That might not be enough in the end. But it was a start. It was enough to earn him a chance to prove this might work.

"I can handle Linus." The moment I got in over my head, I would reach out. I would ask Amelie to sit in on our lessons or move them to Woolly. Surely she would allow Linus to trespass for a few hours as long as I was there to act as a buffer. "I know you mean well." I walked into his arms and wrapped him up tight, his heart pounding furious and wild under my ear. "I know you're protecting me." I breathed him in, his scent so familiar I equated it with being home. "But I need him."

"I know, I know." His arms came around me, crushing me, and he rested his chin on top of my head. "I'm sorry." His sigh rustled my hair. "I worry about you, Squirt. That's all. I hate that I'm not here to protect you." He pressed a warm kiss to my temple. "I'm proud of you. So damn proud." Another brush of his lips attempted to distract me. "I'm a shit friend for robbing you of your pride. I never should have implied your grades weren't earned or that your accomplishments weren't deserved. Forgive me?"

"Consider yourself on probation." I pinched his nipple and twisted until he shouted. He jumped back, releasing me, and I shook my head. "I don't remember you being this possessive. You traded girlfriends like some boys traded baseball cards. I wasn't expecting you to try and cram me into a plastic sleeve in your binder."

He rubbed his chest with the heel of his palm. "Would that work?"

The poor guy sounded so hopeful, I almost hated to burst his bubble. Almost. "That's going to be a hard *no*."

"I don't have a binder," he confessed. "I don't even own a plastic sleeve. I've never wanted to keep anyone."

"Boaz," I whispered, but he must not have heard.

"Amelie warned me I was suffocating you." He palmed his nape and scrubbed a hand over his bristly hair. "Tell me when to poke air holes in the lid, even if you have to poke air holes in me to get my attention." He tried for a charming smile, but his eyes were too raw to make it stick. "The army proved I'm trainable. I'm willing to learn if you're willing to teach me."

"We'll have to figure it out together." One day at a time. "Even if that means figuring out we can't be together."

A fraction of his confidence made a reappearance. "As long as you'll still love me."

"Boaz," I told him with complete honesty, "I would have no idea how or where to stop." Just what flavor of love existed between us required more extensive taste testing. "Are we still on for our date?"

"Do you mean are we still going out on the town, after which I will expect no sexual favors in exchange for providing you with dinner and entertainment? Yes. We are."

"You are a true gentleman, Boaz Pritchard."

"Can I pay you a dollar to say that again so I can record it?" He palmed his cell and wiggled it at me, his good mood restored. "Mom will never believe a girl said that about me without being coerced."

"Except if you give me a dollar, that's bribery. Pretty sure that's the same thing as coercion."

"Hmm." He tapped the phone against his chin. "I could tickle you until you say it."

I took a cautious step out of range. "So now you've escalated to threats?"

"What are a few threats between friends?" He rushed me, scooped me up and dumped me over his shoulder like a sack of potatoes. His fingers proved they still remembered all my most ticklish spots. The crease at the bend of my knee, the spot where my neck met my shoulder. My ribs. Goddess, my ribs. "Am I a gentleman now?"

"No," I howled between bouts of laughter. "You're a holy terror."

"Hey, that's not nice." He smacked my butt, a stinging punishment. "Only my sister gets away with calling me HT." He clomped up the steps with me writhing on his shoulder, and Woolly—the traitor—dialed the porch light up to blinding in greeting. "Aww shucks, Woolly. I missed you too." And because he was an unrepentant flirt who couldn't help himself, even where houses were concerned, he tacked on, "Your foundation is looking mighty fine tonight."

The curtains in the front windows rustled in her version of tittering laughter.

"Woolly," I panted, breathless from laughter and the bite of his hard shoulder in my soft gut, "I could really use a little help here."

The front door swung open before we reached it so he could walk right in, potato sack and all.

Glowering up at the chandelier in the foyer as we passed beneath it, I growled, "That's not what I meant."

Once we hit the living room, he set me on my feet. "Get dressed."

Rubbing my stomach, I noticed he was dressed as casually as me. "Is this the dress code?"

"Nope." A smug grin curved his lips. "I have to go home and pretty up for you before we leave." A trace of his earlier caginess returned. "After Taz texted me about the missed lesson, I figured I should go pry you from Linus's clutches before I changed, in case things got messy."

The idea of things getting messy between Boaz and Linus was laughable. Boaz was a hunk of muscle trained for war, and he was a natural-born brawler. Then again, Linus had a wraith on his side. Maybe the match would be more even than I'd first thought.

Thinking of the wraith left me with the unhappy reminder that Linus would be given a blow-by-blow accounting of our evening thanks to Cletus.

"Shorts, dress, pants, skirt...?" I rolled my hand. "What's appropriate?"

"Wear whatever you want, whatever makes you comfortable." He backed out onto the porch. "I'll match our plans to your outfit."

Woolly closed the door behind him with a sigh from the nearest floor register.

"Okay, you've got a point. That was a dreamy thing to say." I just wished he hadn't had so much practice in saying them. It was hard to know how many of his lines were off the cuff—he really did have a silver tongue—and how many were taken from his well-worn play-book. "I hope he wasn't in the mood for steak and lobster."

After hours spent hunched over a table with a pen in my hand, I wasn't in the mood to be restricted again. Not in how I dressed or in how I ate. Casual suited me just fine. I did give a nod to the fact it was a datelike thing by wearing a swishy navy sundress with moons and stars embroidered on the hem. I kept my shoes flat and my hair down, and I skipped the makeup since I would make a hot mess of it without professional help.

Boaz took longer with his primping than any woman I had ever known, so I decided to wait for him on the porch to enjoy the cool night air. I plopped down on the slatted bench seat and kicked off the planks, setting the chains jangling until they fell in sync. I tipped my head back at the same time I caught movement out of the corner of my eye.

Turning my head, I spotted Linus strolling across the lawn, heading for the curb like he had a ride to catch. The urge to apologize for Boaz pushed me upright, and I smoothed a hand down my dress, pressing all the wrinkles flat. By the time I looked up with a *hello* in my throat, he was gone.

SEVEN

A shrill whistle let me know my date had arrived. Considering motorcycles didn't have horns, I figured this was the equivalent of Boaz parking outside my house and honking. I wasn't sure if I ought to be offended I didn't rate a pickup at the door or relieved that he really was treating this like any of a thousand other dates he'd been on. As much as I didn't want to be lumped in with all the others, there was a certain thrill in finally living what I had fantasized about for half my life.

I took the path leading toward the garage and stumbled at the sight of Boaz. He always had cleaned up nice. His tan cargo pants had been pressed, and his mossy green button-down shirt brought out the warmth of his eyes. With his milk-chocolate irises striated with lighter bands, they always reminded me of swirled caramel. As appealing as he was with his lips quirked up in one half of a knee-melting grin, it was what squirmed in his arms that held me transfixed.

"Kittens?" I couldn't stop myself from rushing over or snatching the miniature orange tabby crawling up his shoulder. "Where did you find them?"

"They swarmed me when I opened the garage." His gaze raked down me, and he moistened his lips. "You look good enough to eat."

"Thank you, Mr. Big Bad." I curtseyed. "Is this the part where you ask if my grandmother is home?"

"Sorry I didn't pick you up at the door. I meant to but..." He lifted his hands, a kitten in each. "I wasn't sure what to do with all this."

A flutter behind my breastbone announced his lumping me in with past girls was forgiven and forgotten, as if that had ever been in question.

"Have you seen the momma cat?" I peered around him into the garage where Jolene and Willie stood together companionably in chromed silence. "We should probably leave the kittens how you found them."

In this neighborhood, with so many Society residents sprinkled throughout, there was always the possibility the momma cat was someone's familiar. If that was the case, the kittens were hereditary familiars and would mature into more powerful foci than their parents. Most likely, the fuzzballs were slated for kids waiting to begin the bonding process.

All High Society darlings were raised alongside their animals. All budding practitioners were expected to bond with their familiar, the true first test of their potential. That connection, once cemented, used a trickle of the child's life force to slow the animal's aging process.

Keet and I hadn't bonded before he died. There hadn't been time.

The upside of having a psychopomp was while other necromancers worried their familiars might die from accidents as mundane as getting backed over in the driveway, mine was already dead. Undead. Whatever. I would never have to part with him as long as I was around to revive him.

"There's a box in the back." Boaz aimed a kitten's pink nose in that direction when he lifted his arm. "Can you get it down? We'll dump the little guys in there then make our escape."

"It depends." I handed him the kitten back and sidled between the bikes to the back wall. "What's in there? Knowing my luck, it'll be your weights left over from high school. Or your football gear. Or your baseball gear. Or your soccer gear. Or—"

"I get it," he grumbled. "I took over your garage."

Among other things. Boaz had been taking over small corners of my life for as long as I could remember.

"I let you do it." I grasped the box and gave it an experimental wiggle. "I could have stopped you if I didn't want your junk all over the place."

A curious note spiked his tone. "Why didn't you?"

I liked having a part of him with me. I liked sneaking out here smelling jerseys that carried his scent, sleeping in them when I could get away with it. I liked knowing he would have to come back, if not to see me, then to dig through his stuff.

"Here goes nothing." I pointedly ignored the question. "Oh, hey. This isn't so bad."

The box was large, but not so big the momma cat couldn't retrieve her babies. Nothing rattled inside, and it weighed much less than expected. It must be an empty waiting to be refilled.

Years ago, I found an outfit from his toddler days used to wipe up an oil spill. Another time I'd found his lion costume from an elementary school play used as an animal skin rug. And once, I found a onesie with his name embroidered on it used to coddle a greasy carburetor.

Odd bits of his life had a way of ending up here, part of my collection, making me the curator of his personal history. I was the world's foremost expert on Boaz Pritchard.

I set the box on the concrete and folded open the flaps. A worn sketchbook held together with rubber bands sat in the bottom. When I lifted it out, I saw there were more pieces of paper stuck to the back. The brand was familiar. Maud had used it. I did too. But we never let them degrade to this ragged state. She was meticulous about keeping her supplies in good repair, and I had learned to retire sketchbooks before they fell apart too.

Flipping it front to back, I spotted no name or signature to identify the owner.

"Have you seen this before?" I held it up in one hand while I carried the box to Boaz with the other. "It looks like one of ours. Maybe Maud left it out here."

It wasn't beyond the realm of possibilities that it could be from when I was younger, something I doodled in for practice. She kept my art, my stories, my scribbles, all locked away in her library. I had blamed sentimentality, but I was beginning to grasp the truth, thanks to Linus.

"Yeah." He nuzzled a kitten and avoided eye contact. "I know who it belongs to."

This couldn't be good news, and I had a sinking feeling I could guess the owner.

"I found Linus up that old oak in our backyard once. He was staring in your window." He toyed with the jellybean pads on one fluffy paw. "I yanked him down so fast he saw stars."

"You're telling me *Linus* climbed a tree?" Try as I might, I couldn't picture him communing with nature by choice. Or committing willful acts of athleticism. "How do you know he was looking in my window?"

"He was sketching you," Boaz answered flatly. "He didn't even try to defend himself."

"*Me?*" There must be more to the story, like a homework assignment or maybe a gift he'd been working on for Maud.

"I was so pissed I stole his sketchbook. I would have burned it, but his mother being who she was, I figured it was smarter holding on to it until she made me give it back." His lip curled at the yellowed papers. "He never demanded to know what I did with it, and he never asked for it back. His mother never called either. I must have forgotten about it and tossed it in with some of my junk at some point."

Well, that explained why the temperature dropped around Linus when Boaz was in the same room.

"Why didn't you tell Maud? Or me?"

"I'm not a snitch." He glanced up, a piece of white fur stuck to his lip, offended. "Besides, I handled it."

"I have to give this back to him." I ruffled the pages with my thumb. "Maybe it will smooth things over between you two."

"I don't lose sleep over what I did," he told the tuxedo kitten determined to use him as a scratching post. "He violated your privacy, so I returned the favor."

Yep, here was the root of their mutual animosity laid bare and left to fester.

"All the same." I heaved a sigh. "It's the right thing to do." I dropped the now-empty box at his feet. "Can you manage the kittens while I put this somewhere safe?"

"Sure thing." He was already tucking each furry body in gently. "Cats love me."

"Mmm-hmm." That's why he looked like he'd lost a fight with a very small demon.

Leaving Boaz to his delusions, I waffled on where to stash my contraband. I considered the carriage house, but Linus wasn't home, and letting myself in while he was gone felt like a further invasion of his privacy. I could leave it leaned against the front door, but I worried dew might damage the fragile papers. After such a long separation, I expected he would be eager to see his drawings again.

When no bright ideas winked into existence above my head, I returned to Woolly. The sketchbook had been missing from his collection for this long. Surely Linus could wait a few more hours for a reunion. The porch light flickered in question, and I patted the doorframe on my way into the living room.

"We found an old sketchbook of Linus's out in the garage. I'm just putting it here until I get back." I placed it on the coffee table, then blew the foyer chandelier a kiss. "Don't wait up."

The crystals tinkled with amusement that put a smile on my face too.

I was determined not to let anything ruin this evening. Not ex-girlfriends. Not kittens. And not old grudges.

By the time I had checked the wards one last time, a nervous habit, and strolled back down the walkway, Boaz sat astride Willie with a helmet dangling from his fingertips. He wore a new leather jacket, this one a matte black that absorbed the moonlight, and I took a minute to zip up my own battered hand-me-down before I accepted the helmet, settled it on my head, and mounted behind him. His wide palm settled on my bare thigh, and a breath shuddered from my lungs.

"You're living dangerously," he murmured. "I like it."

I popped his hand, earning a husky laugh that thrilled, and kept to myself that I'd learned a long time ago I could ride bikes in skirts or dresses all I wanted as long as I wore spandex shorts underneath.

"Arms around me, Squirt." He still hadn't moved his hand. "Don't want you falling off."

He didn't have to ask me twice.

I linked my fingers at his navel then rested the side of my helmet against his back. I held on tight, a grin stretching my cheeks as Willie roared to life between my thighs. The vibrations rattled my fillings when he revved the engine, and a laugh burst out of me. He glanced back, his eyes warm, and I did my best to burrow so deep he would never be rid of me.

This much, at least, hadn't changed. He'd always loved taking me on rides, and I'd always loved going. That's why, financial reasons aside, I had glommed onto Jolene at the first opportunity. Riding her was like wrapping myself in the thickest, warmest blanket of *it's gonna be all right* I could imagine.

Miles flew past in a gust of cool, spring air before Boaz coasted to a stop in front of one of the older bars in the area. Smart man, wooing me with history. This place was steeped in paranormal energy, and the air crackled with possibility.

The Black Hart and its grim past was, on occasion, part of the walking tour at Haint Misbehavin'. As the story goes, the original owner bricked his mistress up in the basement when she tried to leave him. On clear nights after the bar closed, tourists and locals alike swore they heard his wails of grief at having killed the love of his life.

A flicker of doubt crossed his features. "Does this work for you?"

"It's perfect." I smoothed my dress and finger-combed my hair. "They have the second-best burgers in town."

Boaz slid his palm across mine and meshed our fingers. A zing of excitement raced up my arm, but the frantic thudding in my chest eased once I reminded myself we'd held hands a million times for a million different reasons.

Never because he took you out on a date, a gleeful corner of my mind reminded me.

He chose a booth in the back and let me in before capping off the end of the bench with his massive body and throwing his arm around me. "What looks good tonight?"

"I like their loaded potato skins and their big bacon burger." I plucked the lone menu from the salt and pepper stand and pushed it over to him. "It's got jalapeño aioli, bacon, buffalo sauce, bacon, and a honey chipotle sauce along with the usual suspects. And bacon."

"Good call." He was looking at me, heat in his eyes, when he said, "I like spicy."

I dug my elbow in the soft spot above his hipbone, but he remained unrepentant. Being with him was as easy as breathing. Except when I wanted to strangle him. Then it was as easy as him *not* breathing.

Being on the receiving end of his charm almost made me feel sorry for anyone who got hit full force without any preparation. No wonder women tripped over themselves to get where I sat tonight.

"Evening, folks." A red-haired waitress who looked vaguely familiar bumped a hip against our table. "Hey, Boaz. I didn't know you were back in town."

"Hi, Rachel." He didn't glance up from the menu. "Just here for the night."

The muscles in my spine hardened into blocks of wood in my effort to remain unnoticed.

"I can make it a good one," she purred. "You and me always have fun."

This time he was the one transformed, his fingers becoming iron spikes where they dug into my shoulder. As though he sensed my wish to vanish under the table and refused to let me slip through his fingers.

"I'm here on a date," he said, polite as you please. "You remember Grier?"

Rachel's gaze flicked to me. "Oh. Yeah. Hi." She made a vague gesture. "Sorry about..."

"No problem." I always wore a bulletproof vest while in public with him.

"I'm so used to seeing you guys together—not *together*, together—I didn't think." She straightened and rearranged her expression along more professional lines. "You've never dated Grier, so I assumed this was a friend thing."

Since Boaz was in no mood to toss her a life preserver, I cleared my throat. "I'm ready to order."

Rachel wrote as fast as I talked, like her life depended on the cook leaving off the onion slivers. "Boaz?"

"I'd like the lady to order for me." He smoldered at me. "She knows my tastes better than anyone."

Heat scalded my cheeks, and Rachel wasn't faring much better. I doubled my order, and both of us girls slumped with relief as she scurried toward the safety of the kitchen.

"That was rude." Though I had secretly enjoyed him sticking up for my dateability.

"She was rude to make assumptions." He rubbed his forehead with his right hand. "She was right to think you'd never date me, though. You're a smart girl, a good girl."

"I spent five years in prison, Boaz. Whatever I used to be, whoever that girl was, she's not the woman I am now." I was a phoenix thrashing in the ashes of my old life, aching to rise again, to soar one last time, but the cycle exhausted me. "You've got a lot of history in this town, but you were right when you said I know you better than anyone else. It's all old news. I won't hold it against you."

"Then I'll hold it against me for you." Frustration ignited a spark in his eyes. "Hindsight is blinding me right now, Grier. I've been a damn fool."

"Hey, don't be so hard on yourself. You were my hero." Humiliating as that was to admit, it was nothing he didn't already know. "My knight on shining motorcycle."

A faint blossom of pink highlighted his cheekbones, making him adorable in his embarrassment.

"Hindsight is clearer for me too," I admitted. "You were larger than life, you still are. Everyone loved you. Teachers. Students. Old ladies at the supermarket. All the girls wanted to have you, all the guys wanted to be you. Mix in a few other corny one-liners, and you've got how I saw you."

Uncertainty had loosened his hold on me. "You never wanted to tame the bad boy?"

"Not hardly." I laughed at the idea such a thing was possible. "I knew better."

"Then what was the appeal?" Honest curiosity overshadowed any of his lingering hurt.

"I think..." I worried my bottom lip for a minute before admitting, "I wanted to be you."

"*Be* me," he mused. "Not *with* me."

"A little of both?" There had never been a clear line. Boaz was want, want was Boaz. I hadn't put much thought into untangling the mesh of our lives until after he kissed me, until after I grasped how much I stood to lose if a romance between us soured. "Is it wrong to want to be the hero of your own story *and* want to corrupt the boy next door?"

A slow smile overtook his face. "You wanted to corrupt me?"

I expected him to point out I was in no position to corrupt anyone, let alone him, especially not him, but he settled back in the booth with a happy smile, fragile in its hope.

"You can't be debauched in *all* ways." When he didn't answer, I swung startled eyes toward him. "Can you?"

He was spared from answering me when our drinks arrived courtesy of a waitress who was not Rachel. She ignored us almost as hard as we ignored her. Almost, because she still had to serve us to earn a tip.

"Did you play hooky for me?" Boaz stabbed straws into our drinks. "This isn't your usual night off."

"Deflate your ego. It's smooshing me against the wall, and it's hard for me to breathe."

A wicked grin curved his lips. "Consider me deflated."

I doubt he'd ever been deflated a day in his life. And yeah, that sounded bad even in my head.

"There was an incident at work." I guided us back on topic. "A human girl was hurt in an altercation with a poltergeist, so the job site was shut down for the night."

His amusement faded around the edges. "Job site?"

Nodding, I sipped my sweet tea. "She was attacked aboard the *Cora Ann*."

"That old steamer?" A peculiar stillness infused him, and his voice came out hollow. "What does it have to do with being a Haint?"

Fiddlesticks. Apparently my bestie and I had both kept Boaz in the dark on my new job. Probably for the same reason. The girl-ending-up-hospitalized one. The one that guaranteed he would pop his cork and demand I stay home.

"Well..." The truth about how I had spent the previous week elbows-deep in research, how it resulted in a desperation for fresh air that led me to the *Cora Ann*, came tumbling out in a jumble. "And that's about it."

Boaz drew designs onto my skin with his fingertips while he digested all I'd told him.

"You're extra clingy tonight," I added in summation. "I'm not complaining, but I am curious."

He stopped doodling on my arm. "I missed you."

"I missed you too, but you don't see me squeezing you in a death grip with my biceps of steel."

"Squirt, you don't have biceps of steel." He howled when I twisted his nipple. "Okay, okay. You win. What is it with you and my nipples? What have they ever done to you?" When I kept staring, waiting for a response, he caved. "I hate leaving while you're so vulnerable. I hate knowing you're here without protection." He laughed, seemingly at himself. "No, that's not true. Without *my* protection."

As a swoon preventative, I reminded myself, "Taz warned me you tell everyone my panty size."

"I have never once told anyone your panty size." His expression matched every kid who had ever dropped their lollipop. "I've never gotten you out of them, so it's not like I've got firsthand knowledge."

"Are you pouting?" I thumbed his lower lip, right over the indent from his scar. "Again?"

"Depends." He pushed it out farther. "Is it working? Do you pity me enough to wiggle out of your panties and pass them to me under the table?"

A flush rode my cheeks. I couldn't believe for a split second I considered the logistics of getting them off without sacrificing my stretchy shorts. "Has that line ever worked for you?"

"Yes." A cocky grin lit up his features. "I don't recycle ones that aren't effective."

I shouldn't have asked if I didn't want the answer. "You're totally unrepentant, aren't you?"

"I am who I am." He delivered the line with a wink, but it sank to the bottom of my stomach. His eyes didn't sparkle, his skin didn't fold into deep creases. That wink was a lie. "If I started being sorry for everything I've ever done, I wouldn't have time to stay current on my favorite shows or to chase after girls who really ought to know better than to come out alone at night with a boy like me."

Since Boaz had kicked that conversational door wide open, I walked right through it. "How many girls are you chasing these days?"

"Just the one." His other hand found my thigh and rested there, on top of my skirt, not pressing for more, just allowing me to get used to its weight. "She's fast, though. I haven't managed to catch her yet."

The heat from his palm spread up my leg and made me squirm. "Maybe invest in running shoes?"

"Nah. This is the best part." He returned his hand to the table before I got my wriggling under control. As much as I wanted to play it cool, I had never let a man touch me that way, and it showed. "I like working for it. I want to earn it. A woman shouldn't give herself away for free."

"And what happens after you've had her?" Like I needed him to spell it out when I already knew.

He turned his head and locked gazes with me, his expression troubled. "I'll want more."

"How can you be sure?"

"I haven't been with anyone since the night you assaulted me in Mom's garden. I haven't looked at another woman, I haven't touched another woman, and I haven't thought about another woman." The furrow in his brow deepened. "This thing between us has already lasted longer than any relationship I've ever had. Whatever this is, I want more."

Pleasure unfurled low in my stomach, and I allowed myself a moment to just be happy he wanted me at all. I still wasn't convinced this was a line worth crossing between us, the idea of losing him as a friend terrified me, but I couldn't stop myself from toeing the edge of dangerous possibility.

EIGHT

Dinner was nice, the kind of effortless good time that has a girl thinking second-date thoughts before the first one is even finished. Boaz proved he was my soul mate, at least in one regard, by ordering a square of Mississippi mud cake off the menu served with homemade vanilla ice cream and whipped cream. That wasn't the proof, though. No, that came when the waitress asked if we needed two spoons, and he told her he valued his life too much to poach from me.

I appreciated guys who respected my capacity for chocolate intake without flinching.

Dessert was, of course, the best part of the meal. And not only because I played nice and shared my cake with him. Or because he let me feed him and made appreciative noises in the back of his throat I'd probably dream about come dawn. There was an undefinable quality in Boaz that made you feel like if he wanted you, if he wanted to be with you, then you must be special too. That his seal of approval, once stamped on you, made you glow so bright others couldn't help but squint.

"I owe you a dance." Boaz licked the spoon clean then stuck it to the end of his nose where it hung while he waggled his eyebrows at me. "There's a new club on River Street. Interested?" He puckered up like an asphyxiating guppy and leaned close. "Or do you want to cut to the making-out part?"

"Knock it off." Shoving him back, I took the spoon and set it on the table. "Goober."

"I'll have you know I'm at my peak sexiness after dessert, when your body can't differentiate between the sugar rush and *me*."

I covered a snort with the back of my hand. "Oh, I can tell the difference."

I had meant the comment to be flip, but it came out too soft, and he heard the ache.

His voice gentled, probing for open wounds. "How?"

"The sugar rush fades," I answered honestly.

"I'm going to kiss you now." His left arm slid behind my shoulders, and he hauled me up against his side while his right hand cupped my cheek. "Trust me?"

All I could do was nod and twine my fingers in the fabric of his shirt to hold on for the ride.

This was actually happening. My first real kiss. With the boy of my dreams.

His lips brushed mine, a gentle pressure that had me chasing his mouth for more of the delicious taste of him—chocolate and man with a hint of trouble. He let me pursue him, a chuckle in his throat, until I retreated on a frustrated sigh.

I'd spent a lifetime chasing him. It was past time he returned the favor.

"Get back here." With a growl in his throat, he stalked me, pressing me against the wall at my back, unwilling to break contact. The hand on my cheek roved down my neck, my shoulder, my arm and eased under the table where it palmed my hip and rolled me against him. A heartbeat later, he cursed into my mouth and yanked back his hand. "Damn rules."

I laughed at his frustration, and he thrust his tongue between my lips to tangle with mine. He surrounded me—his scent, his taste, his warmth—and my head spun faster than a merry-go-round. I drank in his groan when I nipped his bottom lip, and grinned when he murmured my name in a guttural tone I had never heard from him. That I wished no one had but me.

"The owner asked me to toss some ice water on you," our waitress said blandly. "Can you two behave or do I need to go back and grab my pitcher?"

Ignoring her, he kissed me once more, twice, before resting his forehead against mine. "Why haven't we done this before?"

The answers were all too grim for a moment like this, so I kept thoughts of heartbreak, of Atramentous, of Volkov, locked away so as not to tarnish this perfect memory.

"It wasn't a bad first kiss." I patted his cheek, not about to stroke his ego, then turned to the waitress. "We can behave—"

Boaz threaded the fingers of his left hand through my hair and hauled my lips crashing back to his while his right stroked my hip, tracing the top edge of my panties through the fabric of my dress. Penned between him and the wall, a trap I did not mind falling into at all, I forgot how to breathe.

At least until ice-cold liquid splashed us in the face, and I gasped against the water plugging my nose.

"Worth it." The devil was in his smile, and this time he didn't apologize for breaking the rules. He looked like he was debating when he could do this all over again and wondering if I'd let him. "You were saying?"

"I was saying—" *What had I been saying?*

"That was all the warning you get." The waitress hooked a thumb over her shoulder, indicating a wrinkled gentleman gazing at us with jolly eyes and a sly grin. "I do what the boss says, and he says it's time you got a room, Boaz Pritchard."

The use of his full name snagged his attention, and he eyed the woman. "Do I know you?"

"You knew my little sister for about ten minutes." Her gaze swept down him, clearly not impressed. "If that." Her smile turned mean. "Though you might remember me from the baseball bat I took to your bike when I found you passed out on top of her in the kitchen, we haven't been formally introduced."

"Dana Higgins," he said without missing a beat, and I could tell the woman was stunned he remembered his exes' names at all. "We met our freshman year."

"Sweetheart," she sighed in my direction, determined not to award him points for having that much decency. "He's only going to break your heart."

"Oh, he already has," I assured her. "Smashed it, really." He recoiled so hard from me, he bumped his head on the back of the booth. I reached up to rub away the sting, enjoying the bristly feel of his scalp against my palm before I ruffled the longer strands on top. "But you know what? He's worth it." I held her gaze. "I bet your sister said the same thing."

All the girls who contracted Boazitis understood it was a lifelong condition with no cure. They might yell and cuss and rail at him, they might even hate him for not loving them back, but none of that mattered in the end. Boaz had only to crook his finger, and they would all come running back for seconds. I was terrified, having had my first real taste, that I would be the same.

"She never had a lick of sense." The woman slapped our ticket down on the table. "Guess you don't either."

I used a few napkins to blot my face dry. "Guess not."

Boaz paid, arguing that since he had asked me out, it was his job to cover the tab. I left the tip, and I was generous. It took guts to stand up for your sister, let alone for a total stranger you worried might be in over her head. Plus, knowing Boaz, he probably deserved the ice water.

The owner patted Boaz on the shoulder when we passed him on our way to the door. "Come back any time, son." He hooted. "I haven't seen Lisa that riled up in years. Just call ahead so I can pass out ponchos to the customers in advance. We'll charge extra for folks who sit in the splash zone."

"Looks like you made a new friend." I chuckled under my breath. "I expected him to start yelling for an encore at any moment."

Boaz kept walking, making his way toward Willie. "Yeah."

"Hey." I grabbed his arm. "You okay?"

"What happened in there doesn't bother you?" His stricken expression made me wonder what distressed him most. That the waitress had called him out or that I'd had a front-row seat. "I deserve what I got. I'm not contesting that. But you didn't."

"It was only water. Our clothes will dry." I raked my fingers through my damp hair. The humidity was having a field day with my not-exactly-curls. "Besides, how many girls can say their first kiss was so steamy a concerned bystander doused them with ice water?"

Boaz looked torn between his trademark cocky smile and a vulnerability that pierced my heart like a crooked arrow. "You're not upset?"

"Why would I be?" I took his hand and led him to Willie. "I know you, Boaz. The good, the bad, the ugly."

He didn't say another word, just handed me my helmet and put on his.

I climbed on behind him, certain this would be the end of our night, but he surprised me by aiming for River Street. I was still deciding if dancing would restore his mood when the fine hairs lifted down my arms. I tipped back my head, following a hunch, and spotted Cletus fluttering above me.

Oddly reassured, I held Boaz tighter and let the night wash over me until he found us a parking spot.

Music poured out into the street, soft and inviting, but we didn't head toward the club.

The pensive edge of his mood hadn't lifted, but he put on a decent act. "May I have this dance?"

"Yes, you may." I accepted the hand he offered and let him lead me into a waltz that fit the bluesy music about as well as our soggy attire would fly in a ballroom. I stumbled once or twice, well out of practice, but his steps were sure, and he made a fine partner. "I hope you didn't need that toe."

"Technically, there are no toes on that foot. Squish all you want."

That somehow made me feel worse that my two left feet had decided to tag team his prosthetic foot.

"How are you still so good at this?" I asked through a spin that ended with my back trapped against his chest. "I'm as rusty as barn nails."

Not much use for gliding waltzes in Atramentous. Death was the only partner worth dancing with there.

Maud would be appalled to learn I had let all those years of lessons fester, but I had always hated balls. I had only ever gone so I could bail her out when the sycophants made her tired. But goddess, all the attention had been miserable.

As much as I picked on Boaz, we were warped mirrors of each other, always had been. All High Society boys had wanted to date me, and all High Society girls had wanted to befriend me. Not me, of course, but Maud's ward. The daughter of her heart. The Woolworth heiress.

The Marchands were a fine High Society family, but I was no longer a Marchand. I was a Woolworth.

"Make no apologies for surviving."

Maud had repeated that refrain the way some guardians told their wards bedtime stories. These days, in light of all I'd learned, I wondered what she'd really meant. There was a double meaning there, I was sure of it.

"I practiced with Amelie all morning." A hint of smugness resurfaced. "I had to pay her thirty dollars, but it was worth it to impress you."

"Thirty dollars?" I tsked. "That's highway robbery."

"Hey, I negotiated her down from fifty. I would have paid a hundred."

"How very gallant of you." Amelie must be rubbing her greedy little hands together with glee.

"Not really." He whirled me away from him, until both our arms were fully extended, then stepped back into my space with purpose before we glided together again. "I owed her a hundred bucks for picking up some groceries for me the last time I was home. I forgot to pay her back, so it's her money she's bargaining with either way."

I laughed out loud, and the bright sound lightened his expression. "You really are a terror. I'm not sure how holy you are, though."

"You've called me that twice tonight." This time when he trapped me against him, my back to his front, there was no wiggle room. The song had ended, and so had our dance. "Keep name-calling, and I'm going to think you don't like me."

"I like you just fine." I reached up to ruffle his short hair into careless spikes. "Most of the time."

His snort gusted warm air across my nape. "Do you carry a needle in your pocket to deflate the egos of all your dates, or am I special?"

"This was my first real date." I kept an eye out for Cletus, a black smudge darker than the surrounding gloom, but I didn't spot him again. "I came prepared for anything."

"I don't deserve so many of your firsts. You shouldn't have saved yourself for me," he murmured against my neck. "How can I live up to your expectations?"

"Who says I was saving myself for you?" Living in solitary confinement made romance a tad difficult.

"I'm not good at slow, Grier, and I suck at being gentle." He plucked at my ear with his teeth. "You ought to kick me in the junk and run as far and as fast as you can from me."

"I'll reserve the right to junk-kick you." I angled my head to the other side, inviting equal attention. "How about that?"

"Grier."

"Hmm?"

"Don't move." Boaz unspooled me from his arms, tucking me behind his broad back.

"What's wrong?" I fisted his shirt, imagining vampires bleeding from the shadows. I *knew* it had been too quiet. It was almost a relief that they had finally acted. Now maybe we could get some answers. "What do you see?"

"A wraith," he growled.

"Oh, he's mine." I rested my forehead against his back until my pulse slowed. "Come say hi, Cletus."

The wraith descended in a swirl of ethereal robes that leaked inky darkness into the surrounding night.

"Cletus?" Boaz halved his scowl between us when I stepped around him. "What do you mean it's yours?"

Unlike with Amelie, I had to tell him the truth. The whole truth. He had been in the Grande Dame's chambers at the Lyceum with me. He knew Linus had dispatched his wraith to Woolly and what it had done there.

"He's my bodyguard." That sounded more adult than babysitter, and the last thing I wanted was Boaz jockeying for the title. "He protects me whenever I leave the house."

"This is Linus's pet." It wasn't a question.

"Yes." I flicked my hands at Cletus, and he fluttered away. "Linus gave him orders to guard me. He'll raise the alarm if he can't handle a situation on his own."

"By raise the alarm, you mean zip back to his master's side."

"Well, he is the only one who can understand the wraith, so yes."

"Why didn't you tell me?" He kept an eye on the spot where Cletus had been seconds ago.

"To avoid this?" I would have thought that was obvious. "I was going to tell you, but I didn't want to do it tonight."

Wraiths and romance didn't exactly go hand in hand.

"He'll tell Linus everything we said and did, everywhere we went." His fingers twitched like he wanted to scoop them through the air and sift Cletus from the night. "Doesn't that bother you?"

"I don't want a wraith or anyone else to shadow me, but Cletus is less intrusive than a sentinel would be. Even an Elite. As much as I want to pretend nothing has changed, we both know that's not true. There are powerful people with a marked interest in me." I placed my palm over his spine. "I'm trying to be smart about this, but I don't want to be under house arrest for the rest of my life, and I won't be able to defend myself for a while yet. This is a good compromise." I scratched his back with my nails until his shoulders relaxed a fraction. "I want to be as free as I can be, for as long as I can be."

"There's got to be another way," he murmured to himself.

"Do you want to go for a walk before we head home?" The music had ended, and I wasn't in the mood for dancing, not while calculation gleamed in his eyes. "We could buy churros from Esteban."

"Churros?" He blinked a couple of times, and his focus returned to me in a snap. "You've got room for more sweets?" He reached down and lifted the hem of my dress a fraction of an inch, just enough to make me gasp and dance out of range. "Where do you hide it all?"

"Linus says I..." I clamped down on my tongue, but it was too late.

The fabric slid from his fingers, along with his mischievous grin. "What does Linus say?"

"That I've lost a lot of weight," I answered softly. "That I need calories."

He grunted once and extended his arm. "For once, we're in agreement."

We set out for my favorite booth in River Street Market Place, hand in hand, and soon I was leading the charge toward the scents of fried dough and sugar.

Esteban loomed over his fryer when we stepped through the canvas flaps acting as his doorway, and his smile grew bigger than my head, his teeth as bright white as the wispy hairs floating above his scalp. Everything about Esteban was supersized. When he abandoned his station to hug one of his best customers, I couldn't shake the feeling of a redwood tree bending to greet me. His arms were like trunks all on their own, and I disappeared into the forest of chest hairs peeking from his V-neck shirt.

"*Bomboncita*," he boomed in my ear. "I haven't seen you in weeks." He held me away from him and pinched my arm. "What happened? You didn't juice cleanse, did you?"

"I wasn't well" was the most diplomatic response. "I've come for your help in regaining my curves."

"That I can do." He startled when he noticed Boaz standing behind me. "Are you with my little candy?"

Huh. I'd always wondered what *bomboncita* meant, but I'd never asked because it sounded delicious—like a bonbon—and I didn't want to be proven wrong.

"I am." Boaz shook hands with the giant. "We'll take two of all her favorites."

Esteban slapped Boaz on the back hard enough to wind him. "I like this guy."

"Me too." I patted him on the shoulder. "This is Boaz. He's Amelie's big brother."

"How is *nena*?" He returned to his post and rescued newborn churros from their sizzling oil bath. "She never visits anymore."

"School and work keep her busy." I would have to share some of this bounty with her when I got home. "I'll tell her you asked after her."

"Do that." He took a thick churro in hand and started squeezing it full of whipped filling. "Give me a quarter of an hour, and I'll have your order ready."

"We'll go for a walk," I told him. "To get out of your hair."

"Or perhaps to sink your fingers through his?" Esteban winked at me. "I heard the bike, but helmet hair flattens, not spikes. Your friend here looks electrified."

"We'll just be over..." Pointing toward the street, I cleared my throat and inched out the flaps, Boaz chuckling on my heels.

"The *Cora Ann* docks near here," he mentioned after we'd passed a few darkened shops, all of them run by humans and closed long before midnight. "Is that how you and Esteban struck up a friendship?"

The high from inhaling so much airborne sugar must have gone to his head. The timeline didn't fit, and he should have noticed, but he was distracted again.

"I only worked one day on the *Cora Ann*. Esteban's had his shop here for years. Maud used to dump me on his doorstep with a couple of twenties when she had business in one of the specialty occult shops."

While he lacked enough necromantic talent to rub between his fingers, he was pure magic in the kitchen. Personally, I embraced his chosen vocation. There were plenty of necromancers, but not nearly enough churro stands in Savannah.

"Hmm."

Curiosity led us to where the steamboats loomed high over our heads. I spotted the *Cora Ann*, half-expecting yellow crime scene tape to barricade her gangway, but the quiet boat was no more or less spooky than her two sisters.

A cool brush of fabric against my arm had me turning to find Cletus hovering at my elbow. "What's up?"

The wraith extended its arm, pointing toward the second story.

"That thing's talking to you?" Boaz recoiled at the notion. "Or is Linus speaking through it?"

"Fully bonded wraiths can only do as their master bids them," I repeated what I had been told. Using that logic, Cletus must be channeling Linus, and Linus must have a message or a task for me. "Guess his master must be bidding him."

"What does he want?" Boaz scanned the darkened windows on the upper deck. "That's where the dining room is, right? Where your coworker was attacked?"

"I have no idea. I suck at charades." I tried reasoning with Cletus. "What is it you want me to see?"

His arm remained outstretched, steady, but I saw nothing to justify his marked interest.

"Time's almost up," Boaz announced. "We need to start back toward Esteban's."

"Sorry, fella." I made one last attempt to spot what Cletus meant to show me. "We'll have to work on our sign language for next time."

We backtracked to pick up my second round of desserts, but Cletus lingered at the docks, drifting back and forth, rocking between the boat and me, as though stuck with two objectives he lacked the faculties to prioritize.

A shiver rippled down my arms. Sentience was measured in a lot of ways, but the ability to reason, to appear torn in his loyalties, made me wonder if Linus had told me the whole truth about Cletus or only what would help me sleep easier during the day.

The wraith caught up about the time we entered Esteban's stall and claimed our churro order. Esteban had prepared two filled with rich caramel, two filled with hazelnut-chocolate cream, and two more regular orders that came with an assortment of dipping sauces, including my favorite couverture milk chocolate.

To Boaz's amazement, I managed to polish off one of the caramel-filled churros on the way back to Willie. The rest I tucked safely in their glassine paper bag, which I cradled against my chest, and zipped them up in my jacket. The fit was tighter than usual, and I had to forgo breathing to prevent smooshing them flat, but it would be worth it if I wanted a late-day snack.

The trip home took no time at all, and Cletus stuck close to me the whole way. We parked Willie at the mouth of the garage, and I strained my ears for the mewing sounds of antsy kittens but heard nothing. Either they hadn't realized they had company yet, or their mother had returned for them.

"I'll handle the fuzzballs." Boaz took my jacket and helmet, and he draped them over the seat. "Come on, Squirt." His fingertips brushed the small of my back. "Let me walk you to your door and pretend I have manners."

Woolly glowed in welcome, the electric buzz of her excitement giving me warm fuzzies.

"I had a good time tonight." He attempted to resuscitate his flattened hair. "I'd ask you out again tomorrow, but I'm leaving around noon."

You'll be back in a week. The words sounded too desperate to speak, even in my own head. I turned on my heel, having already paid him his goodnight kiss plus interest, and palmed the doorknob. Better to cut my losses now than remain trapped in this awkward lull where plans for a second date ought to fit.

"I had fun too," I tossed over my shoulder. "Night, Boaz."

Strong arms slid around my waist and linked over my left hipbone. He gathered me against him, my back flush with his front, and exhaled like he couldn't breathe without that contact. He leaned down until his lips brushed my ear. "Would you like to go out again when I come home?"

"I don't know." I suppressed a giddy thrill. "I'll have to check my schedule."

He bit my throat, a stinging reprimand. "Your social calendar is filling up that fast?"

"Amelie did make me promise to go out with her once a week. And Marit—the woman who was injured aboard the *Cora Ann*— invited me out for drinks. She was bummed when you called. She wants a single friend to club with, and now she thinks I'm unavailable."

His breath skated across my carotid. "Are you?"

"Am I what?" Pure cane sugar flowed through my voice.

"Unavailable," he growled.

"Do you want me to be?" I craned my neck around to see him better. "If I'm unavailable, where does that leave you?"

Blowing out a sigh, he rested his forehead on my shoulder. "You're my punishment for every wrong thing I've ever done."

"You say the sweetest things. Why Hallmark hasn't scooped you up yet, I'll never know."

"Grier." Head down, eyes hidden, he let himself be vulnerable. "You didn't ask me."

Expecting another cheeky response, I stood frozen, a riot of conflicting emotions pummeling my heart.

Ask *Boaz* to be faithful to me.

Ask Boaz to be faithful to *me*.

Ask Boaz to be *faithful*...

"I'm scared." And here I'd thought not much frightened me these days, that the worst had already happened. But as long as you loved someone, you had more to lose. "Want to paint a yellow stripe down my spine later?"

"Depends." He appeared to consider this. "Will you be naked? And can I supply my own brush?"

Grateful for the reprieve, I rolled my eyes. "Perv."

For once, he was slow to claim his title, and the silence that followed worried me.

"The truth is I'm scared too." His somber turn gave my heart freezer burn. "Dame Woolworth, and that is your title now, will make decisions going forward the old Grier could never imagine." When I started to argue, he shushed me. "You will make choices to preserve your line, your home, your legacy, Squirt, and you might not have a choice in the matter."

"That's not me." I spun in his arms to see him better. "That's not who I am."

But he had struck a chord, not with the mention of my line, of which I was the last, and not with the mention of my legacy, of which I wanted no part, but the mention of home. There wasn't much I wouldn't sacrifice to keep Woolly safe. Perhaps even myself.

"You do tend to spit on tradition." He closed his hand over mine where it had come to rest on his chest. "It's one of the things I admire about you."

The mention of his admiration set off another round of flutters I worked to suppress. "I wouldn't say spit so much as—"

"Oh, no." He chuckled. "You hock big, juicy loogies in the faces of all those High Society dames, just like Maud."

The comparison warmed me with an odd sort of pride. Maud had been her own woman, and that's what I wanted to be, though I had no doubt the Grande Dame would attempt to thwart my independence at every turn, seeing as how I owed it to her in the first place.

"You like that in a girlfriend?" I was only half serious. "Are you also a fan of grasshoppers and llamas?"

"Spitting doesn't bother me." His lips curled when he said it, and my cheeks exploded in a blast of mortification at what he implied. He lapped up my embarrassment for several beats before squeezing my hand where it rested over his heart. He looked on me like I was sand gliding through his fingers. "I'm all in, Grier." Gravel churned in his voice. "For as long as it lasts."

With neither of us ever having been in a serious relationship, I hadn't expected a romance with Boaz to be anything less than pistols at dawn, aimed at the heart, but his fatalistic outlook blew me away. The heiress I once was, the one well aware I might be called upon to marry for position or wealth or power, appreciated him giving me this time with him no strings attached. But the girl who had walked out of Atramentous with no title, no money, no future, wanted to give her word that she would be his for as long as he wanted her.

After all, the odds were good he would tire of me long before I was ready to give up on him. History was nothing if not repetitive. "Are you available?"

"For you?" His lips brushed the shell of my ear. "I'm wide open."

There was zero chance I could resist asking with that lead-in. "For everyone else?"

"There is no one else."

Eyes crushed shut against reality, I pressed my face into his chest and sank into him, willing myself to believe this was real.

I'm not dreaming, not dreaming, not dreaming. It was still so hard to be sure. *Please, never wake me.*

"I'll be off the grid for the next twenty-four hours." He tugged on my ear with his teeth. "Call me after?"

"Maybe." The sting ignited a path leading straight to my core. "Maybe not."

"Don't sass me, Squirt." His smile pressed into my skin. "I'm trying to be good here."

I let my right arm dangle at my side, and my fingertips traced the seam of his jeans. "Define *good*."

"Good means walking away while I still can, not throwing you over my shoulder and climbing up to your bedroom. Good means knowing my limits and refusing to let a little brat like you push me past them. Good means doing my job. Not holing up with you for as many days as we can go without needing groceries."

"Who needs groceries?" Not I. Not him either. "That's why takeout was invented."

"Please," he groaned against my throat. "Let me do this right for once in my life."

"Okay." I brought my arm up again, held him as tight as I could for as long as he let me, but his body was fighting his noble intentions. The hard length of him pressed against my soft stomach, and I eased back, more to allow him his honor than to preserve mine. "Be safe out there, Elite." I hooked my finger through his belt loop and gave him a hard tug. "Come home in one piece or else."

"I always come home, if not all in one piece." Turning his attention on Woolly, he smoothed his palm down the wooden siding beneath the glowing porch light. "Take care of our girl until I get back, okay?"

The bulb flared in bright agreement. She was, as ever, his humble and eager servant.

Boaz ambled over to the garage, and I forced myself to stop watching. I hated it would be a week before I saw him again. Already tonight felt spun from dreams instead of memories.

I lingered on the porch, the churros cooling in my arms, and reconsidered my plan to share the bounty with Amelie. Following

Boaz home, even if I technically beat him there, smacked of clingy girlfriend vibes, and it's not like Amelie would want me to gush about the moves her brother put on me. Remembering the sketchbook waiting on the coffee table, I decided to share the treats with a different sort of friend. Sugar in exchange for questions about Cletus.

I passed through the living room, scooped up the sketchbook and tucked it under my arm. Remembering the avowal, I picked that up too. I paused to rub Keet's earholes while he hung upside down with a single wing extended. "You're such a little weirdo."

He blinked one red eye at me then returned to his bat impersonation. Leaving him to practice his echo location, or whatever undead parakeets imagined while pretending to be something they were not, I exited the house through the back and entered the garden.

Cold fingers closed over my shoulder as my toes brushed grass.

"Hey, Cletus." I waited for him to unclamp me, but he held tight. "What's wrong now?"

Maybe the wraith really was broken.

"Let her go," a dark voice purred from the shadows. "I won't harm her. Promise."

Dread, cold and sharp, turned to icy perspiration down my spine. "Who are you?"

Cletus, who was not the trusting sort, released me then coalesced before me, an undulating shield of malevolence.

"Grier Woolworth." The man savored my name the way I had that first bite of caramel-filled dough.

"Who are you?" I demanded again over Cletus's shoulder. "Why are you here?"

"Call me Ambrose." His laughter serrated my ears, two bright stars honing their edges against one another. "My reasons and my purpose are my own. I do not answer to you, little goddess, and you would be wise to remember that."

Cletus bumped against me, ushering me back up the steps onto the safety of the porch. His bony fingers lengthened to vicious blades he clacked together in warning, but the man kept circling, a shark scenting bloodied waters.

For a single heartbeat, through the tatters of Cletus's cloak, I glimpsed him.

His skin was as pale as the first full moon in winter, his hair a ravaging flame around his head. His lips were so blue they were almost violet, his eyes full of shadows so deep no light had hope of penetrating them. Mist swirled around his ankles, black tendrils that resembled a wraith's tattered cloak. Having that emptiness gaze back with calm detachment turned my knees to water.

He looked more like the stories I'd heard of ethereal fae princes, as sharp as razors and as lovely as death, than anything born of this world. He twitched his berry lips, and my heart gave a painful lurch.

Behind me, Woolly rang her doorbell in panicked bursts. I glanced over my shoulder as she waved her door back and forth in a hurrying gesture. Gathering my courage around me, I turned from Ambrose and ran. I didn't stop until the wards snapped into place on my heels.

Hands shaking, I dialed Boaz and got dumped straight to voice-mail. I queued up Linus next. No answer. Amelie left me hanging too. I jogged up the stairs and peered out my bedroom window. Ambrose stood on the lawn, his hands shoved into his pockets, head thrown back to see me better, the Romeo to my Juliet. He was electric in the night, alive in the way dreams are before you wake.

And he was wearing a French blue dress shirt.

NINE

Today the nightmare wasn't a problem. I never fell asleep. I kept seeing Ambrose when I closed my eyes.

Smoothing my thumb over my phone's screen, I scrolled through its list of unanswered texts. Amelie had finally replied. Turned out, she had been taking an exam with her phone muted. She hadn't seen my message until after she left campus. Now that the immediate danger had passed, I wasn't in a rush to call her over knowing she would have to cross the yard—and Ambrose—to reach me. Boaz was within his twenty-four-hour incommunicado period, so no help there. And Linus...

Right now, I wasn't sure what to make of the shirt or the resemblance.

"Of all the gardens in all of the backyards in all of Savannah..." Ambrose walked into mine.

Woolly sighed her agreement through the floor registers.

First the ghosts and now an otherworldly trespasser. What the heck was going on in this town?

Slumped at my desk, I gave up on catching shut-eye and hauled out my grimoire. The modified pen Linus adapted for me tipped heavy in my hand, but I refined the foundation wards for Woolly, line by line, over and over, until my vision doubled.

Dusk took an eternity to arrive, but I was dressed and ready to confront Linus in record time.

After gathering the grimoire, the sketchbook, and the avowal, I made a beeline for the carriage house. The front door stood ajar, as usual, and delicious smells snaked out to tempt me across the threshold. Funny, I had never considered bacon as sinister before now. But I had also never seen a man so calm about his head being on fire while dressed in a shirt belonging to Linus either.

I padded inside, leaving damp-grass footprints, and searched for hints Ambrose had been here.

"I made pancakes to apologize for the bagels." Linus glanced over his shoulder and indicated I should sit. "We need to get started on the foundation before it's too hardened to accept sigils."

"I came by last night." I sank into my usual seat. "You weren't home."

"I had an errand to run, as I told you in my text." His movements lost their fluidity, a hitch in his otherwise calm façade, and the pancake he'd been flipping broke over the edge of the pan. "You didn't reply, so I assumed it was nothing pressing."

"Sorry to leave you on read." I picked at my fingernails, still unsure how to play this. I had never been on this side of the interrogation table before. "I got distracted by homework and forgot what I wanted in the first place."

A motion rolled through his shoulders that might have been a shrug or a flip of the spatula.

"I brought you a present." It came out too loud, too bright. "Two, actually." I placed the avowal on the table, but it was the sketchbook I held out to him. "Does this look familiar?"

"I haven't seen that in years." He killed the burner, set the pan aside, and carried a plate stacked high with pancakes to me. There he traded them for the sketchbook. Despite the heat from the stove, his fingers were frigid where they brushed my hand. "Where did you find it?"

"In the garage." I jogged my leg under the table. "I didn't look inside."

The rubber band was so brittle it snapped in two when he removed it. "How did you know it was mine?"

There was nothing for it but to be honest. "Boaz recognized it."

Absorbed by the slow turn of pages, he didn't speak for a long time. "Did he tell you why he took it?"

I toyed with my fork, unable to eat no matter how tempting the food smelled. "Yes."

"Here it is." He paused on a page crinkled more than the rest. "Would you like to see?"

The silverware clanked on the plate when my sweaty fingers slipped. "Sure."

Taking care not to damage the fragile onion-skin paper, he turned the sketchbook around then watched for my reaction.

The drawing was of me, true enough, but that girl had yet to be broken. There were fractures, tiny ones, so small you had to squint to see them. She missed the idea of her mother, but she was loved. She had a family, a home, friends, a life. Try as I might, I could not see myself in her. I could not remember ever being this open, like my heart was a book with hope for the future written on its pages.

The graphite portrait showed me kneeling in front of my open window, almost prayerful, with my arms stacked on the windowsill. I rested my chin on the bend of my arm and stared across the yard, right at the artist. Or so I would have thought if Boaz hadn't told me the story of yanking Linus from the tree that straddled the property line. Linus, despite the angle, hadn't been the recipient of my wistful sighs or my star-crossed gaze. As usual, it all came down to Boaz. I had been daydreaming in the direction of the Pritchard house, and Linus had immortalized that pitiful ache that entered my eyes whenever I saw him.

"You could have drawn that from the ground," I murmured. "Why did you climb that tree?"

"I hoped you wouldn't notice me," he admitted. "The upper limbs concealed the limb where I sat."

I could almost tell from the angle he was higher than I'd first thought. "How did Boaz find you?"

"Bad luck." He grimaced at the memory. "He had a slingshot and a handful of berries. He was going to test his aim and see how many he could shoot through your window."

"That sounds like him." And he had conveniently edited out that part.

"The rest of the story you know." He left no room for doubt that Boaz had told me how it ended.

Linus's candor was why I returned the favor. "I met Ambrose last night."

A brief flicker of—surprise?—played across his features before he sank into the chair across from me. "Where?"

Not *who*? Or *how*? But *where*?

All the niggling doubts skipping through my head all day broke into a sprint.

"He was in the garden. I bumped into him when I went to drop off the sketchbook with you."

"Did he...?" Black threads spooled through his irises. "What did he say to you?"

I cradled the grimoire to my chest, its warm leather a comfort. *"My reasons and my purpose are my own. I do not answer to you, little goddess,"* I repeated, *"and you would be wise to remember that."*

"That's all?" His pupils expanded into gaping voids. "Did you get a good look at him?"

"Yes." I forced myself to hold his fathomless gaze. "He resembled you—" in a funhouse mirror kind of way, "—and he was wearing one of your shirts." As a matter of fact, the style and cut matched the one he wore, if not the color. He probably ordered them in triplicate from his tailor. "Who is he? *What* is he?"

"Let me handle Ambrose." Ice glazed his words until a warm breath would shatter them into a million pieces. Not since that night in the Lyceum, when the Grande Dame named him my tutor, had I heard this imperious tone from him. "He's a dangerous man. Avoid him at all costs."

The warning startled a laugh out of me. "Hard to do when he's trespassing on my property."

"You don't have to trust me," he said, each crisp word making his teeth clack, "but trust me to take care of this."

As much as I wanted to show a little faith after all he had done for me, he had dodged too many of my questions for me to let the matter drop, and I was fresh out of blind faith. I had two eyes and— despite what Boaz thought—they were both cranked wide open. No one got a free pass from me these days. I had written too many in the past, and look where it landed me.

Unwilling to give him my word, I let my silence speak for itself.

"I must secure this." He stood abruptly, sketchbook forgotten, and collected the avowal. "Then we'll get started." On his return from the office, he brought two boxes overflowing with supplies with him. "Are you ready?" The stiffness in his limbs echoed in his speech. "Or would you rather postpone?"

Shoving back from the table, I got to my feet. "There's no time like the present."

Neither of us had eaten, but I wasn't hungry, and he never seemed to be either.

Since his arms were full, I held the door for him, and we trekked over to Woolly together. The old house rustled her curtains in question, and I raised an arm in answer. All was well. No signs of the berry-mouthed Ambrose.

About the time I realized I had been staring a hole through the back of Linus's head, he caught my eye, his expression wary, like he didn't trust my acquiescence. The flat press of his mouth reminded me of the flaps on an envelope as he sealed them closed on the topic still itching my lips with questions.

Without resorting to a letter opener, I wasn't sure how to get him talking again.

"How does this work?" I stuck my nose in the topmost box, expecting to find silvery chisels or hammers. But the contents all sloshed and glistened in the moonlight. Jars upon jars filled with Maud's signature ink waited for us to crack their wax seals. "The old wards were etched into the foundation. Is that what we're doing?" I found a pen and three brushes of varying sizes loose in the bottom. "I'm not sure how steady my hand will be."

"This etching is done with a sigil, not by hand," he explained, not buying my act for a minute. "All you have to do is paint on your design, let it dry, and then I'll walk you through the rest. That's where things get interesting."

Things had already gotten plenty interesting, if you asked me. "Are you going to help?"

"No." He located a sketch pad and pencil in the second box. "This way the wards will be answerable only to you."

"I like the sound of that."

A hint of smile threatened to peek through. "I thought you might."

A dip in temperature announced Cletus's arrival, and it got me thinking. "Last night—"

Linus was already shaking his head. "I told you I'll handle Ambrose."

I bit the inside of my cheek to keep from telling him what I thought about that.

"No, it's not that." I sat and crossed my legs. "Boaz and I were walking after dinner. We passed the *Cora Ann*, and Cletus started acting peculiar. He kept pointing toward the second deck."

"I see." He settled on the grass near my elbow. "Was that the extent of it?"

"He didn't seem to want to leave the boat, but it was late, and we wanted to get home."

Linus rubbed his jaw. "He wasn't aggressive or agitated?"

"No." I smoothed out my design in front of me. "He was protective of me, but he didn't harm or threaten me. He didn't bother Boaz either."

I shook the small vial of ink Linus selected for me, broke its seal, then breathed in the familiar tang of Maud's unique blend. There was no mistaking a necromancer's signature once you learned its scent. Inks were as individual as the necromancers who mixed them.

"I'm glad to hear it." He tapped his pencil against the pad in his lap. "Cletus has been with me for a long time. I trust him as far as you can trust a wraith."

"I thought you said they weren't autonomous." I kept working, kept moving, not giving the words any particular weight. I think that offhandedness was the only reason he answered.

"You can teach a wraith a series of commands, and the creatures abide by them as law. You can give them short-term goals, such as *protect Grier.* Or long-term goals such as *do no harm unto others.*" He scrunched up his face. "They operate within those parameters, even if you're not actively controlling them. Or they should. Accidents do happen, but usually weak summoners are to blame, not the wraiths themselves."

This was different than what he'd told me the last time we'd spoken about wraiths. Then I had imagined Cletus parked in the living room at the carriage house, staring off into space, waiting for his master's command. But Linus was admitting he had given Cletus blanket instructions to protect me as he saw fit.

While he lectured me on wraith theory, relaxing into the safer topic, I worked on laying down my design in neat rows. I had a cramp in my hand when I finished the space within easy reach, but I was pleased with the work I had done. Flexing my hand to ease the pangs, I leaned back so Linus could get a better look.

"You must have worked all day to finish this." His gaze cut to me, a question in his darkening eyes. "I only recognize every fourth sigil or so from your initial design."

Ambrose had robbed me of sleep, but I kept that to myself. I seemed to be bottling up more and more lately. Woolly would not be pleased about that. She would demand I uncork as soon as possible. That meant reaching out to one of my three lifelines.

I had burdened Odette the last time, and Boaz was MIA for the next couple of days. That left Amelie.

I hoped day-old churro still worked as an incentive.

"Yeah, well, I told you I got carried away with my homework." I resisted the urge to test it with my finger. The good thing about ink was it dried almost on contact. It had to bond fast. Skin was a slippery canvas, and that was our most common medium. "What comes next?"

"Choose a dry brush." He passed me a clear bottle sloshing with liquid. "Paint the sigil for grounding."

"What is this?" I sniffed the contents for hints of its composition. "I haven't seen anything like it."

"It's mélange, a mixture of thrice-blessed birch water and horned owl tears."

A sniff test proved there were no binding elements, no blood, so I deemed it safe enough. I swirled on the grounding sigil with a swoop of my wrist, and the effect was instantaneous. A rumble shook the foundation as bits of concrete chipped and flew, pelting my forearms, my cheeks.

"Hey," I yelled. "Give a girl some warning next time."

The window over my head swung open, and the curtains fluttered out into the yard.

"Not you, girl." I patted the siding. "I meant Linus." I touched my cheek where it stung, and drew away bloody fingers. "I could have lost an eye."

"The sigil shouldn't have reacted that way." He wiped bits of dust and concrete off his face. "It was meant to sink the design into the foundation, like pressing a stamp into hot wax, not explode." He removed his glasses and wiped them clean using his shirt. "Your magic must be reacting to the mélange."

Thrice-blessed birch water and horned owl tears. Neither ought to be giving me fits, but owls were familiars of Hecate, and I was goddess-touched. Maybe there was a connection, and my magic reacted more strongly to her symbols. I wondered if we would ever know for sure.

Reaching up, I let Woolly's curtains tease my fingertips. "It's not hurting her, is it?"

He didn't answer straightaway. "Woolly?"

The old house groaned, settling on her foundation, testing its fit, deciding how she felt about what I had done, and then she blasted the curtain overhead like a party horn blown.

"I'm guessing that's approval." I sank down as relief melted me. "We still need protection before we..."

"Hold still." Linus pulled a handkerchief from his pocket, white linen embroidered with his initials, and pressed it to my cheek. "You're bleeding."

Cold seeped through him into me, and the sting lessened the same as if I had cradled a bag of frozen peas against my face. "Thanks."

"Let me fix this," he murmured, assessing me, "and then we'll find protective gear."

The pen he removed from his pocket was familiar by now, and so was the weight of it when he pressed it against my cheek and began to draw healing sigils that made my skin itch and tingle. The pain ebbed as he worked, and when he finished, I lowered the handkerchief to let him inspect his work.

"The wounds have closed." His fingertips trailed beneath my eye, an ice cube skating over skin. "They're shallow. They won't scar."

"What about you?" I passed him the bloodied fabric. "You've got a cut at your temple."

"Do I?" He reached up, smearing crimson, and frowned. "I didn't even feel it. Is that all?"

"I think so." I held out my hand for the pen. "Want me to patch you up?"

There was no hesitation on his part. He seemed to be saying, *I trust you even if you don't trust me.* Though anyone who experimented on themselves had to have at least a teeny, tiny death wish, so I didn't let it flatter me too much. "You remember the sigils?"

"I think so." I pulled the grimoire onto my lap and turned to a fresh page. "It's this combination, right?"

Linus nodded after a moment. "Yes, it is."

"Here goes nothing." He pretended to be a block of uncarved marble while I braced my hand against his cheek. I drew the sigils as precise as possible while my hand grew numb from contact. Even his freckles appeared limned in blue. He hadn't been this cold even a week ago. Maybe whatever was going on in town was affecting him too. And maybe the *whatever* was named Ambrose. "There you go. Good as new."

Linus blinked as though waking from a long dream then unfolded his legs and strode off toward the carriage house. I used the time he was gone to text Amelie an invitation to chat before work. And yes, chat was code for listening to me gush about her brother.

"We shouldn't leave your blood lying around." Linus spoke from behind me, and I twisted to see he had returned with a box of matches. He tossed the handkerchief on a spot of bare dirt then struck a match, letting it ignite the fabric on contact, and my blood turned to ash. "There are enough dangerous things a person could do with anyone's blood. Let's not tempt them with yours."

What a depressing thought, that I was no longer even free to bleed without it causing an incident.

"You'll get used to having power." Linus watched the flames. "Or maybe it's best you never do."

I almost asked him what that meant, but he had disappeared again. This time he returned with two heavy sweaters, two thick scarves, and two sets of plastic goggles that belonged in a high school science lab. He dropped one of each into my lap then sat and started pulling a sweater on over his head.

"I won't lie." I lifted the knitted weight, obviously his, and shrugged into its warmth. "I pictured you as the sweater vest type, but actual sweaters?"

"I get cold," he said softly, and that was the end of that.

Sweating inside my woolen armor, I got back to work. I painted on the sigils to complete one entire side of the foundation before braving the clear liquid a second time. "Are you ready?"

"Remember your scarf." He was coiling his around his throat and head in a makeshift mask he topped off with his goggles. I tried one-handed, but mine kept slipping down around my shoulders. "No, not like that." He took the scarf and slowly bound me like a mummy then slid on my goggles. "Now do it."

The grounding sigil blasted chips in the air that bounced off the plastic covering our eyes and stuck to the wool wrapping our heads. "Much better."

Linus was quick to disagree with me. "This isn't going to work."

I felt my shoulders rolling in before I could stop them. "I did the best I could."

"Your work is superb. That's not the issue. We need better supplies." He looked me dead in the eye. "This is not your fault. Understand? We're both learning as we go."

The tension coiling me inward released, and I regretted he held even that much sway over me. "I want to be better than I am. Faster. I want to know it all before you pack up and leave."

"Time is never wasted when it's spent with a student who genuinely wants to learn."

"More teacher logic," I joked, but it came harder with us still at odds over Ambrose.

Not for the first time, I wondered if his mother had any idea what he was teaching me. Nothing she would find useful. Nothing that would gain her prestige. And then I wondered if that wasn't the plan, to appeal to the rebellious side of me. To feed me what I wanted in tiny bites until I could swallow the whole of what they intended for me.

"There are sigils to keep the concrete pliant," Linus was saying.

"You'll need to paint those on using the mélange before you start sparring with Taz."

The mention of her name forced a groan of protest from my aching muscles. "Show me."

And he did. I hadn't finished cleaning my brush when a boot swung at me in my peripheral vision. I tossed the brush and the solution at Linus, drenching him, and rolled away, hoping the ingredients weren't as rare as they'd sounded. "What is your damage?"

"Oh, I'm sorry." Taz was not sorry. "I forgot vampires and kidnappers always announce their presence before they attack to make sure their victims are prepared to defend themselves."

"Smartass." I scrambled to my feet and got out of range. "I can see why you and Boaz get along so well."

"That's not why." She bounced on the balls of her feet. "Boaz can have most anything he wants, so he wants what he can't have."

The thought mirrored mine so closely, I was stunned. That second of doubt was all it took for Taz to land her first blow. The kick connected with the side of my head, and I went down hard, ears ringing, but I rocked onto my hands and knees.

"Don't let them get inside your head." She squatted beside me. "You have to learn to block the mental hits too. Not just the physical ones. These people research, Grier. They memorize you like a favorite song, and they don't miss any notes."

"What you said..." I panted through the worst pain. "It's true."

"That's why I said it. Lies don't resonate. Only the truth cuts as well as a blade."

I hung my head, letting her wisdom sink in, letting it carve all the way to the bone, but then I stood and braced my legs. "Again."

Boaz was an old wound. From here on out, she could pick that scab all she wanted. I was done bleeding.

TEN

The fight with Taz ended the way all fights with Taz end. I was leaking from places one should not leak, sweaty in places one should not sweat, and grinning at the person responsible through pink teeth. I didn't have to limp far for Linus to doodle sigils on my throbbing face. He had stayed to watch again.

Humiliation got pummeled out of me with each lesson until I was grateful for a medic on the sidelines.

Once I stopped resembling a cautionary tale, I grabbed a shower and loaded a crossbody bag with tools for work and supplies for a rendezvous with Timmy then rushed off to meet Amelie in her yard.

"I hope she bought you dinner first." She clucked her tongue. "Why does this matter so much to you?" A sigh moved through her. "The magic I get, but the fighting?"

"Magic requires time and preparation," I explained. "A fist comes preloaded."

"Sometimes you sound so much like Boaz, it's like speaking to his much shorter twin." She leaned against her car and patted the door in an invitation to join her. "Go on. Get it over with. I can tell you're about to pop. Tell me about your first date. Just not the kissy, touchy, feely parts."

"Honestly?" I had to laugh. "Anything that could go wrong did. It's a good thing I don't believe in signs, or I would think Hecate wanted us to change our names and relocate to opposite sides of the country."

She winced sympathetically. "That bad, huh?"

"There were good parts." I let my tone convey that I was willing to elaborate. "*Really* good parts."

"No details required. I don't want to know about his parts." She covered her eyes with one hand and her nearest ear with the other. "Please. Keep those to yourself. I just ate, and I really don't want to be sick."

"You're always asking me to tell you everything." The car rocked when I leaned against it. "Now that I have something to share, you're going soft on me?"

"Before it was hypothetical." She scowled when I pried her arms away from her head. "Now it's literal. You have more than dreamy-eyed sighs to offer. You've got legit dirt on how my brother..." She made gagging noises. "This is so gross. *So* gross. Worse than pineapple on my ham pizza. It didn't seem all that disgusting until he walked in wearing a goofy smile." A shudder rippled through her. "He's never looked like that after a date. He looked... I don't know. Happy?"

Our date made Boaz happy? A dopey smile wreathed my face.

"Ugh." Amelie made heaving sounds. "That's the look."

"Okay, okay. I won't make you listen to how your brother pressed his lips to—"

Amelie slapped a hand over my mouth. "No."

"—and he pulled my—"

Adjusting her grip, she also pinched my nose closed. "Really, no."

I held my breath until sparks lit my vision, but she didn't back down. I was forced to go in for the kill, which is to say I pulled out the churros and dangled them in front of her nose, trading their lives for mine. She couldn't grab them fast enough, and her eyes crossed with pleasure when she inhaled from the top of the bag. We collapsed on the poured-concrete drive, leaned against her car, and got high on sugar together.

"I really hope this doesn't blow up in all our faces," she said around a bite of dough.

"Me too."

"Just know I'm on your side if this goes south." She gathered my hands in hers. "He might be my brother by blood, but you're my sister by choice. Plus, once you gain back the weight you lost, we'll be the same size again, and I can borrow your clothes."

"I have holey jeans and ratty T-shirts. You've got plenty of those."

"You're Dame Woolworth," she reminded me. "You're going to have to buy some nicer clothes. Camouflage is the only safe way to move unseen within the Society. *Those* are the outfits I'm going to pilfer from your closet."

"I haven't spent any of my money," I admitted. "It doesn't feel real."

"Wait until you start swiping that debit card." She leaned her head against my shoulder. "It's hard to dismiss boxes and garment bags as imaginary, and should you ever doubt, all you have to do is reach out and pet them."

"I hate shopping." I pursed my lips. "Maud always bought my fancy clothes."

"No, she didn't." Amelie was laughing softly. "She hated shopping too. She always palmed the job off on her sister. Literally every stitch of clothing you wore to any Society event you attended was handpicked by Clarice Lawson."

I jerked so hard, I jostled Amelie and sent her crashing into my lap. "How do you know?"

"Please." She snorted and made herself comfortable, resting her head across my thighs while she stargazed. "Her driver would pull in, she would lower the window and snap her fingers at Boaz and say, 'You there. Boy. Run these parcels in to my sister, won't you?'"

My jaw came unhinged as I tried to picture her gall in ordering around another person's child.

"She would tip him twenty bucks and remind him the tree marked the property line and he should stay on his side of it." Amelie linked her fingers at her navel, and they jumped with her laughter. "That's probably why he started peeing on her tires whenever she came over if the driver stepped away to smoke."

"Are you serious?"

"As the grave."

Absently, I raked my fingers through her hair. "Boaz hates the High Society, doesn't he?"

"Yep."

"He's never going to get over it, is he?"

"Nope."

I thumped her in the forehead. "How is this going to work?"

She swatted my hand and sat upright before I tried it again. "He doesn't see you as one of them."

I didn't see myself that way, either. "But I am."

A door shut behind us, and footsteps rounded the vehicle. "What are you doing out here?"

Matron Pritchard wore an ensemble any librarian would envy. Crisp white blouse, emerald A-line skirt with matching cardigan and sensible shoes. She crossed her thin arms over her narrow chest, toyed with the strand of white pearls at her throat, and waited for an answer.

"*We* have to work tonight," Amelie said in a prim voice. "*We* wanted to chat before *we* part ways."

"You have a cellular phone," Mrs. Pritchard replied. "I know. I pay the bill each month. Perhaps next time you could use that instead of cluttering the driveway. It's unseemly to sit out here alone."

The hand Amelie had braced on the concrete tightened into a fist. "Yes, ma'am."

Mrs. Pritchard left without looking at me or speaking to me. Business as usual.

Tonight was a night for revelations, it seemed. "You hate the Low Society, don't you?"

"Yep."

"You're never going to get over it, are you?"

"Nope."

Telling her *I don't see you as one of them* wouldn't be a comfort in the same way the reverse was true for me. That line had kicked off way too many old fights, and we hadn't had a real one since my return. I wanted that trend to continue.

"I'm going ghost hunting tonight." Not the smoothest segue, but it was the best I had to offer.

"Timmy?" She embraced the topic change with a winged eyebrow. "Are you sure that's wise?"

"I brought supplies." I patted my bag. "I'm going to protect myself."

"How's the girl?" She grunted as she stood. "Merida?"

"Close." I joined her and dusted off my pants. "Marit. And she's fine. Or she was fine when her dad left me a voicemail yesterday." I intercepted her questioning look. "No, I didn't visit her at the hospital. She's a daddy's girl, and he blames me for what happened. I think he was trying to use the ghost to spook me off since he pegged me as Cricket's spy. Now Marit is calling me her hero, and he's stuck with me. That doesn't mean I want to rub his nose in it."

"Good call." She shook her head. "Assuming you want to keep the job."

"Of course I do."

"Of course you do," she repeated, then she cleared her throat. "Do you need any help?"

"Something tells me dining room security is going to be airtight on the *Cora Ann*. I doubt Mr. Voorhees lets me or anyone else back in there until the investigation is concluded." I had a plan, but I wasn't sure it would work on water. "Maybe take me to see the Whitaker Street lamppost after? I want to scout the area."

"Oh." Her disappointment was palpable. "Sure. We can do

Whitaker." Her good mood returned in a blink. "That reminds me. We've got another dead zone. The sign at The Movie Rack has gone out."

"Wow." I counted back in my head. "That place has been closed for like ten years."

The consignment shop that moved into the space never replaced the overhead sign. They just propped their own in the windows and let that be advertisement enough. The strip mall manager killed the power to the sign, at their request, but that didn't stop it from blinking on at dusk. He claimed it shared a breaker with the ones for the laundromat on its left and the Mexican restaurant on its right, and that's why he couldn't deactivate one without the others going dark too.

"Yep." She toyed with the handle on her door before shooting a glance over her shoulder at the house. "Hey, I gotta go. Mom is in rare form tonight. That means you gotta go too."

She didn't have to tell me twice. There was a reason our trio always hung out at Woolly. Two, actually. Amelie called them Mom and Dad.

"We meet after work to search for hotspots gone cold." I stuck out my hand. "Do we have an accord?"

"We do indeed." She shook on it. "We can grab takeout from the Waffle Iron while we're there."

"I like the way you think." One of their pecan waffles would more than make up for the pancakes I missed out on earlier.

"Only because it's also the way you think." She twirled a finger in the air. "Poh-tay-toe, pah-tah-toe."

"Toh-may-toe, tah-mah-toe?"

"Exactly!" She blew me a kiss and slid behind the wheel. "This is why we're best friends."

"Well, that and no one else would have us." I waved. "See you later."

A curtain rustled in the window nearest me, and it took a full second to remember the Pritchard house wasn't Woolly to be sending me messages.

"I'll be on my way," I told whichever of Boaz's parents watched me through the split in the fabric.

Paranoia and I were on good terms. Friendly even. But the Pritchards had never treated me like an out-and-out leper. Socially, they couldn't afford to even after I was released from Atramentous. No, they didn't get aggressive in their dislike of me until I got reinstated. What did that mean? And should I ask Amelie or let it slide?

Undecided, I headed for the garage and did a quick check for kittens. Finding none, I pulled on my protective gear and drove Jolene to the *Cora Ann*.

The mood was somber onboard, and no one greeted me as I searched for Mr. Voorhees.

Sneaking in to meet Timmy might be easier than I thought.

"Ah, Grier," Captain Murray boomed to my right. "I worried we scared you away."

"Not at all." I picked my way to him across a pile of dry rotted boards. "How is Marit?"

"She'll make a full recovery." He placed his hand on his heart like any other outcome pained him. "She's such a bright girl. Sean and I have been friends for years, and she dated my son for a while. Marit is very important to me. She's the closest thing I have to a daughter." His eyes shimmered. "Thank you for saving her."

"I'm glad I was there." Though I had probably been the cause of the attack in the first place. Necromantic energy had a way of riling up spirits.

"Tonight you'll be working with Arnold's crew on the downstairs parlor." He indicated a barrel-chested man covered in tattoos. "Come find me if you need anything. Sean won't be back the rest of the week, so until then you will report to me."

"I'll do that." Tightening my grip on my bag, I crossed to Arnold. "Reporting for duty."

"Start peeling paper," he grunted, indicating an interior room. "Bag it as you go. Keep it tidy, yeah?"

Segregated from the rest of the crew, I plucked and tugged and pulled until I finished an entire wall and my fingers pruned from the solvent. The isolation didn't bother me, I was used to that, but conversation would have made the task go faster. Maybe the others thought I was bad luck or cursed. The stigma didn't bother me, either. I was *other*, and I couldn't blame them for their suspicion.

I was admiring my handiwork when Arnold ducked his head in and grunted in my direction. "You're on break."

"Already?" I checked the time on my phone. "I've only been here an hour."

"Twenty-five minutes." He tapped his watch. "Starting now."

After wiping my hands dry on my pants, I set a timer for twenty minutes on my cell then returned it to my pocket. I rooted through my bag for a brush and a bottle of Maud's ink. Linus's pen was handier, but it was a tool meant for flat surfaces. This job called for ink that would flow over rusted metal and warped boards without breaking any lines, assuming I got to that part.

The first step in my plan was to test the obfuscation sigil, so I pulled up my shirt and painted an intersecting row of them across my abdomen where I could hide them easily. The crew would freak if it didn't work and I showed up bloodied again. Humans could only withstand so much trauma without breaking.

With that done, I took a slow lap around the deck. No one looked up or otherwise acknowledged me.

That wasn't totally unexpected, since I suspected they believed I cavorted with knife-wielding ghosts, so I made a point to kick boards and boxes of nails as I went to see if the clatter got their attention. It did, and I almost popped my arm out of its socket patting myself on the back.

Certain of my relative invisibility, I crept up to the second deck. Not a single body wandered this level. A bonus for me, since that meant I could talk to Timmy without being overheard. I lifted my shirt and painted on protective sigils in a tidy line beneath the others, and then I attempted to commune with the dead.

"My name is Grier Woolworth, and I'm a necromancer."

I gave him time to absorb that, to wonder at what it meant.

"What do you want?" I walked the length of the room. "Why are you angry?"

The lights remained sure, the temperature steady, and no projectiles launched themselves at me.

"Who are you?" I made another circuit, this one slower. "How can I help?"

Still nothing indicative of a haunting.

I painted a sigil across my palm to heighten my perception and swept my hand in slow arcs like a treasure hunter swings a metal detector in search of coins. A prickle across my knuckles had me turning, and a small boy appeared before me. Other than his faint blue sheen, he appeared solid enough. "Oh. Hello."

His lips moved on silent words.

"I can't hear you."

His eyes, black and empty, blinked imploringly at me.

Out of ideas, I used the amplification sigil once more on my arm, hoping a signal boost might help.

"The night eternal comes," he said, his voice static like an untuned station on a radio.

On reflex, I glanced out the window at the moon. "What does that mean?"

"He comes." Fat tears as black as tar rolled down his pale cheeks. "The devourer."

"That sounds...bad." I held still so as not to provoke him. "How can I help?"

"You can't," he sobbed. "No one can."

"Will you harm me if I try anyway?" His narrow brow crinkled, and I hesitated. "You hurt my friend Marit, remember?"

"You're...different," he whispered. "I thought you were like him."

"Him?" I kept my voice low. "The devourer?"

Wrong thing to say.

"He's coming. He's coming. He's coming."

Timmy vanished in a gust of cool air that carried with it a lost boy's wails.

No matter how many times I reworked my amplification sigils, there was no calling him back.

The timer on my phone buzzed in warning, and I hit the stairs. I ducked into the bathroom, washed off the blood, and rinsed out my brush then returned to the parlor and secreted away my supplies.

Four hours after I arrived, Arnold cut me loose for the night. No one mentioned I was a part-time hire, but the incident with Marit seemed to have landed me on probation. With hours to kill until Amelie got off work, I decided to drive out to Tybee and pay the visit I owed Odette.

The petite black woman who completed the troika that had been Maud, Mom, and Odette, stood in the driveway leading up to a bungalow that reminded me of peppermint still in the wrapper. A pastel dress that might have been teal in another life flapped around her ankles, torn by the same breeze clacking the coral beads threading the long braids of her white hair. Her bare feet burrowed in the sand, and her arms opened to me before Jolene came to a full stop.

"*Ma coccinelle.*" She adjusted her thick glasses on her pert nose. "I had a feeling in these old bones I would see you tonight."

"I got off work early." I crossed to her and let her gather me close. "I have a date with Amelie later. Do you mind if I hang out until then?"

"Pah." She kissed both my cheeks. "You need no excuse."

Grinning, I followed her inside, kicked off my shoes, and took a seat on her bone-white couch. "I've had an interesting couple of days."

"Do tell." She made herself tea, the hot kind, but I declined. I preferred mine with ice cubes and enough sugar to congeal it. "What adventures have you had since last we spoke?"

With my legs curled under me, I unburdened myself in fits and starts. I told her everything from Linus and the grimoire to Taz and my self-defense lessons to Detective Russo and her suspicions to

Timmy and his fears. Woolly would be so proud. I could feel the warmth of her approval already. She was right, as usual, that sharing my secrets with someone made carrying them lighter.

"This ghost child." She stirred her drink with a carved-bone spoon. "He won't trouble you much longer."

A pang of guilt arrowed through me. He had been so afraid. "Why do you say that?"

"He spoke to you." She sipped and sighed with pleasure. "Self-awareness in a poltergeist is rare. Usually, they're a brute force. They spew whatever hatred has kept their souls tethered and act out whatever revenge they see fit, but they have no higher reasoning. They are loops, as all ghosts are, but they are more powerful and can exist within several loop variations. Each sequence of events, such as throwing silverware, will fade as he dissipates, until all that's left is a wisp of a boy seen from the corner of an eye."

Poor Timmy. "What do you think he meant about the devourer?"

"All necromancers augment their power. Some more than others. There are many ways to accomplish this. Using ink purchased from stronger bloodlines or sigils crafted by better practitioners. Bonding with a wraith or multiple familiars." She hummed. "Staring at the sky is not enough for some practitioners. No, they reach up, pluck the brightest stars from the heavens, and burn as they fall back to Earth. They seek more power than they can wield, and in so doing become wielded themselves."

A shiver tightened my skin. "I don't understand."

"Are you familiar with what happens when the last rights aren't performed on a powerful necromancer after death?"

The Culmination was the sacred ritual the Grande Dame had used to excuse the blood on my hands the night I was hauled to the Lyceum to face justice. Witnesses claimed I showed up drenched in Maud's blood, as tradition demanded, which supported Detective Russo's account. But shock and time and drugs had corroded the truth of my memories until I had no idea what to believe. Except that I was innocent. I had to be. I could never have hurt Maud. Not only because I loved her, but because she was *Maud*. No one was more powerful, especially not in her own home.

"Their spirits become shades." I had fretted over such a wretched fate for Maud, but the silver box on my mantle was proof someone had laid her soul to rest. A similar case held Mom's, yet another treasure lost to the basement. "Shades are the necromantic equivalent of ghosts."

Ghosts belonged only to humans. Shades only to necromancers. Terms like poltergeist and wraith were classifications within those groups.

"Just so," she agreed. "Shades are imbued with the magic of their former life, and that makes them dangerous. That's why we perform the Culmination, to snuff out that spark and send the soul to its eternal rest. When it is not performed, the soul, that seed of potential, is left to drift. Unlike ghosts, who fade once their energy has been expended, shades can absorb other magics. Their hunger, over time, bloats them on power until they grow strong enough to possess the living."

Humans could be possessed. Necromancers, not so much. Our innate magic gave us a natural barrier, Low and High Society alike. "Are we talking voluntary possession here?"

"The necromancer must be open to such an arrangement, yes."

"So, the voluntary joining of a necromancer to a shade creates this..." I rolled my hand, "...thing? This devourer?"

A nod sent the beads in her hair clacking. "The dybbuk."

Though I could guess the answer, I asked her all the same. "What are the odds of one roaming the streets of Savannah?"

"The Society chose this city as its American seat of power for a reason." She removed her glasses then gazed into her teacup as though scrying for the answer. "The atmosphere is rich with old magic, the ground steeped in old blood, and the old grudges between classes carry more weight here."

Meaning there was a large candidate pool and the means to fatten them up before approaching potential victims.

"What you're telling me is a possessed necromancer is prowling the streets of Savannah, preying on its supernatural energies." I wondered if he got off on calling himself Ambrose. "Ghosts only?" That would explain why the Society wasn't in an uproar. "Is that as high up the food chain as they reach for victims?"

"Oh, no, *bébé*." Without the magnification of her thick lenses, her squinted eyes appeared lost among her wrinkles. "The more powerful ones will hunt rogue vampires too. That's where the hunter legend originates."

"Huh." That was news to me, which, honestly, ought to be my motto. "Are they dangerous to necromancers?"

"Only if a necromancer opens their heart to greed."

Well, that was a yes. *Necromancer* was synonymous with *greed*.

While I turned over what I had learned in my head, I revisited one final topic while I had time.

"What should I do about Russo?" I wiggled my toes against the cushion. "I mentioned her to Linus." There was no way to avoid it since Cletus had been present during our confrontations. "The Society will bury her if they think she's a threat, but if she knows how Maud really—"

"Hush." She flapped her hands. "Do not give voice to treason. Not here." Her eyes darted around the room. "I am watched as often as I watch. Remember that." Lifting her teacup, she took a sip and grimaced as she swallowed, the contents having gone cold. "Boaz is with the Elite, yes?"

"Yes." The hot rush of blood in my cheeks tattled on all the things I hadn't told Odette, namely about my date with one Boaz Pritchard. The odds were too good she had glimpsed a possible future for us, for him, from the corner of her eye while delving into someone else's life. This thing with him might go nowhere, or it might go everywhere. Wherever it went, I wanted it on our terms. "Do you think I should report her?"

"Yes." Odette didn't mince her words. "There are three types of humans. The type content to believe there are no monsters under the bed, the type who are content to pretend there are monsters under the bed as long as they aren't real, and the type who will grab a flashlight and climb under the bed to hunt down the monster and make sure it can't scare them again."

Thanks to my years working as a Haint, I had seen all types, and I had to agree with her analysis. "You think Russo is carrying a flashlight."

"I do." She hesitated a moment. "You should also ask yourself if this Cricket is a pretender or a hunter."

"I would have lumped her in with the hardcore nonbelievers until Russo." I unfolded my legs. "I'm still not sure what to think. I had no idea she cared I had gone missing. She's not the touchy-feely type. But, if she sought out Russo a second time, years later, there must be a connection."

No bones about it. Someday soon, I would have to confront Cricket and get her side of the story.

"Talk to Boaz," she urged. "He has access to resources you don't."

"I'll do that." I got to my feet. "Do you want to go for a walk?"

"You heard my heart singing for the ocean, did you?" She laughed, delighted. "These walls can no longer contain me. I must have sand between my toes and the spray misting my cheeks to feel alive."

Happy to listen to her prattle on about her conversations with the sea, I walked beside her until it was time for me to go. I left her standing ankle-deep in frothy water, smiling up at the moon, blowing kisses to the gulls who cried out overhead in welcome.

AMELIE WAS BEAT. I didn't have to ask how her night had gone, it was etched into every line on her face when she showed up at the *Cora Ann*. I took pity on her and drove us on our rounds in her car instead of forcing her on Jolene, but the plush seats and the ability to recline weren't helping. I had to pinch her every few minutes to keep her awake.

"Why are you so tired?" She had plenty of reasons. I just wasn't sure which to blame.

"Finals, remember?" She flung her arm across her eyes. "My life is studying and tears."

"I hear you." For once, I knew exactly how she felt.

She glanced toward me. "How are things going with Linus?"

"They're going. We're making progress."

She snorted. "Give me all the juicy details, why don't you?"

"There's nothing to tell. He works me until my brain starts smoking, then he sends me packing with homework." I belted out a sigh. "He's also started watching my training exercises with Taz."

"I wasn't aware it was a spectator sport." She sounded far too interested in joining him.

"It's not," I grumbled before she got any ideas. "I'm so ready to be self-sufficient."

Her gaze touched on the side mirror. "Where's your tail tonight?"

"He's around." I hadn't spotted Cletus since I left Woolly, but he was never far.

She grinned at me. "Is he cute?"

"Uh, no." *Sorry, Cletus.* "He's bony and...no. Not cute."

"Oh, well. You can't blame a girl for trying."

"You should ask Boaz to set you up with one of his friends."

"Have you met my brother? Oh, that's right. You're the kook currently dating him." She winked at me to show she was joking. Mostly. "I don't want to date my brother, and all his friends are carbon copies of him. They're all chest-beating knuckle-draggers."

"Does that mean you think I enjoy being clubbed senseless and dragged into caves?"

"I do worry about brain damage." She patted my head. "How many times can you fall for the old *want to view my cave etchings* line?"

"It's not the etchings," I purred. "It's the way he looks in his saber tooth cat fur thong."

Amelie rolled down her window and made retching noises that might not have been faked.

When we turned onto Whitaker Street, I spotted the absence immediately. I parked under the light, racing the dawn, and we examined the lamppost. I painted an amplification sigil on my palm, and when that got me nothing, I tried a more complex design on my forehead. Nothing I tried earned me the slightest tingle. There was no energy here other than the manmade, electrical kind.

"I don't understand how the residual energy can hang around for years," Amelie said, "and then *poof*."

I chewed on my bottom lip for too long, and she caught me at it, forcing me into a confession. "I don't think this was random."

"What do you mean?" She darted a glance up and down the street like *poof* might be catching.

While I filled her in on my visit to Odette, I pulled out wet wipes and started cleaning off my hand and scrubbing my forehead. I watched for Cletus, but he was too well hidden for me to pick him from the evaporating shadows.

"I think you're right," she said when I finished. "I'm not supposed to say anything." She gestured for me to get back in the car and waited until we had both settled in to talk. "Mom got a message from Clan Peterkin two days ago. Her youngest brother's wife was High Society, but she gave up the title for my uncle. She's a classically trained practitioner, and she's continued to practice even though she commands a much lower price these days. She performed a resuscitation for the Peterkins about three years ago. It was textbook. They got a new vampire, we got gold. Everyone was pleased."

"I'm sensing a *but* here."

"All made vampires come with a fifty-year guarantee from the matron of the practitioner's family, and the Peterkins called to demand a full refund from Mom."

I twisted in my seat to face her. "What happened?"

"They found his corpse in his bed. He was a husk, they said, drained of the magic animating him."

"It does happen," I allowed. "How certain are you of your aunt's talent?"

"She's no Woolworth," Amelie said, a trace of bitterness tucked between the words. "But she's competent. She was well-regarded until she married down."

And there was the rub. Any shine on her family's name from having a practitioner in its ranks was dimmed by her association with them. "What will your mother do?"

"Fight." There was no hesitation. "Even if the family was at fault, she would fight for our reputation."

"Hmm." I considered the problem. "How did the dybbuk get to the vamp without his clan noticing?"

The defensive cant to her shoulders eased, and apology was written all over her face. "I don't know." She twisted her hands into a complicated knot. "That was about the time Mom remembered she wasn't home alone and that her daughter studied very quietly. That's probably why she came down so hard on you tonight. We'd already been fighting before you got there."

Eager to draw her out of her misery, I cranked the engine. "Let's check The Movie Rack."

We did, and it was much the same. The spirit energy that had animated the sign for so long was gone as though it had never been. No wonder Timmy was frightened. Though, I had to wonder, if the dybbuk knew where to find him, and there was no mistaking he was a supercharged poltergeist, why hadn't he been, well, devoured?

And did I really have to keep thinking *dybbuk* when I was ninety-nine percent certain the culprit was Ambrose?

"What now?" Amelie yawned until her eyes squinched closed. "Food?"

"Food," I agreed. "You can stay here. I'll run inside the Waffle Iron and grab the usual."

"You are an angel," she murmured, curling against the door. "Remember pecan waffles are how you get into heaven."

Necromancers didn't go to heaven. We were buried beneath yew trees under full moons and returned to Hecate. But pecan waffles sounded good, so I placed the order.

Amelie was out cold when I returned, so I parked in her driveway and divvied up the food.

"What about Jolene?" Her eyes kept drooping. "You can't leave her out all day."

"I'll catch a cab and drive her home after I eat." I walked Amelie to her house then nudged her inside before shutting the door and carrying my food to Woolly. "Hey, girl. Quiet night?"

The porch light flickered, the equivalent of a shrug.

"How are the wards treating you?" I kicked off my shoes and climbed on the porch to reach for them. A few stanzas of beautiful music flowed through my ears before scratching and dissolving into a muted whine. The discordant noise threatened to give me a headache. I hated that Woolly was stuck with it for the day. "I bet that's uncomfortable, huh?"

A few more blinks signaled her agreement.

"I promise to finish the job tomorrow, even if I have to bail on Taz and call out of work."

A warm glow bathed my face, her gratitude like sunlight on my cheeks.

"I'm going to sit out here and stuff my face," I told her, plopping down in the swing. "After that, I need to catch a ride back to HQ to pick up Jolene."

Woolly dimmed, her disappointment clear. She was still not a huge fan of me leaving, though she was better about letting me go.

"It's all right," I soothed her. "I won't be gone long, and I promise to make no pit stops."

A whistled note had me checking the trees for wind, but the branches were still, the predawn quiet.

I set my carryout container aside and munched on a rolled-up waffle as I went in search of the sound. I wasn't surprised when it led me around the side of the porch that faced the carriage house. I wasn't surprised when a flash of movement, the pop of a white button-down caught my eye. But I was surprised when the luminous creature stalking through my garden in another borrowed shirt sketched a courtly bow in my direction before he vanished as a sigh on a nonexistent wind.

ELEVEN

I studied the spot where Ambrose pulled a Houdini like he
might pop back into existence and let me question him if he
noticed me staring too long. I didn't make the conscious choice
to go knock on the carriage house door, but I shocked back to awareness when my knuckles hit wood.

Suddenly it mattered that Linus answer.

But he didn't.

I tested the knob and found it unlocked. This time I didn't hesitate and invited myself into Linus's temporary home. The living
room still held an assortment of trunks. I smelled maple syrup and
pancakes and, below that, bacon and sausage, like breakfast was the
only meal ever cooked here. The dining room table contained the
same clutter as always. The addition of Linus's sketchbook was new,
and he'd left the book open to the drawing of me. Or Ambrose had.

I didn't want to think too hard about that last possibility.

The bedroom I saved for last, and its pin-neatness worried me.
The bed was made, the quilt tucked snug against the pillows. It didn't
look slept in at all. But Linus was an *everything in its place* kind of

guy. Just because he made the bed didn't mean he never slept in it. I was being ridiculous. Right?

I accepted there were no clues to find about the time I got a handful of Linus's cotton briefs. I shoved his underwear back in the drawer I had no business searching and left the house before he caught me being a creeper.

I wasn't a fan of cabs, but I called one all the same. I couldn't bear leaving Jolene in a parking lot all day. The driver who pulled up to the curb wasn't the chatty sort, and I appreciated that. It wasn't until I was straddling Jolene that Cletus appeared.

His somber outline sharpened, dark against the lightening sky, and he hovered above me, looking forlorn.

I watched his sullen flutters for a full minute, but he didn't perform any tricks. "Where have you been?"

The fabric of his hood rustled as he lifted his head and turned his facelessness toward the fading imprint of the moon.

"I appreciate your discretion. Amelie is..." I hesitated, unable to put my finger on the reason why I had kept Cletus a secret from her. "I'm not sure what she would make of you."

Cletus appeared to have no opinion on the matter, which suited me fine.

When I cranked up Jolene, instead of heading home as I'd promised Woolly, I found myself idling in the empty street in front of the *Cora Ann*. Morning was on the rise, and the lights onboard were all extinguished. Only the dock remained lit. There was no movement, no sound. It was gloomy, its splendor unraveling, the way a boat with a ghost ought to look.

The wraith gazed after it with what I could only describe as longing, but he stuck to me.

An early morning runner breezed past, a reminder I ought to be heading home. "What is it with you and that boat?"

His skeletal arm raised, and his bony finger pointed to the second deck, at the window I was certain belonged to the dining room.

"I don't get it." I sighed. "I'm sorry. I would take you there, but you can't cross water."

Cletus neither agreed nor disagreed, as was his way. Again, I was struck with a resounding certainty that Linus had misled me about his wraith. Cletus wasn't all black smoke and claws, and I didn't buy that he was operating within set parameters, either. Moments like this betrayed him.

Quick as a rattler strike, a black-clad arm snaked around me and twisted the key, killing Jolene before coiling around my waist. A small palm clamped over my mouth as I sucked in air to scream, and a smooth cheek brushed mine. *"Boo."*

Adrenaline roaring in my ears, I bared my teeth then bit down hard enough to taste blood.

"Goddess, Grier." Becky leapt back, flinging her hand. "Is that any way to say hello?"

"Hello, Becky." I spat pink on the sidewalk. "How do you want to die?"

Who did that? Tackled people on the street? She could have gotten herself killed.

"I have a very specific fantasy, if you must know," Boaz drawled as he crossed the street to join us. "It involves me at age ninety-nine, a bottle of oil, and—"

"Cletus could have hurt her." I dismounted Jolene and advanced on him. "*I* could have hurt her." I glared at him. "I might still hurt you."

"No offense, Squirt, but your wraith might be defective. And you wouldn't hurt me." He winked, and the morning warmed. "You like my face too much to wipe the floor with it."

Aware I was only reinforcing bad behavior, I couldn't help smiling as he stroked my ego. Brownie points were awarded for pretending I was a threat to him. Smart man. Maybe he realized one day I would be. Plus, he was right. I did like his face. Especially now that I knew what he could do with his lips.

Boaz was staring at my mouth like he'd done the same math and wanted to check our answers against each other.

"Becky, never sneak up on Grier. It's not fun or funny." His flat delivery left no room for argument. "Not when you've been where she's gone and survived."

"Sorry, Grier." Becky was sucking on her wound. "I spook the guys all the time. I didn't think."

"No problem." My heart would stop attempting to blast open my chest cavity and escape at any moment, I was sure. "It happens."

Boaz shot her a pointed look, and she backed off to give us privacy.

"Where is your shadow?" Boaz tipped his head back. "I haven't seen him."

Cletus, a wraith of few moans, joined us then. Late to the party, he nonetheless billowed menacingly, swiping out with his claws and catching Boaz on the forearm. The kittens had done worse, but Boaz got with the program and took a healthy step away from me. His job done, Cletus returned to watching the *Cora Ann*.

"Maybe you're right," I conceded. "I'll talk to Linus about him."

Hooking his thumbs in the back pockets of his tactical pants, Boaz rocked on his heels. "You haven't asked the obvious question."

I rolled a shoulder. "I doubted you'd answer me."

"I could tell you," he said, playing along, "but—"

"—you'd have to kill me?" I finished for him.

"I was thinking more along the lines of chaining you in the basement at Mom's." His fingers closed over my wrist. "I have manacles in just your size."

I bit the inside of my cheek. "I'm not going to ask."

"It's probably best you don't." He pulled me closer and dropped a kiss on the tip of my nose. "I don't want to scare you off."

"I'm a necromancer." I huffed. "I don't scare easy."

"Then what were those cute panicked mouse noises you made a minute ago?"

I narrowed my eyes at him. "What panicked mouse noises?"

"The ones you breathed the second before you bit through

Becky's middle finger. How is she supposed to flip people off now?"

"A, those weren't mouse noises. I was sucking in oxygen to scream bloody murder, and her hand caused air to whistle—not squeak—through my nose." I caught his wrist and examined the faint scores in his skin. "And B, it's rude to flip people off."

"Well, doc?" The fingers of his other hand tangled in my hair. "Am I going to live?"

"Don't be a baby. He barely broke the skin." I reached for the pen in my back pocket and drew a healing sigil beneath the wounds. The skin knit together before my eyes, and I capped my weapon of choice. "There you go. Good as new."

"What was that?" He gawked at the pen, then the sigil, and then me. "I've never seen one of those."

"Um, can you continue to never have seen one?" I winced at my careless mistake. "It's an invention of Linus's. I shouldn't have used it on you without his permission."

"So that's how he makes his money, huh?" He tapped the end of the pen, but his voice lacked the edge I had come to expect when he spoke of Linus. "I can respect him wanting to earn his own keep."

"I'm sorry. I seem to have gone momentarily deaf." I wiggled my right pinky in the corresponding ear. "Were you just civil to Linus?"

"It is easier to be civil to Linus when Linus isn't here, but yes."

Hmm. Maybe he could be trained after all.

Boaz winced and tapped a device hugging his ear I hadn't even noticed he was wearing. "Yes, sir."

"Look at you all mannered up," I teased, but a burst of insight had my jaw dropping. "You're hunting the dybbuk, aren't you?" There was absolutely no other reason for him to be playing Man in Black with an Elite unit in Savannah otherwise. "Admit it. I'm right."

"How did—?" He touched his earpiece again. "Yes, sir." He bent down, lips brushing my throat. "Meet me in Forsyth Park in two hours. I can sneak away then."

"Care to be more specific?" Forsyth Park spanned thirty acres. And then it hit me. "The playground."

"The playground," he agreed, and then he was gone.

A cool hand brushed my arm, and I found Cletus half-formed beside me. "Ready to go home?"

The wraith didn't answer either way, but he did drift toward Jolene.

Woolly's disco light reception as she flickered in panicked bursts made me feel like dirt for breaking my word to her, so I played a card guaranteed to earn her instant forgiveness. "I'm sorry." I gripped the doorknob she wasn't allowing me to twist. "It turns out Boaz is still in town on some kind of covert mission. He spotted me and came to say hello."

The brass spun in my palm, the door opening in her eagerness for details.

"He's hunting the weirdo that's been hanging around in our back-yard." I should have outed Ambrose to him, but there hadn't been time. And, okay, I owed Linus one last chance at explaining their connection before involving the authorities. "He wants to meet at Forsyth Park."

The floor register exhaled a dreamy sigh that had me rolling my eyes.

I called Linus, but it dumped straight to voicemail. Exiting Woolly, I made the trek across the garden, already certain of what I would discover. I knocked, and no one answered. I called out, and no one answered. I kicked the door, and no one answered. Sensing a theme, I braced my forehead against the wood and debated my options.

"Far be it from me to interrupt, but can I perhaps be of assistance? Whatever it is you want, the door is in no position to give it to you."

That voice.

I whirled, putting the door at my back. "Ambrose."

Cletus materialized in front of me, a shield forged of churning nightmares, and hissed at the garish interloper.

"Ah, she remembers." He kept to the far end of the garden, where the deepest shadows clung, but the living flame masquerading as hair cast flickering light across the sharp planes of his face, too bright for Cletus to douse. "You remember so little, I'm flattered I made the cut."

The barb struck, but it was a flesh wound. I'd suffered worse. "You're trespassing."

"Oh, I think not." He chuckled, and the sound was made of sparkling moonlight. "What is it you want, little goddess?"

After swatting Cletus aside, I bared down on Ambrose. "Where is Linus?"

The angle of his jaw hid the cut of his smile. "Unavailable."

The sound of my molars grinding ought to have warned him of my mood. "When will he be back?"

Ambrose cocked his head. "Do you want him back so badly?"

"We need to talk." *About you* I left unsaid.

"Alas, I am not his keeper. I do so hate leaving a woman unsatisfied, but I fear I must."

Turning on his heel, he marched toward a section of fence like he planned on walking right through.

"Wait."

"No." Ambrose halted the length of a heartbeat and glanced over his shoulder. Dawn bathed his face in reds and oranges that sparked off his hair, and my first unobstructed look at him made my heart stutter. His flame-bright hair crackled, and the blue of his irises tipped into black while he stared at me, but what caught my eye was a cluster of freckles under his left eye that formed the petals of a daisy. "You have no power over me."

I took a halting step after him. "What are you?"

"The night eternal."

And then he was gone.

And I had my answer.

Ambrose was the devourer. And, upon a second viewing, I was certain of his identity.

Oh, Linus. What have you done?

I retreated to Woolly and slumped on the front steps. I couldn't resist checking the carriage house one last time before I set out for the park, but Linus hadn't returned. Neither had Ambrose. Though I supposed one couldn't very well travel without the other.

———————

FORSYTH PARK WAS ROUSING itself when I arrived. Runners mostly. Some joggers. A gaggle of elderly power-walkers. All eager to clock their miles before it got too hot. I was sweaty, and I hadn't done anything but stroll beneath the moss-hung oaks down the walkway leading to one of the city's most iconic sites.

The cast-iron fountain burbled happily despite the hour, a pristine white that popped bright against the dark foliage of the surrounding trees. The robed woman atop its upper tier gripped her staff and held court high above the other denizens of the park. Wading birds and rushes lurked beneath the curling lip above which the figure stood. In the basin, swans spouted water over their heads while mermen blasted water from the shell horns lifted to their mouths.

I stood there a moment, gripping the black wrought iron railing circling the fountain until it bit into my hands, enjoying the cool spray on my face.

Hello, procrastination, my old friend.

I pushed off the fence and made my way to the playground. I didn't have to look far for Boaz. It was hard to miss him decked out in black tactical gear even if he hadn't been sitting in a swing that looked ready to cry uncle.

"I was starting to think I'd been stood up." He patted his lap. "Do you remember how?"

"You've got to be kidding me." I walked up to him, so close our knees bumped. "That chain is about to snap from holding you. I'm not adding my weight too."

"Aww, come on." His eyes twinkled. "For old time's sake."

"I know this game." I tsked at him. "You just want to get your boy bits near my girl bits."

"Maybe."

"Do *not* tell your sister I fell for this." Saying no when he was being playful had never been my strong suit. "She'll never let me live it down."

He mimed zipping his mouth shut. "My lips are sealed."

"Mmm-hmm." I got a death grip on the chains above his head and lifted myself up, letting him thread my legs to either side of his hips so that I sat in his lap, facing him. "This was a lot easier when I was ten."

Boaz started rocking us, his hands fisting the chain below mine. "It's a lot more fun now, though."

"Is that what this is? Fun?" I darted a glance at the frame above us. "I feel like the chains will snap at any moment."

"I won't let you fall." He linked his arms around my waist. "See? Snug as a bug."

I cleared my throat, striving for a casual tone that was impossible with him wedged between my thighs. "So you're in town to stake out the *Cora Ann*."

He just smiled. "Am I?"

"Yes, you are." I traced the shape of his lips with my finger, thrilled that I could, that he let me. "You're using Timmy as bait to lure the devourer."

"You lost me." His forehead creased. "Who's Timmy?"

"The ghost boy marooned on the *Cora Ann*."

"Ah. Him." He snapped his teeth at my finger, and I squeaked. "You really should talk to a doctor about that whistling sound your nose makes."

I cradled my hand against my chest. "Stop trying to distract me."

"Spoilsport." He sighed. "Savannah is experiencing a flux of energy that led the Society to believe a dybbuk had manifested. We got confirmation when it stepped up its game from extinguishing spectral hotspots to devouring ghosts to desiccating vampires."

"Vampires," I echoed, as in more than one.

"You don't sound surprised." His gaze sharpened. "What do you know about this?"

I divulged what Amelie had overheard and waited on him to thunder about eavesdropping, but he appeared to be on his best behavior. Too bad I was about to poke him in a tender spot. "One of the deaths implicates your aunt. Doesn't that make this a conflict of interest for you?"

"Desmond Peterkin was the third victim." He studied me. "I was already on the case by the time he was killed."

"Dybbuk are possessed necromancers." I studied him right back. "That means you're hunting one of our own."

"My duty, as an Elite, is to protect the Society and all its members. Even if I'm protecting it from itself."

I gripped the chains for support. "Do you have any idea *who* you're hunting?"

"Grier," he groaned my name like a curse. "Your white-knuckled grip tells me you already know or think you do. Spill, Squirt."

While the Society might look the other way when ghost lights extinguished, vampires were paying customers. The Society was built upon their ability to deliver the promise of immortality. Necromancers didn't play around when it came to money. One refund could dent a reputation. More than one could sink a family for centuries.

Not even a Lawson was immune from crimes of this magnitude.

"I met a man calling himself Ambrose in my garden," I said softly. "He was wearing one of Linus's shirts."

"I'm sorry, Squirt." He covered my hands with his. "I know you wanted Linus to be your anchor, but from here it looks like he's the one sinking."

I dipped my chin. "Does his mother know he's involved?"

"The Grande Dame has been kept out of the loop for obvious reasons. She's aware of the disturbances, and she's been informed there are Elite on the ground in Savannah, but she's not privy to the specifics." He rubbed his thumbs over my knuckles. "The only way this works is if we catch him red-handed. There can be no mistakes. Not with a Lawson. Our case must be airtight. We only get one chance. The Grande Dame will vanish her heir to protect him."

The Grande Dame's fury if her son was exposed was too great for me to contemplate so late in my day. "How do you know the dybbuk will come to the *Cora Ann?*"

"We're hedging our bets. We've been seeding the local papers for weeks with updates on the supernatural disturbances in the hopes we might flush out our perp. We've secured television and radio coverage to get the word out about the poltergeist aboard the *Cora Ann.* We've done everything but tack up a neon sign that says *All You Can Eat,* but we haven't gotten a nibble so far."

"That explains a lot, actually." I hauled myself up by the chains and wriggled free of Boaz. The urge to pace struck me as soon as my feet hit the ground. "But it doesn't explain why Timmy chose now to lose his marbles. He was a benign entity by all accounts until recently. The escalation of his behavior from spooking guests in empty halls to impaling them with silverware isn't normal progression, even for a poltergeist of his strength."

"We amped him up," Boaz admitted. "It was a last resort."

"Timmy will die." I whirled on him. "Okay, so he's already dead, but this will vanquish him for good."

There was no guessing if his energy would burn out before the dybbuk finished the job, but it felt cruel.

"We had to bait our trap somehow."

"He's a little boy." A scared little boy who had no explanation for his wild fits of violence.

"He's not sentient," Boaz protested.

That argument was holding less and less water with me these days. Cletus was *more.* Why couldn't this little boy be too? I had no idea what made them different, but they were not just electrical charges and smoke.

"He told me the devourer was coming." That counted for something. He hadn't been stuck in a loop murmuring stock phrases. He heard me, and he responded. "He understands he's going to die. Again."

"I'm sorry, Grier, I really am, but I'm a cog in the machine, and the machine only cares about the bottom dollar. Vampires are worth more to the Society than ghosts. This operation will move forward, and there's nothing I can do about it."

"I need to get back home." Giving up Linus felt like a betrayal, even if Boaz had already locked him in his sights. And learning the violence about the *Cora Ann* had been orchestrated to lure in the dybbuk made me sick when I thought of poor Marit and all the other victims viewed as acceptable losses because they were human. I backed toward the path. "I have a big project to finish tomorrow."

"Don't walk away angry."

I shook my head, unable to articulate the problem. "I'm not angry."

His fist closed around one chain, and I imagined it gasping for breath. "Will you still call me?"

"Yeah." I wrapped my arms around my middle. "I will."

"Help us get him on that boat, Grier."

"Help you...?" The true reason for this meeting smacked me in the face with enough force to turn my cheek. I should have known a career soldier wouldn't break cover during a stakeout for anything so paltry as a kiss. "How am I supposed to do that?"

"He trusts you," he coaxed. "The sooner we end this, the better it will go for him."

"I have to go."

The walk back to Jolene did nothing to improve my mood. I had forgotten to mention Russo to him, and I regretted not hugging Boaz goodbye or telling him to be careful. His job was dangerous, and there were no guarantees in life, but either I was going nuts or there was more to this than met the eye.

TWELVE

I slept so deep not even the dream could touch me, and I woke without fanfare in my own bed.

A flashback of the last time I'd woken in a bed hit me between the eyes so hard I whimpered.

I'm home. I'm safe. I'm home. I'm safe.

I was in my own bed, in my own room, wearing my own clothes. No eager maid dressed in frilly strawberry layers was poised to burst through the door to feed or water or pet or brush me. Volkov was locked away. The master was in the wind, but he wasn't in my house, and right now that felt like a small victory.

Woolly started the shower, and I didn't fight her over the necessity. I got clean, dressed, and then clutched the grimoire across my chest like a talisman as I went in search of Linus.

The carriage house door stood open, and the smell of coffee coiled around me in the entryway. "Linus?"

He appeared, immaculate as always, and passed me a brown paper bag with the vulpine logo of a local coffee shop. "I had a craving for horchata and brought kolache for you."

"Thanks." There was no horchata in sight, and I wondered if

melding with a wraith meant you no longer had to eat or drink to survive. "I haven't had kolache in...a long time."

The circular pastries came in a variety of flavors, and he had selected poppy seed and cream cheese for me, two of my favorites. One day I really would stop being surprised by what he remembered about me.

"Eat up." He poured me a glass of milk, sank into his spot at the table, and began flipping through a notebook. "You need to get started soon if you're going to finish Woolly tonight."

I joined him and forced myself to bite into the sweet dough, to chew, to swallow. All the while I examined him for signs of Ambrose lurking beneath his skin and came up empty. Other than the dark circles under his eyes, there was no evidence to suggest he wasn't simply a tutor enjoying a sabbatical in his home town.

"You're staring," he mused without glancing away from his papers. "Do I have milk on my upper lip?"

"No. Sorry. No." I redoubled my efforts to stuff my mouth so full I couldn't let the cat out of the bag. I crammed in the last bite and chased it with a gulp of milk. "Done."

Linus startled at my chipmunk cheeks and the dribble on my chin. "All right."

He gathered the remaining box from yesterday, and we walked to Woolly together. I was gripping Eileen so hard, the grimoire squinted. I willed my fingers to relax and settled on the ground in the spot where we'd left off last night.

"Are you sure this is soft enough?" I smoothed my hand along the foundation, but it felt solid to me. "I should have sucked it up and finished this yesterday."

Ambrose would still be a mystery if I had, and Timmy would be just another ghost, and I wouldn't feel so torn.

"You couldn't have finished it in a single night," Linus assured me. "I was overly ambitious when I suggested it was possible." He snapped his fingers. "I almost forgot. I bought us a few items that ought to make this go more smoothly."

"Oh?" I sat in the grass and started arranging my workspace while he disappeared back into the carriage house. "Are you ready for this, Woolly?"

The nearest window opened and shut in an affirmative.

"The design is a bit loud," Linus was saying as he approached, "but it ought to do the trick."

I twisted to see what he was talking about and goggled. "Oh, um. Wow."

He had bought us matching welding helmets. One was chili-pepper red, the other lime green, both with black and white scroll detail that flung out like spider webs across the back before dissolving into curling vines that snaked over the front. The name of the manufacturer had been stamped beneath all that in neat rows in an easy-to-read font. A sticker glued to the visor boasted automatic lens adjustment.

"This was all they had in full helmets. I figured we might as well invest in case your magic holds more surprises we've yet to discover." He dropped buttery-soft leather gloves in my lap as well. Their thin-ness reminded me of driving gloves. "These are cut and puncture proof. I bought them from a local law enforcement supply store. They're strong enough to protect your hands from debris, but flexible enough not to impede your work." One final item pooled across my knees after falling from his hand. "The jacket is reinforced with precurved sleeves and water-repellent zippers. It's fully lined, and there are several interior pockets. There are also armor plates in the shoulders, elbows and back."

"This is a motorcycle jacket." I couldn't bring myself to touch what must be hundreds of dollars' worth of leather and flash. "I can't accept this." My treacherous fingers slid over the supple black leather without permission, and I might have whimpered. "Okay, I *can* accept this." I brought it to my nose and inhaled that new-leather scent like a dork. "But I'm paying you back."

"I'll forward you the bill if that means you'll use it." His lips twitched as I rubbed the jacket on my face like I was one of the kittens from the garage. "You needed a new one. This way it can do double duty."

"You're using logic against me." I caved to temptation and shrugged into the new love of my life. "It fits."

"You have your friend Neely to thank for that. He was happy to select the cut and provide measurements."

Since Cruz worked for the Society, and I had confided in Linus about Neely, there was no mystery about how he had known where to go, but it still shook me how he mentioned my friend so casually.

"Why am I not surprised he would use my measurements for evil?" I zipped up and flexed my arms, which probably looked like a chicken trying to take flight. "He knows I'm allergic to spending money."

"I told him we're family, that it was a gift."

Dread ballooned in my chest at his kindness. I didn't fool myself that I knew Linus, but I couldn't picture him murdering vampires without Ambrose as a monkey on his back. Before I thought better of it, I hooked an arm around one of his thighs in half of a hug. "Thank you."

The tips of his cool fingers skated over my hair. "You're welcome."

After disentangling himself from me, he sat at my elbow to observe the final stretch. That's when I noticed he wore a jacket similar to mine, insurance against any protest I might make against such a lavish gift, proving yet again how well he knew me. He removed a pair of gloves from his pocket and put them on then settled the helmet in place.

Following his example, I pulled on my gloves and practiced sigils inside the grimoire for a few minutes. Certain that Linus was right, that my penmanship wouldn't be affected, I set back to work applying the warding. When I finished the second side of the foundation, I popped on my helmet, and we braced ourselves as I swiped on the grounding sigil.

Chunks of concrete pinged off our helmets and hit the ground as the design sank into the foundation.

"Woohoo!" I crowed after double-checking that neither of us was bleeding on our arms or torsos. His precautions had paid off in spades. We removed our helmets and clanked them in a toast before strapping them back in place. "Success."

Settling into a rhythm, I finished up the pattern on the third side then painted on the grounding sigil. Cocky after that success, I completed the fourth then added the mélange with a twist of my wrist.

An explosion rocked Woolly that sent us flying across the garden to land in a miniature rosebush with delicate apricot-colored blossoms. Thanks to the protective gear, their fragile thorns failed to pierce my leather-clad skin, but they tangled the ends of my hair and scratched at my ankles.

"That was...unexpected." I rolled my head toward Linus. "You okay?"

"Yes." He extracted himself from the pointy limbs with care not to damage it more than we already had then offered me a hand. We stripped out of our gear and dropped it in the grass. "We need to check on Woolly."

The sound of her name set off a chain reaction of panicked impulses that set my pulse sprinting. I got my feet under me, thorns be damned, and ran to the back porch. The planks hummed under my feet, electrified. I tapped into the wards, and a lush symphony filled my head. Each note swelled into the next, *allegro, allegro, allegro,* and then—*crescendo.*

Tears wobbled in my vision as I swung my head toward Linus, our gazes clashing as magic sang through me.

Woolly was flush with power, the combination a strange mixture of Maud and me, a blending that felt right, that said *home.*

The back door flung open as Woolly trumpeted her glee via smoke alarm.

I stuck out my hand for Linus, inviting him up to join us, and I pulled him into a silly dance that made the tips of his ears flush red as he jangled in my arms like an anatomical skeleton on a faulty stand. I spun and whooped until I was dizzy. Linus, not willing to get near another of Woolly's doors, guided me to the steps and helped me plop down without face-planting.

"She's so..." I waved my arms. "So..." I grabbed him and shook him. "*Alive.*"

He let me rattle his marbles without complaint. "I'm glad."

"I forgot how good this feels." The wood beneath me thrummed with potent magic, and I felt more alive than I had in years too. "We used to be so connected. She could ping me when she needed me, and I could sense her when I was in town. This feels like that." I took his hand and placed it on the plank under my feet. "Can you feel it?"

"I do." His fingers spanned the wood. "I can't imagine what it's like for you."

"Drinking liquid sunshine," I told him with a smile. "That's how it feels." I collapsed back across the porch and let the magic flow over and through me. "All of it, everything, was worth this. Having her back."

Linus relaxed his perfect posture, twisting around to watch as I made a fool of myself by creating paint-chip angels on the peeling back porch. "This, all of it, was worth it for me too."

The urge to ask what, specifically, he meant pursed my lips, but I feared how it might come out sounding. Did he mean leaving Atlanta, his job, his life, for this chance to observe me? Or did he mean the things Ambrose had done, the energies he had consumed, the power he had given them both?

"What are you doing tonight?" The question popped out before I made the conscious decision to save him from himself. "Are you up for taking a fieldtrip?"

"Nothing I can't postpone." He considered my face, and I wondered what he saw there. "Is everything all right?"

"Remember how we talked about the ghost boy aboard the *Cora*

Ann?" I laid my trap with such care, I might have walked into it myself. "He's exhibiting odd symptoms."

"Oh?" Curiosity replaced his wariness. "How so?"

"He spoke to me. Not *at* me, *to* me." I wet my lips and sat upright. "He mentioned the night eternal coming for him."

"Loops can be convincing." Linus shook his head. "He might have drowned in the dark. The river may be the eternal night that claimed him."

"He also mentioned the devourer was hunting him." I placed no emphasis on the title. "He claimed that's why he attacked Marit and me. He thought I was one too." Ghosts were drawn to necromancers like bees to flowers, so it made sense I would read as *other* to him. "That doesn't sound like a fear a six-year-old boy would have, not even one who drowned."

Linus hesitated a beat too long. "Did he say anything else?"

"Only 'He comes,' followed by tears and a vanishing trick." I couldn't look at him anymore. "I'm not sure if there's anything we can do, but I've never encountered a ghost that self-aware."

"Consider my interest piqued." He arched an eyebrow. "What time do you want to go?"

"I have a lesson with Taz and then work." Neither appealed to me, but routine was important to maintain the illusion. "I'll grab a bite on River Street after work and wait until the boat is empty. I'll call you with the all clear."

"I'll be here," he said as he stood. "I have some reading to catch up on."

"Great." How much damage could he do between now and then? "See you later."

Movement teased the corner of my eye, announcing Taz's stealthy arrival. I was tempted to stay seated and let her take a free swing at me just to see her face when Woolly zapped her into next week for attacking me on warded ground. Thanks to the new sigils, I was safe even sitting on the bottom step with my feet resting in the cool grass.

"You look like someone fed your parakeet to a cat." She braced her feet apart and tapped her boot, the one usually flying at my face. It was weird seeing her use it for standing. "What happened?"

"Doing the right thing sucks," I confided. "It sucks hard."

"How is that a newsflash? People do wrong because it's the path of least resistance. It gets them what they want without them putting in the work to earn it." She popped her knuckles. "Being a good person is hard. Doing the right thing is hard. That's why only masochists keep a clean nose."

"That's the most I've heard you speak," I marveled. "It's also the first time I've been called a masochist."

A roll of her shoulders dismissed the conversation, and a curl of her fingers invited me to dance.

Too bad this wasn't the happy dancing I'd done earlier. Maybe I'd get lucky and Linus would patch me up one last time before I marched him off to the gallows.

THIRTEEN

Halfway through my lesson, Taz accused me of stepping into punches I could have deflected. Our earlier conversation left her convinced I was punishing myself, and she refused to be an enabler. She spat at me on her way out and informed me lessons were over until I got my head on straight. I wanted to fight her, and that more than anything convinced me the bare-knuckle brawl I craved was my dumbest idea yet.

I had no business fighting with anything tougher than a plush bear.

Taz would yank out my stuffing, gnaw off my button eyes and rip me apart at the seams if I kept pissing her off.

Work didn't go much better. I was tucked away in the same parlor on the *Cora Ann* and given another task to complete alone. I sneaked upstairs on my break, but I found Mr. Voorhees already there. He stood in the center of the room, his arms at his sides, flexing his hands into fists. I left him to whatever he was doing and slinked back to my post before he could pressure me to talk to the police. I almost tried again when Arnold dismissed me for the night, but I figured there was no point when Linus and I would return within a few hours.

With that happy thought in mind, I drove to HQ and went in search of Amelie. But it was Neely who intercepted me in the hall with a wrinkled nose and reddening eyes.

"What do they have you doing over there?" He sneezed three times fast. "Cleaning out sewers?"

"I'll have you know the perfume I'm wearing is eau de mold, not sewer."

"That explains it." Another sneeze ripped through him. "You can't stay here. I love you, but no. You have to leave. My allergy medicines can only do so much."

"I'm looking for Amelie." I took a healthy step back. "How booked is she tonight?"

"She's not. At all." He gave me a funny look. "She called in last night and tonight. She didn't tell you?"

"You must have your days wrong." I frowned. "She picked me up after her shift last night."

"I can check her timecard if you'd like, but I'm telling you she wasn't here. Cricket almost blew a gasket. Even after she shuffled the girls around, she still had to lead a tour herself to make up the difference. She was not pleased." He dashed beneath his watery eyes and darted around me to hold open the door. "Sorry about the eviction notice, but you've got to go. Call me if you want to finish this conversation later."

A prickling sense of foreboding raised the hairs down my arms, but I wouldn't let him see me rattled.

"I understand not everyone appreciates the bouquet of a good vintage mold the way I do." It was a miracle that fungi-encrusted wallpaper hadn't sent the *Cora Ann*'s passengers screaming long before Timmy. "We'll have to catch up this weekend. Promise. I owe you a drink for getting me the job with Mr. Voorhees." I fluttered my eyelashes. "Unless you don't want the scoop on my date with Boaz."

Neely rolled in his lips, but a whimper escaped. "Begone, temptress!"

"Oh, I'm going." I winked at him on my way past. "And I'm taking the details of our playground rendezvous with me."

"You're killing me." He thumped his head on the door. "I'm in actual, physical pain."

"Yeah, if you'd stop banging your head, you wouldn't have that problem." I sashayed toward Jolene, grateful to Cricket for all her lessons as I played my part to the hilt. "Toodles."

Lost in thoughts of Amelie, I didn't notice Detective Russo until she stepped into my path.

"Ms. Woolworth." She raked her avaricious gaze over me. "You've got your color back."

The distance to HQ and the safety it promised helped me stand my ground. "Can I help you?"

"You can tell me the truth." Her expression sharpened. "What really happened to Maud Woolworth?"

"I told you she suffered a heart attack." The Society would back that lie, though it tasted foul in my mouth. "Check the medical examiner's report. You'll find it matches my account."

Just that fast, she changed tactics. "Where did you go after Ms. Woolworth died?"

Air solidified in my lungs, making breathing about as possible as taking flight. "Away."

"Can you be more specific?" She pulled out that damned notepad and checked one of its earliest pages. "Your mother is deceased. She died in a car accident when you were five. That's when Maud became your guardian. There's no mention of your father, so you couldn't have gone to him. You were a minor. Someone had to care for you."

Care was not the word I would use. I had been fed and clothed and sheltered in the broadest sense, and that was all.

"Given Ms. Meacham's concern over your latest disappearance, and the signs of physical abuse present when we met, I must now consider her account in a new light." The pen in her hand tapped against the pad, eager to record my miseries. "The blood at the scene

—did it belong to you?" She whirled her pen around my face, the healed evidence of my latest bout with Taz still clear. "Who hurt you, Grier? Was it Maud? Or someone else? Are they still hurting you? Do you need help?"

"Maud was my mother's best friend. She was a second mother to me. She never raised a hand against me, and she would have ruined anyone who dared to try. Financially, socially, emotionally." I set my jaw. "No one has abused me." *Lies, lies, lies.* "I stayed with Clarice Lawson, Maud's younger sister, until I came of age." *Lies, lies, lies.* "That's it. That's all there is."

She set her mouth into a mulish line. "I don't believe you."

"You asked me questions." I shrugged. "I can't help you don't like the answers."

"What are you hiding?" Her hand snaked out to shackle my wrist. "Tell me the truth."

A black figure coalesced behind her, his bony fingers spread wide in anticipation.

"Let go." The clench of her hand made cold sweat blossom down my spine. "Or I'll make you let go."

This woman had made an enemy out of me by invoking Maud, but it still wasn't smart to go around roughing up Savannah's finest. Not unless I wanted to bring the Grande Dame down on me.

"You heard the lady." The door to HQ swung open, and Neely strolled out with his phone lifted. He was recording the whole thing. "Let her go."

"Turn that off." Russo's fingers twitched on my arm, but she held tight. "Erase it. Now."

"That's going to be a hard no, but thanks for asking." He kept filming. "Oh, and in case you try to smash my phone, I maybe should have prefaced this by telling you this is live. You're streaming to the world's most popular social media site as we speak." He flipped the camera to face him. "Hi, Mom!"

Jaw clenched, Russo released me and backed away. "I will have my answers."

I wondered if our virtual audience heard the threat as clearly as I did.

Neely killed the feed then zoomed in on Russo's license plate as she sped off in her nondescript sedan. The *click, click, click* told me he had snapped photos before he pocketed the phone and swooped down on me.

"Are you okay?" He trembled around me. "I was watching to make sure you got to your bike okay, and then I saw her blindside you."

"I'm glad you were here." I sank against him. "I don't know what I would have done without you."

"That's the same cop who came to see you before, right?" He rubbed up and down my back like enough friction might soothe his shakes too. "What does she want?"

"I'm not sure." That much was the truth.

"I tagged Cruz in that video." He pulled back to look at me. "Is that okay?"

Sure. Yeah. The more humans, the merrier. *Goddess.* The Grande Dame was going to have a dying duck fit. At least Cruz was on the Society payroll. They ought to be able to handle the damage control without me. "It's fine."

"Oh, God, Grier." He dropped his forehead to my shoulder. "I should have asked you first. I should have—"

"You did fine." It was not ideal, but it was done. "I'm fine. It will all be fine."

A phone chirped somewhere on his person, and he checked the display. "It's Cruz. Do you want to talk to him?"

"No, that's okay." I started making my escape. "I just want to go home and take a hot bath." His face fell, and my heart ached. "Tell him to call me with any questions tomorrow, okay?" That would give the Grande Dame or whoever fed Cruz details time to sort out a cover story. "Tell him thank you from me in advance."

"Are you sure you should take Jolene?" The phone quivered in his grip. "I can drive if you need me."

"The fresh air will clear my head," I promised him, since he was in no better shape than me. "I'll call you when I get home and let you know I made it."

"Deal." He toyed with the screen. "Be safe. Call if you need me."

I waved him off, straddled Jolene, and made my escape before we attracted more attention.

Jittery from my encounter with Russo, I hit a coffee shop and texted Amelie. She didn't reply. I almost called, but I didn't want to push her. She must have had a reason for not telling me she was taking the weekend off. Knowing her, she wanted to cram before taking her last finals.

Depressed over what I was about to do, I proceeded to make a bad situation worse by drinking roughly my weight in iced caramel macchiatos. There might have been a donut or two involved. A bear claw. Possibly one of those cream horn things too.

I was clinging to Linus's belief I needed to carb up like gospel.

Linus.

It was almost time to call him. I really, really didn't want to lift my phone. But I couldn't turn the other cheek, either. People— granted, they were undead people—were dying. Permanently. That was wrong, and it had to be stopped before the dybbuk claimed another victim.

After sloshing my way to the restroom, I did my business and washed my hands until they sparkled.

Procrastination was a serious talent of mine.

Heart a weight in my gut, I dialed up Linus. "Hey, are you ready?"

"I have a bag packed. I'll grab it and be on my way."

Carrying luggage sounded fitting since he wouldn't be going home after this for a long while.

"I'll meet you there." I ended the call before guilt leaked into my voice then rode Jolene to River Street. I parked in the same spot where Becky had accosted me and listened to the night sounds. "Cletus, you with me?"

The wraith drifted down to keep me company, and I had to wonder when his presence had become a comfort. Probably about the time he started acting unwraithlike. Yet another mystery in need of solving. Linus had chosen a piss-poor time to go on a killing spree.

A crimson sedan pulled alongside me and ejected Linus. He wore another pair of dark-wash jeans, a gray button-down shirt and work boots. A worn leather satchel crisscrossed his body. He murmured to the driver then turned to me.

The spark of excitement in his smile nearly slayed me. He might not believe Timmy was the real deal, but it was clear he wanted it to be true. He was eager to see the ghost boy with his own eyes. "Are you ready?"

I wished he hadn't asked me that. "Can we duck in your car for a second?"

"An obfuscation sigil." He read me easily. "Good idea."

"I haven't noticed any security or cameras onboard, but it's not like they would tell me if preventative measures got installed after Marit was attacked."

Not when I was under suspicion as far as her father and much of the crew was concerned.

Linus climbed back in and pulled a pen from his pocket, but I struggled to do more than perch on the edge of the bench seat. I was okay as long as I kept my feet planted on the ground, but swinging them onto the floorboard seemed as impossible as roping the moon. I tried, I really did, but the car was the same make and model as the one Volkov had stuffed me into weeks ago, and...

The second the thought registered, I bolted and almost knocked over Jolene in the process. "I can't."

"I understand." He exited again and cast his gaze around the market. "Where is the shop you mentioned? The churro one?"

"Esteban's stall is that way." Relief blasted through me when I realized I wouldn't have to sit in the car. "He won't mind if we use him for cover."

The man himself greeted us at the flap, smelling of sugar and fried dough, his arms dusted with white powder.

"Back so soon?" He rubbed his hands together. "Good. You should come back every day until you've put on at least twenty more pounds. You're too thin. You're like a papery layer of phyllo." He noticed Linus and drew him into the lecture. "Men like women with meat on their bones. Tell her."

Linus flushed a shade of red normally reserved for checkered picnic tablecloths. "Grier is lovely as is."

"You don't have to defend my honor with Esteban." I patted Linus on the shoulder. "He's not saying anything you haven't already told me."

"See?" Esteban crowed. "Men know what men like."

"Men must like this look." I lifted the hem of my shirt to flash ribs. "It's on magazine covers everywhere."

"Bah." He swatted the notion of pop culture perfection aside. "Real men know the value in a woman who embraces her curves."

"The reason we're here—" I cut in before he got too wound up, "—is to borrow your kitchen long enough to paint on obfuscation sigils. Do you mind?"

"What are you up to?" He folded his arms over his chest. "You tend to disappear on old Esteban. I can't be party to that nonsense. I don't have so many regular customers I can afford to lose even one."

"We're sneaking onto the *Cora Ann*, the boat where I'm working." I pasted on my best sheepish expression. "There's a ghost boy there I want Linus to see."

"Linus," he echoed. "Clarice Lawson's son?"

The son in question inclined his head. "It's a pleasure to meet you, Esteban."

"Your aunt was a good woman." He turned fond eyes on me. "She raised another good woman."

"I agree on both counts." Linus rubbed the skin over his breastbone. "I miss Maud every day."

"Me too," I murmured.

"All wounds will heal." Esteban leaned down from his great height to press a kiss to the top of my head. "You will see her again one day. Though not too soon, I hope." He gestured to his kitchen, a rectangle of canvas panels laced together. "Go do what you must." He spared a second look at Linus. "Take care of her. She is a precious treasure to me."

"I do my best," Linus assured him. "She is precious to us all."

Heat prickled in my cheeks that I rubbed away. "I can't take all the flattery, guys."

"Learn to take a compliment," Esteban chided. "The older and more beautiful you become, the more men will toss them like flowers at your feet. You must become familiar with the varieties so that you may distinguish between the hothouse stock, the wild ones, and those that are garden-tended."

Never would I have classified compliments in such a way, but he knew Maud, and he knew me. Our language was flowers. Or it used to be. "I'll see what I can do."

I scuttled into the small kitchen and pulled out my pen. Linus joined me, and we each drew on our own sigils but for a single line and then, by silent agreement, compared them. The root of the design was the same if you looked hard enough, but they shared few similarities in execution.

"The way your mind works never ceases to amaze me." He tapped the cap of his pen against his bottom lip. "I wonder if it would work the same if I drew your sigil on me."

"An experiment for another day." I kept my voice level. "We should get out from under Esteban so he can work." We completed our sigils then and disappeared from each other's sight. "Coming through." I skirted Esteban, who just smiled at empty air in the direction my voice originated. "Thanks for letting us borrow your kitchen."

"Anything for you." He straightened a display placard. "Next time, bring the other boy, the blond one. He spends his money."

"I'll do that." I chuckled. "Night."

The scuff of boots across cobbles told me Linus was near, but gauging distance was hard when you couldn't see the other person, and they couldn't see you.

"Was I rude?" His steps slowed. "Not to make a purchase in exchange for Esteban letting us use his kitchen?"

"Nah." The thought never would have crossed his mind. "He was just teasing me for bringing two guys to see him in as many nights."

We walked on while he digested this, and in minutes we stood before the *Cora Ann*.

"Stick close to me, and watch where you step," I warned him. "There's debris everywhere."

Prickles marched up my nape when he fell in step behind me on our trek across the gangway.

"Grier..." he began. "Have you experimented with this sigil over water?"

"Yes." Two or three times. "I tested it out while I was at work."

"Check your sigil."

A quick check of my forearm revealed the problem. The design was flaking. "Fiddlesticks."

"Crossing from land to water must have broken the seal." He pressed against me, skin a few degrees shy of normal through the layers of his clothing. "We need to hurry up and get onboard."

Nothing prevented us from leaping the locked gate. It was only waist-high, and there were no obstructions on the other side. Mr. Voorhees must have been counting on the boat's reputation to protect it. In hindsight, I was stunned that I hadn't heard anyone mumbling about break-ins or fanatics attempting to commune with Timmy. Then again, the answer to both those problems might be found squatting in the bushes a dozen yards away. Voorhees might have hired the Elite to act as extra security. I could see them finessing that type of job to maintain their cover. And that meant they were in a prime position to keep the curious from climbing aboard for a look-see and ruining their dybbuk hunt.

I led Linus into the first deck parlor responsible for my moldy perfume, and we swiped on new sigils.

"I really hope there are no hidden cameras," I mused. "I'm not sure if what we just did made it better or worse."

"The Society has plenty of experience burying this type of thing if we do get caught."

I was glad he couldn't see the look I shot him. Had the Society, his mother in particular, been covering for him long? Or was this a recent development? I wanted to ask as much as I didn't want to know the answer.

"The boy is upstairs you said?"

I heard him moving toward the doorway. "Yes."

"I'll go first," he offered. "In case he starts throwing cutlery again."

"That's not necessary." He might as well have knifed me in the gut offering to act as my shield. Of all people, I expected Linus to trust I knew my limits. Ironic, I know. "Timmy and I have an understanding." Okay, so that wasn't exactly true. "He'll recognize me, so I don't think he'll hurt me. If he does, then that proves your point, and I deserve what's coming."

I'm not sure how he located me, but Linus closed his chilly fingers around my wrist. "You've been hurt enough, Grier. You don't deserve to so much as stub your toe again in this life."

"You're kind to say so, but we both know life doesn't work that way." The sentiment was so bittersweet, I smiled, though he couldn't see. "Come on." I slid from his grasp. "Time for you to make a new friend."

We entered the dining room together and stood close enough our clothes touched at the shoulders.

"Timmy," I called. "I brought a friend for you to meet."

Linus scuffed a piece of carpet foam from under his shoe. "Does he come when called?"

I never met a kid who did, let alone an undead one. "Is anything ever that simple?"

"I suppose not." Footsteps paced away from me. "What do we try next?"

"I painted on a sigil for perception then amplified the crap out of it last time."

"That's as good a place to start as any."

Pen in hand, I got to work marking up my forehead with the perception sigil. Maud told me once it was a nod to opening our third eye. But she followed that up by claiming it was a bunch of hooey. Considering we were necromancers who turned our own blood into ink capable of resurrecting dead humans, I wasn't sure she had a leg to stand on. She was Maud, though. No one argued with her. No one ever dared. There was no point. She was always right. Or so it had seemed. Her brilliance had a way of blinding anyone around her. Only after her death had I acquired the ability to stand up to her, but glaring at a box on the mantle just wasn't as satisfying as railing at her in person would have been.

Goddess, I missed her. I was mad at her. I was hurt. Crushed really. She had lied to me. All my life. And she was so very good at it no one had suspected the truth. The more I tugged on the strings of my memories, the more my past unraveled.

Maud Woolworth hadn't spooked easy, but she must have been terrified to bury my identity so deep.

"I'm ready," Linus informed me, snapping me back to attention. "I'll follow your lead."

"Hi, Timmy." I started walking the length of the room. "I came back to visit you earlier, but you had company."

No answer.

"Why are you here?" Linus spoke from the opposite corner. "Why haven't you moved on?"

Still no response.

"I spoke to a friend about the devourer." I wasn't sure if sharing that news would terrorize him or spark a hope I had no right to claim, but I was running out of ideas fast. "I might have an idea how to protect you."

Right now, that idea involved throwing myself on Boaz's mercy, but Timmy didn't have to know that yet.

The pale outline of a boy dressed in a sailor suit appeared before me. "You can't."

I checked the urge to tug one of his blond curls, uncertain if it was even possible. "Will you let me try?"

The tremor in his little voice slayed me. "How?"

"I brought someone to meet you. His name is Linus." I waved him over until I remembered he couldn't see me. "Linus, I think we better do this next part sans sigil." He blinked into existence an instant after me. "There. Now we can all see each other."

"He looks mean," Timmy whispered. "Is he?"

"He's a teacher," I whispered back. "They all look that way."

The ghost boy wobbled his head in eager agreement.

"Grier and I grew up together," Linus said, crossing the room to stand with us. "We were...friends."

The slight hesitation shamed me. I should have made more of an effort to befriend him when we were kids. I'd had Boaz and Amelie and Maud and Woolly, and I hadn't needed anyone else. All Linus had was his mother, and it sounded like he'd learned more life skills from the people in her employ than he had from her.

"We were friends," I assured him. "We're even better friends now."

Which explained why burying the hatchet in his back was going to hurt me as much as it hurt him.

Linus smiled, humanizing him, and Timmy relaxed enough to stop inching behind me. "I'm pleased to meet you, Timmy."

"My name's not Timmy." His square chin hit his tiny chest. "It's Oscar Horrigan."

Linus and I exchanged a look over the boy's head before he asked, "How did you end up here?"

"I don't remember." His feet drifted above the floor an inch or two. "I woke up in this room one night, and I can't leave. I've tried."

Fascinated, Linus tugged on his ear. "What's the first thing you recall?"

"All the fancy people were sitting at tables, but nobody was eating." Oscar scrunched up his face. "They were all looking at a couple across the room, and I looked there too." He drifted in the opposite direction until he stood where he had attacked Marit. "A pretty lady was crying that her son was missing. A man was holding her. He told her they were on a boat, and he could have only gone so far."

"Oh, Oscar." His story plummeted my heart into the soles of my feet. The poor kid was remembering his death. The small mercy seemed to be he didn't recall the event itself, only the aftermath. The specifics he'd shared, paired with a name and his clothing, would make locating his identity easy as pie. But what good would it do him? Or his family?

"Are you happy here?" Linus gentled his tone. "Do you want to stay?"

"No." Oscar hiccupped on a sob. "I want to go home."

"Oh, sweet pea." I squatted to put me at his eye level. "I wish I could make that happen."

Tears rolling down his cheeks, the boy flung himself into my arms. I didn't even try to catch him. There was no point. Unless he used anger to hone his focus, he had no substance. Only his fury enabled him to lift weapons and wield them. Without their rage, poltergeists were impotent.

So you can imagine my surprise when he smacked into me bodily and knocked me onto my butt. Oscar didn't miss a beat and curled up in my lap, his arms linked around my neck, sobbing. He was too old to be held this way, but he hadn't been held since the early 1900s, if his clothes were any indication.

"Grier," Linus breathed, his eyes as round as the moon beyond the window. "This isn't possible."

While I held Oscar and rocked him, I stared up at Linus. "This isn't a loop. He's not repeating. He's here with us. He's aware." This close his neck smelled of boy and linen. "How do we help him?"

"We'll have to report this." His lips pursed. "There hasn't been a documented case of a sentient poltergeist in…" He blinked. "I can't think of a single instance."

"Are you sure involving the Society is the best thing for him?" I held Oscar tighter. "I don't want him to become someone's science project."

The bubbling excitement that had been animating Linus fizzled. "It's the only way to keep him safe."

"I don't know." This had all been so much easier before Oscar became a bundle of child in my arms. "What can they do for him?"

"They'll give him protected status for starters. I'm sorry, Grier, but they will want to know how he works. I can't stop that. They'll confiscate this boat so that his tether is secure."

"Meaning Cricket will lose out on her haunted cruise idea." I attempted to unclasp my poltergeist necklace and settled him more firmly in my lap. "She won't be happy, but she'll live."

The more he expounded on the protective measures for Oscar, the lighter I became, until I should have drifted off the floor with him.

This fixed the problem. The Society would stamp their name on Oscar and the boat. The Elite couldn't touch him now. They would have to find another ghost to…

Blasting out a sigh, I had to stare the truth in the eye. This fixed nothing. This might save Oscar, in a way, but it would condemn him to living in a test tube for the Society. Would he prefer that to acting as dybbuk bait? And who got to pick the replacement sacrifice? Who was to say the next spirit was any less worthy of salvation? Not to mention this threw a monkey wrench into the works as far as the Elite were concerned. How could I say this boy, who was already dead, was more valuable than a vampire living an equally undead—if a substantially more normal by our standards—life?

Philosophy had never been my best subject. All this noodling was giving me a headache.

And then there was Linus. He hadn't smacked his lips or licked his chops once. He was intrigued. He was fully invested in Oscar's future, and not as a main course. So what did that mean? That dybbuks were great actors? That Linus had no idea about its murderous leanings? Or that Boaz and I were wrong about him?

Except I had seen Ambrose wearing his shirts, and the resemblance to Linus was uncanny.

A clatter below yanked me out of my head, and I set Oscar on his feet. Or I tried to, but it turned out he was stickier than the saltwater taffy sold in Savannah Candy Kitchen, and he clung to me even as I stood. The kid weighed nothing. I was boosting ether onto my hip, but it was super clingy ether. His arms never left my neck, and his face burrowed against my shoulder.

"Linus," I hissed. "We have to disappear."

"Allow me." He leaned over and swiped an obfuscation sigil on my forearm before doing the same to himself. "Hide in the alcove. I'll stand guard at the door."

The sound of approaching footsteps ruled out further conversation, so I tiptoed into position and hid, trusting the sigil to do the rest. Linus was nowhere in sight, and I had to believe his skill would keep us safe.

"No," Oscar whimpered. "*No.*"

I stroked his hair, soothing him as best I could without using my voice. It was too late for whispered reassurances. Holding him tight, I rocked a little, the way you calmed babies. It seemed to work for six-year-olds too, until the footsteps entered the dining room with us.

Up to that point, I'd had control of my pulse, but one glance at the doorway had my heart galloping right out of my chest. It was a miracle Ambrose wasn't leveled in the stampede. But there he stood, clearly not trampled. The twisted version of the Lawson scion, hewn from midnight and flame, licked his berry lips as his nostrils flared. Shutting my eyes, I sent up a prayer to Hecate.

We were going to need all the help we could get.

FOURTEEN

"**C**ome here, child," Ambrose crooned. "It's time. I spared you for as long as I was able."

Chills dappled my arms as the power in his voice swept through the room.

Suddenly facing the dybbuk alone didn't seem like such a hot idea.

Had Linus engineered the noise downstairs to throw me off his scent? Once we both agreed to be invisible again, there was no telling what the other was doing. He could have transformed into a slavering beast and been steadily prowling toward me. I wouldn't find out unless the sigil failed, or his jaws snapped closed over me.

"*No,*" Oscar yelled. "I won't go with you."

"No?" The clarion ring of Ambrose's voice twisted my heart until it seemed my blood would be wrung out on the floor. "Who are you to say no? Who are you to say anything at all? You're a bit of inconsequential energy the universe has yet to consume. You're a snack is what you are, and no one likes it when their food talks back."

The boy struggled until I set him on his feet. "I'm going to be safe." His tiny hands formed equally miniscule fists. "Grier told me so."

The sound of me smacking myself in the forehead with my open palm got devoured by Ambrose's silken laughter. Thank the goddess for small mercies.

"Her involvement would explain the curious predicament we find ourselves in," he mused. "Tell me, boy, did she share blood with you? Is that why you have the sense to be afraid when others of your ilk drift into oblivion without a spark of terror to flavor them? Only a goddess such as she could rouse a soul such as yours."

The dybbuk had made it no secret he was aware I was goddess-touched. He had teased me with it all along. Yet another box checked off in favor of Linus being his vessel.

"Go away." Oscar stamped his foot, and it shot him into the air like a rocket. "Leave me alone."

"Would that I could, dear boy, but no." Ambrose watched him with the patience of a spider waiting for a fly to land in his web. "I can't."

Oscar shot me a panicked glance that sealed my fate. All I could do was scramble for a plan.

The dybbuk was grinning now, hungry, his teeth chips of moon-light. "Who's hiding with you?"

The boy realized what he'd done and blanched, quite a feat considering his usual pallor. "No one."

"Good effort, but I don't buy your performance. It smacks of too little, too late." Ambrose didn't sound upset by the fact, merely intrigued. "Come out, come out, whoever you are."

There was nothing for it. He would find me now that he knew to look. The sigil didn't make us invisible so much as it made us uninteresting, forgettable. If I let him look too hard, he might find Linus too. Assuming it wasn't Linus I was about to stare down in order to buy a few extra minutes to think of a plan.

Stupid, persistent hope. Here I thought I was all out, but it seemed I was unwilling to give Linus up as a lost cause just yet.

Seeing him with Oscar poked holes in my theories and stretched my nerves thin to breaking. Hope truly was the worst thing that could ever happen to a person. Maybe the Grande Dame had been right keeping her silence until I was freed.

"Ambrose," I said as I scrubbed off the sigil and stepped from my hiding spot. "What brings you to the *Cora Ann*?"

A nail rolled behind him from the vicinity of the doorway. I scuffed my shoes to cover the sound and tried not to get my hopes up when any number of things might be to blame, including the poltergeist who was working up a head of steam over his imminent demise.

"We are in a dining room, are we not?" His gesture encompassed the space. "I would have thought my purpose self-explanatory."

"I'm afraid Oscar is a friend of mine." I extended a hand, and the boy clasped it hard in his clammy grip. "You can't have him."

"You've been making promises too big to keep," he tsked. "You can't take a meal from my mouth without offering me a replacement." His luminous eyes fastened on Oscar. "I'm afraid there's no other spirit in Savannah on par with our friend— Oscar, did you say his name was? You awakened him. Your blood opened his eyes. Unless you're willing to do the same to another spirit, then you have nothing to barter. And since your objection is no doubt due to his sentience, I doubt you'd condemn another soul to a waking slaughter. So I say again, you have nothing with which to barter."

"You act like you have a right to him." I pushed the boy a half step behind me. "You don't own this boat, this boy or this city. What right do you have to prey on its citizens?"

"I was invited into this city, and that makes it mine. I was invited into one of its citizens, and that gives me the right." The flames in his hair roared higher, almost licking the ceiling. "I was awakened with a promise, and I will see it manifest."

"No."

"No?"

"This is my city." Sweat dampened my palms. "The people here are under my protection."

"Ah." That amused him all the more. "Who granted you sovereignty here?"

"A Woolworth stood alongside General James Oglethorpe at Yamacraw Bluff. A Woolworth was present at the founding of this city."

A cruel smile cut his mouth. "You're no Woolworth."

My Marchand bloodlines were no secret, but I was surprised the dybbuk was so well-informed. He was definitely pulling facts from his vessel to know me so well. "I hate to break it to you, but my adoption paperwork says otherwise. I am Maud Woolworth's daughter in all ways except blood."

"Blood is what defines you." He glanced between me and Oscar. "In your case, it is *all* that defines you."

A twinge I couldn't hide left him grinning. Only my blood had granted me freedom. The Grande Dame measured me by its potential, but I refused to let it define me. "What do you know about my blood?"

"More than you do." His hair returned to its usual corona. "More than you ever will at the rate you're going."

"It's been a hard few years. Sorry if I'm not up to snuff."

"Atramentous," he breathed with profound reverence, "creates diamonds from the rough."

"We'll have to agree to disagree."

"You wouldn't be the woman you are today without the time you spent there."

"You're right." I awarded him the point. "I would be normal, well-adjusted, and I wouldn't wake screaming in the mornings. I would be working toward a degree, hanging out with my friends, and generally doing all the things average people do with their time."

Instead I wasn't on speaking terms with normal, screamed myself hoarse in my sleep, worked toward the level of proficiency most practitioners acquired around age ten, and looked over my shoulder every time I left the house, making it hard to pal around with friends when my mind was elsewhere.

"Normal," he spat. "Average." His hair sizzled around his face. "Ordinary is a death sentence."

"Again, I gotta disagree with you there." I would trade my eyeteeth to have my old life with Maud back.

The unnatural cant of his head alarmed me. "Say that louder next time."

"Say...?" *Oh.* Oh crap. "You heard what I was thinking."

"How else do you think I hook them so deep?" He chuckled. "I'm a tradesman, Grier, an entrepreneur."

"Are bargains offered the only thoughts you can detect?"

"I don't have to read your mind to know what you're thinking. It's written all over your face. But alas, I'm only privy to what's offered to me. I can't take anything from anyone. All I am, all I have, is freely given."

"I doubt that." I kept watch from the corner of my eye for any motion that might indicate a rescue was underway, but no Elite boots pounded up the stairs, and Linus remained a big question mark. Guess it was up to me to squirm out of this on my own. "Who bargained with you?"

"Ah." He touched a finger to the side of his nose. "That information comes with a price. Will you pay it?"

"Nope." I had enough chaos in my life, thanks. "Just making conversation."

"You can't save him." Ambrose was well aware of what I was doing. "You might as well stand aside. The longer you drag this out, the more hope you give him. That's crueler than anything I will do to him."

There wasn't much of Oscar to start with, but I used him for cover while I eased a hand into my pocket. Fountain pens were so much stealthier than using a brush and a jar of ink. Talk about your combat applications. Linus was a genius. Whether or not that genius was evil remained to be seen.

Trembling with urgency, I scribbled a row of sigils across the back of Oscar's hand. I figured if I could feel him, I could affect him, and my theory was proven correct when he jolted as the magic snapped into place around him. That power was a pale echo of the symphony playing through Woolly's eaves, but the soft melody of this ward told me it had anchored despite the water sloshing far beneath us.

"A pen," Ambrose marveled. "How fascinating. Wherever did you get it?"

Nice how no one assumed I had made it myself. "From a friend."

A fresh trickle of doubt dripped in the back of my mind. If Linus was his vessel, wouldn't he know that too? The way he seemed to know everything else about me?

The dybbuk crossed to us and placed his hands against the invisible boundary that protected Oscar, and gave it a shove. "Impressive."

"Glad you like it." Now that I'd bought us a few seconds, I pulled ink and a brush from my pack and knelt at Oscar's feet. For some applications, you couldn't beat traditional. I dusted the area beneath him as clean as it was going to get then went old school on the circular ward I painted over the warped boards. "Walk away now, and I'll ask my friend to make you one too."

For the span of a blink, he looked tempted, but then it was gone. "I'm afraid I must decline."

"Stay put," I warned Oscar. "No matter what happens, don't move from that circle."

"All right." His wide eyes tightened at the corners. "I can do this."

"Yeah, you can." I stood and faced Ambrose, who appeared too preoccupied with the problem of the ghost in a warding circle to pay much attention to me. Good thing too, as my current plan involved sprinting from the room, down the stairs, and across the docks until I caught the attention of the Elite.

I waited until his back was facing me, his absorption in Oscar complete, and then I ran.

Wild laughter trailed me, and footsteps pounded behind me. Ambrose was fast. But I was desperate.

I hit the first deck, leapt a roll of carpet and dodged a stack of boards. I made a beeline for the gangway, took that first step over water, then wiry arms closed around my middle and snatched me off my feet.

Fiddlesticks.

"Forgot about the water, did we?" He chuckled in my ear. "You are so forgetful, aren't you? It's rather charming, actually."

"Bite me."

"I'm not that flavor of undead." He shook his head, the heat from his hair singeing the peach fuzz on my cheek. "How is it you're allowed to wander about without a keeper?" He hauled me back onto the boat. "Ah, that's right. Your wraith. Not much good all the way over there, is it?"

The dybbuk had a point. "What are you going to do with me?"

"That depends on you." He shackled my wrists and started frog-marching me back up the stairs. "First, you're going to convince your friend Oscar to step outside his wards, and then you're going to rub off the sigils you painted on his hand."

"I won't help you," I snarled, thrashing in his hold. "He's just a kid. Let him go."

"He's just a source of nourishment." We reached the landing, and he paused there, out of Oscar's sight. "Either you convince him to sacrifice himself, or I bleed you until he offers himself to save you. No matter how this night ends, Oscar ends with it. You have about five steps to make your decision before I make it for you."

We took the five steps. My answer didn't change. Neither did his mind.

Ambrose curved his fingers around my throat, and each one bit into my skin with the eagerness of a honed blade. Warm blood slid down my neck to saturate my top. Struggle would have sawed off my head, so I held still, barely daring to breathe, and prayed Oscar held tight to his self-preservation streak.

"Surrender, Oscar, and I won't hurt her." Ambrose forced me into the room ahead of him. "Grier is your friend, isn't she?"

Oscar's knees gave out, and he dropped onto the floor. "D-don't hurt her."

"You can stop this at any time," Ambrose soothed. "Come to me, and I let her go. A life for a life."

"*No*," I managed before his hand tightened, and fresh warmth eased down my chest.

"I told you," Oscar said, a lost boy who had lost hope. "I told you he was coming for me."

The black streaks raining down his cheeks broke something in me, and I used the only move Taz had taught me that might help in this situation. I brought up my knee and stomped his insole with everything in me. When he hissed and loosened his grip, I broke free, skin tearing, and ran to Oscar.

"Stay." More words wanted to come out, but my throat wasn't working right anymore. "Stay."

Boaz would come. He must have seen me. The Elite had been staking out the *Cora Ann* for days. All I had to do was hold on a little longer, and then—

I screamed as one of Ambrose's elongated fingers pierced my side, skewering me on his curving nail.

"I swore I wouldn't do this, but here I am, forced to break my vow." Ambrose yanked me closer, ripping open the tender skin above my hip. "My vessel will not be pleased, let me tell you. You're making both our lives far more difficult than they have to be. This is one child. Let him go."

"You...won't...stop," I gasped as his finger twisted clockwise. "You'll never...stop."

Vicious mirth unspooled in his laughter. "How well you know me. It's almost like we're friends."

I was out of words and out of time. Out of air and blood too if the spinning room was any indication.

A radiant blast of searing agony spooked my hindbrain into retreating down the warren I had created during my time in Atramentous. I was safe there, apart from my body, separate from the pain, curled up in the back corner of my mind where no one could find me. I was in the process of slamming the door shut on my heels when a shout echoed across the distance. I hesitated, hands on the locks, and listened.

"*Grier.*"

The voice sounded so familiar, but it came from too far away to be sure.

"Wake up. Grier. Wake up."

The name it called rang a bell. Grier. I had no name here but...

"Please, Grier," he begged, and it was a man's voice. "Wake up."

I lingered in the doorway, torn between safety and reality, uncertain which way to turn.

"I can't do this without you," he said. "Help me, or Oscar will die. *You'll* die."

Oscar. The boy. The ghost aboard the *Cora Ann*. Oh, no. *Oscar.*

I slammed back into my body so hard I seized in Linus's arms.

"Shh." He cradled me gently until the worst of the shakes passed. "You're all right. I've got you."

"Linus," I rasped. "I thought..."

"I know what you thought." His fingers traced a cool line across my cheek, probing for injuries. "I should have told you the truth, but I wanted to see if..." He shook his head. "It doesn't matter now. You must help me contain the dybbuk."

Pain hammered at me until my bones felt poised to shatter. "My side..."

"You were out for a solid minute." He eased me upright. "I've staunched the bleeding in your throat and side, but you must help me. I set a containment ward. Ambrose tripped it when he got too close to Oscar. You have to help me reinforce it. This magic requires two casters."

Focus was impossible when it felt like my head was hula hooping. "What?"

Linus cradled my face between his palms, the cold like diving into icy waters. "Help me."

"Okay." I shut my eyes and tested what hurt most. "I can do this."

"How dare you," Ambrose thundered. "I was summoned."

"Where is my ink?" I winced as Linus braced his shoulder under my arm and guided me to my feet. Together, we limped to the wards set into the floor precious inches from Oscar, where Linus lowered me onto my knees. "Brush?"

"Here." He pressed my brush and ink bottle into my hand. "Copy my sigils exactly. One mistake, and he'll shatter the ward."

"No pressure," I panted, getting into position.

"Your wards won't hold me, Eidolon." Ambrose paced, a caged tiger, his cruel fingers clashing against air as he hacked at the wards. "Release me now, or feel my wrath."

"Eidolon," I echoed. "Which of us is he name-calling?"

"Me, I'm afraid." He forced his gaze from me with visible effort and began. "There's a stigma to bonding with wraiths, even among shades. Perhaps especially among them since they must barter for their hosts while wraiths are free to bond as they will."

While he spoke, he laid down a swirling design that cramped my fingers thinking about copying it. I steadied myself on my knees, leaving a bloodied handprint behind, and let my mind drift just enough the pain stopped knifing me.

Linus came full circle before I hit the halfway point. He stood watch against Ambrose while I struggled to close the wards before tipping into the darkness awaiting me on the fringes of my consciousness.

Who are you? Let him pick that thought from my head. Who had invited this creature to share their mind, their body? Who was so desperate for power they would welcome this disease? Had the summoner not understood the dybbuk would use them as a means to its own ends? Or had the person simply not cared as long as they were taken along for the ride?

The last flick of my wrist sealed the wards, and Ambrose bellowed in agony.

"Get back." Linus hooked his arms under mine and dragged me. "The ward isn't supposed to—"

Light exploded across the room, searing the memory of its layout across the backs of my eyelids, and the boat began rocking beneath us like the *Cora Ann* was riding out a hurricane instead of anchored in a quiet berth. I scrabbled toward Oscar, using his ward as flimsy protection and dragging Linus with me.

I'm not sure how long we huddled together, but eventually my teeth started chattering from having Linus curled around me, and my eyes, so sensitive to light, began to register my surroundings.

"No," Linus warned, his arms a gentle cage around me.

I had broken free and crossed the room before his warning registered. Even then, I ignored him. This was wrong. This was a mistake. This made no sense. Something had gone wrong. Horribly wrong. There was no way. None. She would never...

Amelie huddled in the center of the wards. Linus's shirt hung off her shoulder, and his pants pinched her waist and stretched past her toes. His shoes were boats on her feet, and they tipped off as she tucked her legs beneath her.

Hands pressed to the wound at my side, I collapsed inches from the warding ring. "Amelie?"

Linus joined me, setting restraining hands on my shoulders. "You can't set her free."

"How do we know it's her?" I sat down hard. "He looked like you before and—"

"He was a caricature of me," Linus said gently. "Look at her. She's flesh and bone. She's Amelie."

"You must have suspected," she croaked in his direction. "You were too good at hunting us."

Unable to contribute more than my unhinged jaw to the conversation, I sat there and listened, hoping that sanity and understanding might collide to explain how this had come to pass.

"The night you came to the carriage house to retrieve Grier you had traces of zinc sulfide on your hands." Linus tucked me closer when I listed forward. "Most people require a black light to see the effect, but the wraith I'm bonded to perceives it in its own unique way."

"The clothes." A brittle laugh strangled her. "You dusted the laundry Ambrose had been stealing from your hamper."

That explained why I kept bumping into Ambrose in the gardens. He had been pilfering new outfits from Linus before he went out for the night. Having his suspicions confirmed also explained the frosty reception he gave Amelie. "Why did he choose Linus to mimic?"

Amelie flinched at the sound of my voice and huddled deeper into her stolen outfit. "Ambrose wasn't powerful enough to manifest his own form for some time. Mostly he used me to..." She blanched. "He must have bumped into Linus and liked the look of him. Or maybe it was easy access to his clothing and supplies that appealed. I don't know. I never asked, and he wouldn't have told me if I had."

Meaning I could have spoken to Amelie, visited her, and been talking to Ambrose. No wonder he knew me so well. He had access to the mind of the person who knew me best. Thanks to the dybbuk, she was privy to all my secrets now. "Tell me this was an accident. Tell me someone forced you. Tell me anything that will let me erase these lines between us."

"I can't do that." Tears spiked her lashes. "This is all on me, Grier. I welcomed him in."

A million questions jostled for position at the head of the line, and my thought process was lost amid all the shoving. "No." That was all there was to it. "He manipulated you. He forced you to bond, and then he—"

"We lost you once." Amelie stared into her lap. "I couldn't lose you again." Her throat worked over a hard lump. "Boaz—" She shook her head. "He was so furious with the system, he was coming unhinged."

A vicious twist set my heart pounding. "What are you saying?"

"After you were sentenced to Atramentous, we saved all we could from Woolly. We held on to it in case you ever..." Her eyes closed, releasing fresh tears. "I found a grimoire. I read a few of the spells, but I didn't understand them." Her fists curled in her lap. "Why would I? I'm Low Society. We're taught nothing except the history of the High Society."

The acerbity in her voice carved my bones, but it had always been this way. She had always felt like she was on the outside looking in, even when I had been standing on the outside looking in right beside her. Envy was a seesaw we both rode from time to time, but none of her lows had been this, not rock bottom. She had always touched off the ground and gone soaring again. There must be more to it, there had to be a reason why she had chosen this path.

"You found a summoning spell in the grimoire." Linus saved me from asking. "That's how you knew what to do."

"I spent the last five years figuring out the language of sigils." Her glare dared him to belittle her accomplishment. "I tried warding and other small magics, but I couldn't work them."

"That's when you started researching ways of increasing your power by using that newfound understanding."

Again, he stole the words from my mouth, and I could only be grateful not to have to speak them.

"There was nothing I could do that wasn't permanent," she answered, "so I did nothing."

"Ambrose is not nothing," I rasped. "Why would you bind him to you?"

"Volkov took you." Her gaze swung to me, full of pleading. "I had to do something. I had to save you."

"No." Linus slashed his hand through the air. "You don't get to lay the blame for this at Grier's feet. You made the choice. You had years to grasp the implications. This wasn't a lark. This was a calculated decision, and the consequences are yours to bear."

"Do you think I don't know what I've done?" Rage blistered her cheeks. "I begged him to give me strength. I threw myself on his mercy so he would keep her safe from the vampires, but he twisted my words. He lied to me." Her voice broke. "Bonding drained him until he was useless. Grier was home again before I noticed I was missing time, before I caught him stealing my body."

"What did you expect?" He stared her down. "There is always a cost for power."

"Perhaps the High Society ought to educate the rest of us on the price of the dream they sell us." Her shoulders drooped, the fire draining from her. "We're fed stories of power and magic from the time we're born until we're grown and left to hunger after scraps from our betters' tables. How can we value our contributions when we're kept ignorant of them? How can we make heroes of ourselves when we're told no stories of our champions?"

"No one can save us from our birthrights." His chill sigh whispered past my ear. "We're all trapped in the net cast around us by fate the moment our eyes blink open. Whether the net is woven from silk or twine doesn't matter. When you struggle against its pull, it cuts all the same."

"What are we going to do?" I looked to Linus, the lifeline I didn't deserve. "What will the Elite do to her?"

"Ambrose murdered nine vampires." Linus resettled me against his side, supporting me so I didn't tip forward to kiss the rusted floor. "She's an accomplice. She will be held responsible for those deaths."

"Godsdamn it, Amelie." A worthless sob choked me. "What were you thinking?"

Amelie rested her chin on her knees to prevent further conversation.

Craning my neck, I peered around Linus. "Why haven't the Elite stormed the castle?"

"Ward," she mumbled. "On the road, not the boat."

Well, that explained why the light show hadn't brought them running.

Linus pinned Amelie with his stare when he asked me, "Will you be all right waiting here?"

Until he moved me and a pang shot through my side, I hadn't

noticed I was almost collapsed on his lap. "Yeah." He laid me down easy. "I'm not going anywhere."

In the stillness after Linus left, a small throat cleared. "What about me?"

"Oh, Oscar." I turned my head toward him since the rest of me was dead weight. "I'm sorry we forgot you."

"I'm used to it." He flashed a cheeky grin. "You saved me, just like you said."

"Linus helped." Linus, who I owed an apology. Linus, who had been doling out second chances too, hoping I would scrounge up enough faith to believe he wasn't a murderer despite the evidence mounted against him. Linus, who really ought to have come back by now. "You can break the ward now."

"I think I'd rather stay here." His gaze darted to Amelie. "Until your friend gets back."

"Suit yourself." I focused on taking the smallest breaths possible. "I'll be right here."

I wish I had blacked out, but oblivion is never so merciful. I was wide awake when boots pounded up the stairs, and I had a front-row seat when Boaz entered the room. He glanced from Amelie to me, torn in his loyalties, rocking back and forth the same way Cletus had all those days ago. I won the coin toss, but it's not like he could have reached through the warding ring to hug her. He had no magic to break ours.

"We've got a medic on the way, Squirt." He trailed his knuckles down my cheek. "Can you last that long, or do I need to carry you out?"

"I can manage." Whatever Linus had done seemed to be holding. "Where's Linus?"

"We detained him. We didn't know what we were walking into, only that you were on the boat with him, and you were in distress." He grimaced. "Godsdamn, I'm a fool. I never should have asked for your help."

"I'm glad you did." I leaned into his touch. "I know you see me as some High Society princess in need of rescuing—"

"Your title has never interested me much," he said plainly. "I would have married you the first time you made goo-goo eyes at me if all I wanted from you was prestige or fortune."

"Okay, you made your point." A tingle ignited in my cheeks. "I wanted you bad, and you knew it."

"I didn't take advantage of you then," he pressed on, determined to make his point, "and I won't now."

The message was clear. He wasn't sure what part Amelie played in all this, but he must suspect her role. Separating himself from her must be killing him. They were always a unit in my mind—the siblings Pritchard. I loved them equally, if in different ways, and they had each been a staple in my life up to now.

"Medic," announced a tall black man who ducked into the room with a red bag slung across his shoulders. "Medic."

Boaz lifted an arm, and the man jogged over and knelt at my side. "Take care of my girl, Heinz."

"Your girl?" The medic blasted me with a megawatt smile. "You're Grier?" He peeled up my shirt and got a look at my side. "You're too pretty for an ogre like him." He palpated my abdomen. "Have you considered seeing other people?" He examined my throat next. "And when I say *other people*, I mean *me*. There's no need to talk. Just blink once for yes."

After his examination moved south, I asked, "What happened to twice for no?"

His chuckle was warm and genuine. "I didn't want to leave you any wiggle room."

"Stop hitting on her before I start hitting on you," Boaz grumped. "What's her status?"

"She's stable enough for transport." He checked with Boaz. "Meet us there?"

"I have to handle this." Boaz scrubbed his palm over his head, his posture weary, but he pressed a lingering kiss to my lips. "I'll join you as soon as I can. Do *not* leave without me. That's an order, Squirt."

"Aye, aye, Captain." I saluted him as Heinz gently lifted me in his arms. "Shiver me timbers."

"Best get her out of here." Boaz caught my hand. "She's clearly delusional."

"She must be if she's dating you," Heinz agreed. "Come on, gorgeous." He angled us toward the doorway. "Normally, I wouldn't sweep a girl off her feet until I'd at least bought her dinner, but the corners are too tight for the stretcher, and the boat is trashed. Are you sure this is a steamboat and not a garbage barge?"

"Boaz." I trapped his hand in mine. "We're going to fix this."

"We'll try." He kissed my forehead and then my nose and then my lips. "I'll see you soon."

"That's enough pecking, lovebirds." Heinz carried me away from Boaz and down the stairs. "Now that we're alone, tell me all the embarrassing stories you remember about Boaz from childhood. He's got serious dirt on me, and I need to find a shovel before he buries me with the other guys in our unit."

And so I told him the story of the second time I saw Boaz naked. It involved a case of beer he polished off single-handedly, a wide-mouth glass bottle (some fancy brand of tea his current girlfriend had favored that smelled like grass), and a jar of Vaseline. It went down-hill from there.

FIFTEEN

Heinz strapped me on a stretcher his partner had waiting for us in the street, and I grunted when they slid me into the idling ambulance. Necromancers use the same hospitals as humans, so it was a short drive. Most High Society types weren't thrilled with sharing a communal medical facility, but most Low Society families lacked the funds for private healthcare, and there were also concerns over emergency care. It was better for us all if we could be rushed into the arms of our own kind for treatment rather than ending up in an all-human hospital after a wreck or other mundane accident.

The compromise was a private floor warded against humans and staffed with exclusive doctors. The Society kept key personnel scattered throughout each department to clean up after supernatural patients, and other factions did too. The staff was close to sixty-five percent nonhuman the last I heard.

The comingled system had worked for decades, and it saved the Society money by piggybacking off the human healthcare system. The High Society worshipped wealth and prestige in equal measure, so it was a tradeoff for the elitists. Saving money at the expense of rubbing elbows with commoners. But none of them were willing to pony up the cash to fund the startup costs of an affordable alternative so...

Basically, if it ain't broke, don't fix it.

"So you and Boaz have history." Heinz clamped an oximeter on my pointer finger, wrapped a blood pressure cuff around my upper arm and stuck leads to my chest. "How long has that been a thing? You guys high school sweethearts or something?"

"No." I shut my eyes to block out the glare from the overhead lights. "More like childhood friends exploring our options."

"There's nothing wrong with just being friends." Heinz's smile flavored his voice. "Maybe it's best if you don't explore this thing with him."

His teasing was doing its job, taking my mind off Amelie. A little. Okay, not really, but he was trying. I awarded points for effort. "You'd rather I explored a thing with you?"

"Absolutely."

"As flattered as I am by your offer, I have no choice but to see where this leads now that he's got it in his head to do something about it, or I'll never get another moment's peace." Oh, to have a time machine. Or a smidgen of discretion. "Good thing you're pro-friendship."

"Now I see the attraction." He chuckled. "You keep him on his toes while other girls fall at his feet."

"Oh, I fell at his feet. I was probably the first girl who did, but I had an unfair advantage." If that's what you wanted to call it. "When he stepped over me and kept walking, he didn't have far to go since he lived next door. Fall down every day, and you start building scar tissue. Get enough scar tissue, and the falls stop hurting. Once the falls stop hurting, you work up an immunity. After you get immune, there's no more reason to fall, is there?"

Heinz was cackling at this point. "I'm so glad I was on duty tonight."

"Me too." I enjoyed meeting people who saw other facets to Boaz or who had different perspectives on the ones familiar to me. "Just don't tell him who ratted him out."

"I won't breathe a word," he promised as the ambulance rocked to a halt. "Even if he tries to beat it out of me."

"That's all I ask." I was smiling as they wheeled me into the hospital.

———

I MIGHT HAVE LIED about having an allergy to anesthesia when the nice doctor asked me. Drugs were a hard no for me. I would rather suffer than be trapped behind my eyelids. I also might have invented an entirely new language of swear words that appeared to impress even the most seasoned nurses with the depths of their vulgarity when the doctor reopened the wound on my side to repair the internal damage. There's even a slight chance I blacked out, hurling myself into the safety of my mind, to escape the sting of the needle and the pull of the stitches in my skin.

The temptation to linger in that place, too far away for pain to touch me, was great.

But then I heard singing.

"*The night birds are calling, calling, calling. The princess she's falling, falling, falling. A stone for a heart and a blade for a tongue, fair beauty she slayed all her suitors but one. His armor was love, and his weapon this tune. Their battle was fierce, the casualties great, but fair beauty, she smiled as she lowered her gate.*"

"I always wondered if that was a metaphor for sex," I murmured, eyes closed.

"Lowering her gate?" Linus mused. "I never understood why you loved that song so much."

"Maud had a beautiful voice, but that was the only song she knew start to finish." I blinked the room into focus and exhaled with relief that Linus had dimmed the overhead lights. "She sang it on a loop. I was forced to love it or go mad hearing it on repeat."

"I never knew that."

"It took me a while to figure out too, so don't feel bad." I turned my head on my pillow and got my first good look at him since Ambrose attacked. His long hair gathered at his nape, but limp strands plastered to his neck with dried sweat. "Are you okay?"

"Minor cuts and scratches." He flashed his hands and forearms at me. "I treated myself on the drive over to see you."

"You saved my life." The bald statement hung between us. "How did you trap him?"

"While you provided the distraction, I painted as many concentric traps as I could around Oscar." His lips, full and hard, turned downward. "I've been asking myself if I acted logically, staying behind after you ran downstairs, or if I was a coward for not chasing him." He pulled his hair down and ran his fingers through the auburn tangle. "I still don't have an answer."

"There's a joke in there somewhere about the teacher not having all the answers, but I'm fresh out of snark." I shifted onto my uninjured side to see him better. "You trusted me to take care of myself, and that's no small thing."

"I've watched you train with Taz." His lips pulled to one side. "I knew you could handle yourself."

"Shush," I warned him, though his praise made me glow. "I'm not finished yet."

He inclined his head. "Yes, ma'am."

"You did the smart thing. Your quick thinking saved all four of us." I might have invited him there for all the wrong reasons, but my lack of faith is what saved us in the end. "I couldn't have lived with myself if we'd had to resort to violence to bring down Amelie. Hurting her that way would have killed me, so thank you."

The tips of his ears reddened adorably, and he cleared his throat. "You're welcome."

Though I longed to ask after Boaz and Amelie, I didn't want Linus to feel unwelcome, so I bit my tongue.

"I brought you a gift," he began, reaching into his pocket.

"This is starting to be a habit with you," I chastised. "You don't have to buy my friendship, Linus. You're earning it. Brick by brick. Literally, in the case of what you've helped me do with Woolly."

"I think you'll want this one."

"Okay." I held out my hand. "Gimme."

He placed a dented brass button on my palm. "This is the first half."

"You shouldn't have?" I examined the raised anchor pattern for clues before turning it over to inspect the shank. "Is this a memento from my latest near-death experience?"

"Not quite." He penned a sigil for perception on my hand. "This is the second half."

Oscar flickered into being at the foot of my bed, his round cheeks stretched to capacity. "Hi, Grier." He launched himself at me, and I grunted at the impact even though he weighed nothing. "I thought you were going to be a ghost like me. I didn't want you trapped on that boat. It's no fun there."

"I'm fine, little guy." I kissed his curls while staring at Linus. "How is this possible?"

"You woke a ghost, Grier, an unprecedented feat, and you're asking me about a simple relocation?"

Relocations seemed pretty magical from where I sat covered in squishy ghost boy. "Yes?"

"Oscar's recollection was correct. He died onboard. He vanished during a cruise, and he was never found. I searched the boat and located his remains walled up in the engine room." He looked so tired all of a sudden. "I collected his bones to return to his family."

Spirits could only drift so far from their remains. Oscar's first undead memory held the clue as to why he ended up haunting the dining room instead of below decks. His soul had been drawn to his parents in that moment of elasticity after death when he stretched his tether to its limits. Once it snapped into place, there was no going back. He was stuck. Anchored to the spot where his parents' world fell apart.

"I don't know anybody anymore." Oscar clenched his fingers in my gown. "I don't want to go back. I want to stay with you. Can I?"

Adopt a ghost child? As an adoptee myself, I understood what a gift it was to be wanted by a second family, but I was too young to be mothering a ghost more than five times my age. And yet... I had woken him. He was my responsibility. At the very least, he was already dead, so it's not like I could kill him.

"Sure, if you want." I gasped when his arms closed around my throat, cutting off my oxygen. "Okay, pal, let's tone it down a bit. I really don't want to get stuck haunting a hospital because you suffocated me in my bed." I checked with Linus and held out the brassy token. "How does this work?"

"I bound his spirit to a button from the shorts he was wearing when he died. That anchor ought to satisfy his needs since past violence imbues objects with more power." Linus shook his head. "Frankly, I'm amazed it worked. Relocations are more like small-scale banishments to rid particular areas of spiritual energy. All it does is move a ghost into another room. But, in this case, he was relocated into a button."

"We make quite a team." I sank back into the pillows and shifted Oscar against my good side. "What did you tell the Elite?"

"I didn't disabuse them of the notion we were too late to stop Ambrose from consuming Oscar. They'll believe me since there's no trace of him aboard the boat, but Amelie might out us if Ambrose gets control of her again."

"They weren't interested in Oscar except as bait," I reminded him. "I doubt they care what happened to him as long as they got their man. Woman. Whatever." A pathetic huff of oxygen masquerading as a laugh escaped me. "I still don't believe it. I saw it with my own eyes, and I..." I mashed my lips together, swallowed hard once. "Where is she?"

"Amelie is being held in a cell at the Lyceum until sentencing. They can't proceed with the trial until all the affected clans have been notified and given a chance to attend. They'll also have to gather documentation proving the vampires belonged to them, who made them, and how much they paid for the service and when."

"So it all comes down to money." How typical. A life's worth reduced to a figure on a ledger.

"That's how these things usually go. Vampires are less sentimental than necromancers, but there's always a chance one of the clans will have had a human turned for love rather than simply allowing a wealthy addition to tithe their way into the collective. The age of the victims will be the biggest determining factor. Older vampires are more revered, but they grow distant with age and lose touch with the modern world and their contemporary kin. Such a loss might be considered a profitable write-off, since a vampire's clan is its sole inheritor. Younger vampires, however, cling to their humanity. A clan would be more upset to lose such potential." He noticed the look on my face and sighed. "I'm sorry, Grier, but that's the way the Society works. You asked me a question, and I answered it using the same formula I learned at my mother's knee."

"I didn't mean to be judgmental, it's just this whole situation is surreal."

Linus parted his lips, pressed them together, then opened them again. "You never suspected her?"

"Of being a cross-dressing ghost eater?" I leaned back against the pillows. "No. I thought she was tired from work and school. She explained it away as studying for finals. I have no idea now if that was true or not." But when I shut my eyes again, I recalled each time the voice in my head warned me away from sharing secrets with her. Why listen if I trusted her? Maybe, after all this time apart, the most obvious answer was...I didn't. And this newest betrayal only made me feel that much worse. "We've had trouble reconnecting since..." I waved a hand in the air. "I didn't push. I thought this was more of that. Us finding our way back to each other. Discovering our new normal."

"I'm sorry," he said plainly.

"Me too." I curled around Oscar like he was a plush toy, and he didn't seem to mind. "Let me know if there's anything I can do. I have money. I can pay whatever tithes are leveraged against her."

"You understand this isn't your fault."

"I..." Words failed me. "That's how it feels."

"You can't help who or what you are any more than she can. You grew up together. She had plenty of time to come to terms with the disparity between your classes without embracing possession as a coping method."

A tiny spark of anger on her behalf threatened to ignite my temper. "Tell me how you really feel."

"She cast blame on you," he kept going, taking me literally. "She knew you would bear the weight, and she cast it off her shoulders onto yours. She considered this for a long time before she reached a tipping point. I won't dishonor her by implying she had no intentions of using her newfound powers as she claimed, but your abduction was a spark next to a powder keg. If Volkov hadn't happened, then there would have been another trigger. She was a loaded gun waiting to go off in a crowded room."

His earnest argument doused the worst of my irritation. "I can't cut her out of my heart."

"I'm only asking you to be careful. Her family won't take this well. They're going to side with her, and they're going to blame you." His fingers pressed into his eyes. "You haven't been dating Boaz long, and he's the Pritchard heir. They're going to come down hard on you and hope he breaks things off before it gets serious. You need to harden your heart against what's coming."

A single tear escaped my eyes in acknowledgment that he was right, that I knew he was telling me the truth, but I didn't want to say it out loud. I didn't want it to be real yet.

The Pritchards had never been fond of me. His parents had made their stance on my romantic feelings toward their son clear. A union between a High Society dame and a Low Society scion would muddy the waters for both our bloodlines. Our children, if we had any, would struggle to find their place the same way I did thanks to my unorthodox upbringing.

Except, in my case, I had been playing human alongside the Low Society kids. At any point, Maud could have tired of the charade and dropped me into a new life that glittered diamond-bright before me. Linus might have filled the role of older brother or raging crush had I been schooled alongside him and my High Society peers. But I hadn't been.

Our children wouldn't have the option of choosing. Our children would be Woolworths. They had to be, or Maud's line would end with me. I lacked her reputation to protect them. The family name would have to do that, and that meant Boaz renouncing his position as Pritchard scion and assuming an almost consort position. And since Amelie was about to fall from grace, the future of their blood-line would rest on the youngest Pritchard's shoulders.

Macon was a good kid, but he hadn't been groomed to lead the family since birth like Boaz. He hadn't been nudged along as a spare like Amelie, either. Life as he knew it would end. His dreams would be cut from his head and new ones whispered in his ears. And the worst he could do was what Boaz had done—rebel. For all the good it would do him. There were different rules for male scions. Even Boaz's rebellion hadn't done more than earn him a title as a modern-day rake. All his acting out hadn't saved him from his familial obliga-tions, and it wouldn't spare Macon either.

"I'm tired." I made a valiant effort to keep my eyes dry. "I'm going to nap if you don't mind."

"I'll wait out in the hall." He pulled a faded blue crochet blanket over my shoulder. "I'll leave Cletus with you."

Eyes already shut, I pretended to sleep while he strolled out the door.

SIXTEEN

Ice spread through my chest, cutting a path between my breasts, and I gasped fully awake. "Cletus?"

"I'm insulted you called out another man's name during foreplay," Boaz drawled, leaning over me as he braced his elbows on the bedrail. "The ice cube move is a classic."

I shoved upright, my heart attempting to catapult from my throat, but the brass button was cold in my palm, and Oscar was wherever Oscar went when he wasn't here. Odds were good Boaz couldn't see him without help since I struggled with his perception too, but I didn't want to find out like this. Or at all. Not yet.

The Elite had been ready to sacrifice the kid to get what they wanted, and I was happy having him off their radar.

"That was foreplay?" The front of my gown was soggy and cold from the ice cube he'd stuck down my neckline. "Huh. All this time, I thought I was missing out on the whole sex thing, when foreplay with you is the equivalent of dumping a cold drink down the front of my shirt. I've done that plenty. Guess I'm less virginal than I originally suspected."

"It doesn't count when you do it," he teased. "Dumping ice down your shirt is fun, sure, but having someone else do it is life changing."

"Hmm." I blotted my chest dry. "Are we talking about masturbation or sex?"

"I have a one-track mind, but self-pleasure is an activity I'm willing to explore with you." His smile made my heart twist. "All couples need their hobbies."

"I expected you to kiss me awake. You're such a fan of the classics, I figured you for a Prince Charming come to wake his Sleeping Beauty."

"What's romantic in theory can come off as lecherous in practice." He traced my bottom lip with his pointer finger. "I don't have much pride, but I can say I've never had nurses pry me bodily off an unconscious woman in her hospital bed."

"Um, ice cubes?" I flicked water at him. "That's classier to you?"

"You *are* High Society." He sniffed. "I had to up my game."

"Standards," I teased. "It's important to have them."

"You'd think so." He picked at the sheets. "Not all folks share that view."

Finally the elephant in the room trumpeted, and both of us took notice.

"Talk to me." I caught his hand and held it balled against my chest. "How are you holding up?"

"I'm numb." He stroked his thumb over the wet spot on the front of my gown. "I can't feel a thing. Maybe I was hoping playing with ice would burn enough to wake me."

"I didn't know." I had to put it out there. "I keep thinking I should have known."

"Me too, Squirt." The bed creaked from taking on his weight when he sat near my feet. "I haven't been home much in the last few years. That's on me. I should have been there for her after she lost you, but things between me and my folks haven't been great since I got old enough for them to list me on the meat market." A sarcastic twist bent his lips into an unfamiliar shape. "I couldn't stomach living in Savannah after the trial. You were a kid. An innocent child. And no one could be bothered to save you."

"You tried."

"Not hard enough." He grunted. "Now Amelie's head is on the chopping block, and it's her own damn fault. I don't know what to do with that. I want to protect her, but I can't when she got caught in the act by the Grande Dame's own son. His word is gold."

My fingers uncurled from his. "Mine's more nickel-plated, huh?"

He cursed under his breath. "That's not what I meant."

Except I kind of thought that's exactly what he meant, though he would never have said so if he weren't so stressed over Amelie. It wasn't that he doubted me. Boaz's faith in me was as solid as the chests stacked in the living room of the carriage house. But he was working among the Elite, with fellow necromancers, and they would be buzzing about my pardon and release. He was a far more trustworthy barometer for public opinion on me than any I had. Clearly the masses weren't convinced my release was more than scraps my aunt tossed under the table to me.

At least no one suspected her true motives. Yet. But that day would dawn all too soon.

"When do I get to go home?" I touched the bandage covering my side and winced. "Woolly will be frantic if I don't get back soon."

"I stopped on my way here and explained things to her," he assured me. "I worried she might hike up her foundation and waddle over here after me, but I think I talked her into staying put. You can rest easy."

"Thanks for thinking of her."

"She's your family." He peeled my hand off the healing wound. "Notifying them is SOP."

"It's not standard operating procedure for most people to soothe the fears of an old house."

"Woolly's my second-best girl." He kept hold of my fingers, exploring their length, the way they flexed, like he'd never seen knuckles a day in his life. "I couldn't leave her hanging."

"I'm going to attend the trial." The Pritchards might not want me there, but I was going all the same. "I hope that doesn't cause friction between us."

"But I'm a fan of friction." He slid our palms together. "Especially between us."

His gambit nearly worked. I almost smiled. "Be serious."

"You're going to be called as a witness. It's unavoidable." He arranged my hand on my lower stomach. "You were there, and they'll want you to corroborate Linus's story."

"Oh, Goddess." I slumped against my pillows. "How can they expect me to help condemn her?"

"She killed people, Grier." Pain throbbed in his words. "She must be held accountable."

Nodding, because he was right, because I couldn't pardon her, because this was life, I closed my eyes. "I'm tired." I used the same line on him since it had worked so well earlier. "I'm going to nap if you don't mind."

"Nah. You should rest." He pressed a tender kiss to my cheek, right in the path of a tear I couldn't manage to call back. "I'm leaving my number as your emergency contact. I hope that's okay. I couldn't remember Odette's, and Linus went to get coffee, so I can't ask for his." And Amelie, my first choice, was a nonstarter. "I'll be back after you're released to give you a ride home."

"Mmm-kay."

The tears came after he left, each drop emptying the well of my soul, but it was for the best. I couldn't face the Grande Dame with grief in my heart or desperation in my eyes. Better to purge now than risk breaking down in front of her.

Oscar popped into existence beside me after the hiccuping sobs ended and offered me his linen handkerchief. I took it and daubed my sore eyes with the chill impression of fabric then pressed the red button on the bedrail. "I'm ready to go home."

"The paperwork has already been started, Ms. Woolworth," the nurse informed me. "Your private physician is consulting with our attending. She'll be in to collect you shortly."

I clutched the sheets like their paper thinness might protect me. "I don't have a private physician."

"Mr. Lawson made the arrangements," she said quickly. "I assumed…"

Well, that explained his coffee run. It's not like he drank the stuff, or much of anything else.

"I'm still muddled. Ignore me." I forced a laugh. "Of course Linus can handle my affairs."

I had no idea who this mystery doctor of his was, but I wasn't above taking any out I was given.

THE THIRD TIME I woke in the hospital, I was alone. It gave me time to think about how short my list of potential visitors was since I had few friends, and that number seemed to be dwindling. Woolly and Keet were family, but they weren't people. It's not like they could stroll in and ask to see me. Neely was a good friend, but he wouldn't be admitted to this floor even if I called him. And if I did call, how would I explain getting stabbed by our mutual friend while she was under the influence of a shade?

This might be Savannah, one of the most haunted cities in the U.S., but even locals had their hard limits.

Miserable, I tugged the blue knit blanket higher on my shoulder. I hadn't felt this alone since Maud died.

Depression was an old coat I sometimes wore. It fit too tight in the shoulders and pinched as I moved, but taking it off required herculean effort, and I wasn't feeling even demigoddess-touched at the moment.

I was debating another light nap, too shallow for the dream to find me, when the door swung open.

"Ms. Woolworth." A vaguely familiar nurse bustled into the room. "I have some papers for you to sign, and then you're free to go."

Gingerly, I turned onto my back and used the controls to raise the head of my bed. "Where's Linus?" I took the clipboard, gave them my blessing to extort me, then passed it back before the nurse set about unhooking me from all the thingamabobs and doohickeys beeping and flashing behind me. "And my, um—" too late I realized I hadn't asked for a name, "—private physician?"

"Dr. Lecomte will be along in a moment." Linus strolled into the room with his hands in his pockets, head angled down like he was unsure of his welcome. "She stopped to visit another patient."

"Dr. Lecomte." I rolled in my lips to keep from laughing. Odette was many things, but a doctor she was not. "I hear you're to thank for contacting her."

His shrug reduced him to the shy boy who used to fumble the butter when I asked him to pass it to me.

"*Ma coccinelle.*" Odette swept into the room with her arms wide open, dressed in baggy jeans and a white tank top. Sandals peeked from under the hem she'd had to roll up a few times, and a scarf in seafoam blues fluttered behind her. "Must you insist on fraying these old nerves?" She pulled up short when she noticed the nurse's incredulous expression. "Why are you looking at me like something you scraped off the bottom of your shoe? Are private physicians not allowed their private time?" Her haughty glare made me chuckle. "Perhaps I should have worn a white coat for the occasion?"

"Apologies, ma'am." The nurse paled. "Ms. Woolworth is cleared to leave as soon as she's ready."

"I'm ready." I swung my legs over the side of the bed then slid until my toes brushed the floor. A cool draft across my backside had me bunching the fabric closed in my hands. "Okay, so pants first. *Then* we hit the bricks."

"Your clothes were ruined," Linus informed me. "I asked the staff to dispose of them."

The whole outfit might have been worth ten dollars, but dang it, those clothes were comfy.

"I didn't want to leave you here alone." He lifted a bag with the hospital's logo emblazoned on the front. I hadn't noticed it in his hand. "I bought these to get you home."

My mouth seesawed until deciding on a smile. Comparing Linus to Boaz was the same as comparing apples to oranges. The apple might have stood watch over me and bought me new clothes to wear home, but the orange had made certain Woolly knew not to fret, and he had taken time away from his family tragedy to ensure I was okay. So, yeah. There was really no comparison. No matter how my brain scrabbled to tally each of their deeds like friendship was a contest to win or lose, it was a tie.

"Do you need help?" Odette shooed the nurse from the room, and Linus left with her. "Sit, sit. Let me do this." I dutifully turned around and let her work the ties free on my gown. "You're so thin. Bony. Do you eat air?"

"Not you too," I groaned. "Last I checked, my name was Grier, not Gretel. Stop trying to fatten me up."

"Save your cheek for one of your boys." She popped my bare bottom, and I yelped.

"Yes, ma'am." I accepted the sweatpants she passed me and pulled them on under my gown before letting it slide down my arms. An oversized T-shirt came next. Its front was emblazoned with a drawing of the hospital, but that was it for clothes. "Panties I don't mind going without, but I have no bra."

"You're like me." She smoothed her hands over her small breasts. "We have knots on a wooden plank."

"Hey," I protested. "I have boobs." I glanced down at jutting ribs and protruding hipbones. "Okay, so I used to have boobs."

Damn it. I missed having curves. Skeletal was not a great look for me. In my line of work, the last thing I wanted was to be mistaken for a corpse.

After tugging the shirt over my head, I finger-combed my hair.

The final item in the bag was a pair of mesh shoes, almost like slippers with a flexible sole. I tugged them on, grateful for the barrier between my feet and the chill linoleum.

A knock sounded at the door followed by Linus's muffled, "Are you decent?"

"Yes." I crossed my arms over my braless chest. "You can come in."

He entered, pushing a contraption unlike any wheelchair I had ever seen. Flowering vines crawled down the sides, engraved into the silvery metal I suspected might be sterling. Each lush petal was accented in gold so rich I suspected they were twenty-four-karat inlays. Those touches I could stomach slightly better than the honest-to-Goddess red velvet cushion for my sitting pleasure, complete with gilded tassels. This chair screamed High Society, and I wondered how my transportation would have looked had I not been Maud Woolworth's daughter.

"It's not that bad." Linus crossed to me, cupped my elbow, and helped me get into position. He also palmed the brass button so I could grip the armrests and lower myself. "You only have to survive the ride down two floors."

"This chair is ridiculous," I grumbled. "Riding in this is embarrassing."

"Then you'll love this." He leaned over me and spread the matching red velvet lap blanket across my knees. His icy fingers skated over my nape, and I started at the unexpected contact. "I also bought you this from the gift shop. It cost me ninety-nine cents. I'll add it to your tab if I must."

The necklace was a length of black rubber cord with a brassy clasp that almost matched the antique button dangling between my nonexistent boobs. I closed my hand over the talisman, and suddenly the throne on wheels wasn't so bad. Still, I couldn't resist adding, "You couldn't have splurged on a hoodie?"

"Hoodies were thirty-six dollars. The T-shirt was only fifteen." He took position behind me while Odette held the door open for us.

"I decided it was safer to buy a lot of cheap items than invest in one expensive one."

Thirty-six dollars was pocket change to him, to me too, really. But I appreciated that he honored my budgetary restraint. "I don't mean to sound ungrateful." I reached up to brush his fingertips with mine where they gripped the handle. "Thanks for being here."

Odette looked on with a twinkle in her eyes I chose to ignore. Whatever she was seeing, or had seen, ignorance was bliss as far as I was concerned. And with Odette, there was always more to the picture than the rest of us saw.

Once we hit the hallway, I propped my elbow on the armrest and braced my forehead against my open palm. I hoped people would assume I was shielding myself from the harsh overhead lights and not trying to hide my mortification over riding in a gilded throne pushed by the equivalent of a High Society prince.

"The night birds are calling, calling, calling," Odette sang softly. *"The princess she's falling, falling, falling."*

I twisted to better see her from the corner of my eye, but wherever her vision had taken her, she was no longer with us for all that her body kept pace with the wheelchair. She snapped out of her fugue as we exited the sliding glass doors and placed a hand over her heart. Though I had been taught it was rude to ask, I couldn't help wondering. "What did you see?"

"A hard road and worn shoes at the end of it," she murmured. "Poor little feet."

As usual, I was sorry I'd asked.

Until we hit the circular drive out in front of the hospital, it hadn't occurred to me to ask how we were all getting home. My tender gut roiled as I waited for the familiar Lincoln Continental Linus favored to pull around, but it was a white van that stopped in front of us. The driver was a grungy young man dressed in pajama bottoms and a dirty tee. He leaned across the passenger seat and flashed us his phone. "You guys call for a lift?"

"We did." Linus worked to suppress the curl of his lip and mostly succeeded as he wheeled me closer. "Let's get you settled in the back." He pulled open the sliding rear door, and a sigh moved through his shoulders. Pizza boxes and empty soda bottles littered the floor, but he swept them aside then helped me climb onto the bench seat where he fastened me in as snug as a bug. "Where do you want me?"

The rear seats had been removed to make room for stereo equipment, so that was out. There was room on the bench seat beside me, or the front passenger seat was empty. "I hate to do this to you, but can Odette sit with me?"

"Of course." He eased out of the van and took her hand, helping her settle in beside me. "This was the right thing to do?"

Unsure which of us he was asking—himself or me or even Odette —I answered, "Yes."

I couldn't believe it. Linus Andreas Lawson III had downloaded a ridesharing app and used it to get me home.

This latest thoughtfulness had spared me from stepping into his hired car. I would take pizza stains on the seat of my gift-shop pants and gunk on the bottom of my water shoes over that misery any day.

SEVENTEEN

rriving home beat any medicine the hospital could have
prescribed. Woolly welcomed us, her glow the beacon I
remembered from childhood, our link so ironclad I didn't
require extra perception or contact with her to discern her
mellifluous wards. The old girl beamed out at us, and I couldn't help
smiling back.

I hobbled onto the porch unassisted, looped my arms around the
nearest of Woolly's columns, and sagged with relief as her magic
swept over me, absorbing me in the protection of *home*. Odette stood
on the bottom step, allowing Woolly to perform a risk assessment, but
Linus kept his feet planted firmly in the grass. I was about to ask
Woolly if she might reconsider granting him porch access when the
crimson car I had been expecting at the hospital glided into the
driveway.

Mr. Hacohen, my quasi-lawyer, a man employed by the office of
the Grande Dame if not by the woman herself, popped out and held
open the door. "Hey, ladies and gent." He tossed our gathering a
wave. "Hate to be a drag, but your presence is formally requested at
the Lyceum."

"Can I change first?" I tugged on the front of my T-shirt. "I can't attend a trial dressed like this."

"The other parties are all assembled." He spread his hands in an apologetic plea. "We have to get you there yesterday." He nodded at Linus. "You two are our star witnesses."

Bile rose up the back of my throat as he cheerily ushered me on toward Amelie's doom.

"Odette is a friend," I reminded the house quietly. "Let her in if she asks."

The planks under my feet grumbled in reluctant agreement.

"What happened with Volkov isn't your fault. Your wards were failing, and they caused you to make a bad call." I curled my toes against the wood. "Do you trust Odette?"

Woolly flicked the curtains in the nearest window in a shrug.

Clearly, I wasn't the only one still suffering trust issues. "I have to go." I took the first step. "Do what you think is best."

That earned me a flicker of doubt from the porch light that made my chest hurt. I hated her uncertainty.

"Go on." Odette ushered me toward the waiting car. "Woolly and I are old friends. We'll sort out our differences and be sipping tea over gossip before you get home."

After a quick embrace that made me grimace when she squeezed me around the middle too hard, I left her to win or lose Woolly's endorsement on her own. I stepped into the grass and joined Linus, who held his phone to his ear. I huddled in his shadow like it might protect me from the car, and when Mr. Hacohen blanched and retreated inside the sedan, I realized the shadow was Cletus, and he had reacted to my fear.

The squeal of breaks heralded the return of the pizza van. The driver lowered the passenger window, leaned out and grinned. "You guys call for a lift?"

"We did," Linus passed the man a fifty-dollar bill before turning to me and offering his hand. "Grier?"

I accepted his chill fingers and kept going until I was hugging him. "You're not half bad for an enemy spy."

"There was no whooping." His hands settled on my shoulders, as light as feathers, the safest part of me given my injuries. "Your early-warning system failed."

"Sorry about that. I'm too tender for whooping and hopping around. You'll just have to give me a pass this time."

"All right." He disentangled us then opened the sliding door and tucked me back on the bench. "Are you sure you wouldn't like Odette to come along?"

"No." She made a point not to make waves, and arriving with me was more along the lines of a cannonball. Linus had the door closed halfway when the walls started pressing in on me. "Linus?"

He held still, like any sudden movement might startle me out of the vehicle. "Yes?"

"Sit with me?" I patted the bench. "I really don't want to be alone with my thoughts right now."

After a quick exchange with the driver, he joined me and sealed us in the back of the van.

We didn't talk during the short drive, and he kept a polite distance between our bodies, but it was a comfort having him there. Maybe it had to do with how students viewed their teachers as protectors, or maybe it had to do with how all his small kindnesses were adding up, or maybe it had to do with the fact there was a yawning void in me I was looking to fill. Whatever the reason, I was as grateful for his presence as I was terrified of what came next.

Thanks to Ambrose, I'd learned I had a new secret. Making vampires, true immortals or not, was one thing, but awakening ghosts? And, if Cletus was any indication, wraiths? That was quite another.

The dybbuk had shined a spotlight on my new talent, and the glare had caught Linus right in the eyes. His zeal had overtaken his expression, the rush of a new discovery animating his features, and I worried. He could betray me. Or he might choose to study me himself. While I couldn't see a way to monetize my new talent off the top of my head, I was certain the Grande Dame would have compiled a list a mile long by the time the words left Linus's lips.

Before I had time to work myself into a panic attack, Pizza Dude cozied up to the curb a block away from city hall. "Keep my number handy." He grinned at Linus in the rearview mirror. "For the right price, I can be anywhere you need me to be."

"We appreciate your availing yourself to us." Linus passed him another fifty before helping me out of the van. He waited until the taillights flashed before taking my arm. "Well, that was an adventure."

"At this rate, he'll be able to buy an all-new van." I leaned on Linus a little since all the bending and shuffling getting in and out was pulling on my stitches. "You can't keep dropping money on me."

"You're Dame Woolworth," he reminded me. "The Society is responsible for any and all expenses resulting from travel required to attend mandatory functions. I'll fill out a voucher for reimbursement if you like. Make sure you do too going forward."

From his tone, it was clear he valued his time more than the hundred dollars he'd dropped on our ride. I wasn't a fan of paperwork myself, so I sympathized. Besides, he probably used fifty-dollar bills as tissues when he got allergy eyes, so the expense meant nothing. The thought behind a gift mattered far more to me than its cost. When you grew up able to ask for and receive anything, a quick debit of funds for a bauble soon forgotten amid towering piles of the same, you learned appreciation when people proved your worth by spending time *with* you instead of money *on* you.

Linus was still figuring out my preference. He spoke the language of plastic best, but there was hope for him yet. All good friendships changed the people within them to a better version of themselves. Maybe he would bring me a step closer to embracing my heritage. Maybe I would impart my couponing skills on him.

The massive limestone building towered over us, its clock tower a distant shadow swallowed by the darkening night sky. We entered together and made our way toward the bank of elevators. Linus ushered me inside the first booth then used a key from his pocket to open the control panel. He pushed the button for the subbasement that held the Lyceum and let the doors close before pulling the emergency stop.

"Tell me you've got a good reason for stopping the elevator, because I've got to tell you—" I swallowed hard. "There's literally never a reason good enough for stopping an elevator."

"I was going to offer when we arrived at Woolly, but there was no time, and I couldn't risk our driver getting curious." He removed a pen from his pocket. "Would you like help closing those wounds?"

I touched my side. "The doctor said—"

"Allowing you to heal naturally would be best, but the doctor had no idea what awaits you." He spun the cap with his thumb. "The choice is yours, but you need to be at your best. Amelie's freedom depends on it."

"That's a low blow." I lifted the hem of my shirt, careful to keep the edge from exposing the underside of my breasts. "But you're right. It's bad enough going in there looking like what the cat dragged in." Though that was becoming a norm for me. "I don't want to have to lean on you if I can manage on my own." I winced at how that sounded. "No offense."

"None taken." Linus dropped to one knee in front of me. One cool palm spanned my left side and held me still while the other rested against the puckered, angry edge of my stitches and began to draw a perfect set of interconnected sigils that washed relief through me. "The only way to survive the Society is to conceal who you are, what you love, how you feel, beneath your title. Never let them glimpse the real you. Show them what they want to see, tell them what they want to hear, and keep your ears open. Collect their weaknesses like cards to play against them at a later date."

The urge to balk against his advice was tempered by his absolute concentration. "Is that what you do?"

"It's what we all do." He examined his work then nodded and capped his pen before rising. "Mother was a strict tutor." He hit the button again, and the elevator shuddered back to life. "The Pritchards will come after us both." He adjusted his clothing and hair before we hit bottom. "However this ends, remember none of it is your fault."

The doors rolled open, and Linus strolled out first. The transformation was instantaneous. Gone was the casual slouch as his shoulders corrected themselves into perfect alignment. Gone was the amusement in his eyes as his gaze hardened to granite when he glanced back to make sure I followed. Gone was the stride that welcomed me to fall in step with him as his gait turned ravenous, devouring the red marble tiles of the Lyceum as he prowled into the center where the assembly awaited us.

I toddled after him in my gift-shop apparel with my two-day hair pulled back in a messy bun that looked like a squirrel had died on the back of my head and kept my arms crossed to cover my bralessness.

Before us stood the opulent box seat where the Grande Dame presided over proceedings. Her throne was an antique, a solid gold and gem-studded eyesore. It was exactly the kind of flamboyant bauble that got ships sunk by pirates looking for an easy score. The kind that sent divers looting wreckage for decades after the resulting cannon fights left the cursed thing on the ocean floor. Plain silver chairs were good enough for the representatives who sat at each of her elbows. A High Society Dame sat to her right, a Low Society Matron to her left.

For a few blessed steps, I distracted myself wondering how many tassels must be decorating the red velvet cushions beneath them, and then we were standing in the center of the amphitheater staring up at our would-be judge and her pet jurors.

I wanted to vomit.

"Linus, dearest, there you are." The Grande Dame flushed with pleasure. "I was beginning to worry."

"Apologies, Mother." He executed a practiced bow, one that reminded me of Ambrose's mocking imitation. "Grier was only just released from the hospital."

A growl worthy of any momma bear poured from our left where the Pritchard family gathered around a shackled Amelie whose chains bolted her to an anchor set in the marble tiles. And below that, in the lowest seating level, a dozen made vampires, almost hidden in the shadows, chittered between themselves.

"This is a blatant ploy for sympathy," Matron Pritchard snarled. "Look at her. Look what she's wearing."

Dread splashed in my gut like a cold stone dropped from a great height. Linus had made the first move in this game over an hour ago, and I was only now grasping how well I had been played.

"She was admitted to the ER for treatment of wounds sustained aboard the *Cora Ann*." He took great care to cast no blame. "I escorted her home myself, and a car was sent for us before Grier made it inside to shower or change her clothes."

The Grande Dame drummed her fingers on her armrest, a tiny smile curling her lips, but she didn't interfere.

"We are ready to hear the charges brought against our daughter," Mr. Pritchard announced, "so that we might defend against them."

The dame on the right lifted a scroll from her lap and unrolled the creaking parchment. "Your daughter is accused of consenting to a third-level possession by a fifth-level shade. She is accused of willfully conspiring with the shade, who self-identifies as Ambrose Batiste, to murder nine members of the Undead Coalition."

Fifth was the highest measurable level for a shade. A third-level possession wasn't much better. It might be worse if you viewed it as the halfway point where the vessel ought to have had some measure of control. But wasn't a partial possession by such a powerful shade more devastating than a full possession by a lesser one? Where would the line of culpability be drawn?

The Pritchards paled, and Matron Pritchard almost collapsed before her husband gathered her close. "No. It's not possible. Not our Amelie."

"Scion Pritchard," the matron on the left intoned. "You were part of the Elite team dispatched to detain Amelie Pritchard, correct?"

"Yes and no." Boaz jutted out his chin. "My team and I were already in position. We'd had the *Cora Ann* under surveillance for several days. We had a suspect in mind, but it was not my sister. Finding her in the warding ring..." He shook his head. "I didn't believe it was really her. I thought the shade was playing another trick."

The dame leaned forward a fraction. "What do you mean *another* trick?"

"Ambrose borrowed clothes from Scion Lawson. He also tailored his appeared to resemble him." Boaz ground his molars. "I thought—I *hoped*—when we came upon Amelie, that Ambrose was using her face to manipulate Grier into releasing him."

"Shades can only manifest one aspect per bonding," the matron informed him primly. "They can choose how they appear, but they can only tailor their look once. Your commanding officer should have briefed you on the dybbuk to prepare you for what you might encounter in the field. Did he fail in his duties?"

"No," he all but growled, "but Amelie is my kid sister. I was in shock. I still am. So you'll have to forgive me if I suffered a lapse in judgment."

Matron Pritchard had recovered enough to bristle as the matron picked at him. "I think we can all sympathize with my son, considering the circumstances."

"Yes, the circumstances," the matron mused. "I understand your son is romantically involved with Grier Woolworth. How peculiar to find both your son, his girlfriend and your daughter all in one place at the same time. One might think the meeting prearranged."

The implication, that Boaz and I had colluded with Amelie, stung. I'm not sure why. I had no reason to expect better from them.

"Scion Lawson was also present," Matron Pritchard was quick to point out to the assembly. "He's living with Grier on the Woolworth property."

The dame gave up all pretense of detachment and leaned

forward, eyes hungry. "Are you implying Dame Woolworth is also in a relationship with Scion Lawson?"

"I don't know what they get up to over there." Matron Pritchard sniffed. "Maud made clear to me some years ago that it isn't my business what Grier does or who she does it with in the privacy of her own home."

Mortification stung my cheeks, and I blanched as our gazes snared one another. *How could you?* That's what I wanted to ask. I had never done a thing to her, and goddess knows my reputation was already in tatters, yet there she stood with shears in hand, snipping away at what scraps remained.

"No," Boaz boomed. "Leave her out of this."

"She's in this up to her neck," his mother spat. "They claim Amelie was captured on that boat. Amelie, who is a straight-A college student. Amelie, who is the Low Society ideal. Amelie, who lives at home under my watchful eye where I would see if something was wrong." She seethed in my direction. "Murder is far more believable of that one. After all, she's been convicted of it once already."

I had expected the accusation, of course, but not its source. I knew Matron Pritchard didn't like me, but I'd had no idea until that moment that she hated me.

"Are you questioning my judgment?" The Grande Dame uncoiled from her chair, a cobra ready to strike. "Do you truly believe I would release a murderer on a lark? Or is this simply an attempt at establishing precedent through slander in the hopes I will show your daughter the same imagined leniency?"

Matron Pritchard gaped in stunned comprehension of her misstep, but the snake she had stomped on was already fanning its hood. She had crossed the Grande Dame, in a crowded amphitheater, no less. Her wide eyes swept the row where other Low Society matrons gathered, but no one could save her from herself. It was one thing to believe I had killed Maud and that the Grande Dame had pardoned me since I was family. It was another to hurl the accusation in her face during a full assembly.

The spectacle made me sick, and I clutched my stomach, afraid it might spill.

Only a minute shake of Linus's head gave me the strength to lower my hands and correct my posture.

The trial resumed, but try as I might, I couldn't shake the ringing in my ears. Or maybe it was all the hateful words and insinuations I couldn't escape. I stood beside Linus, a perfect statue, while inside I thrashed and wailed as I was put on trial once more right alongside Amelie.

Linus, a talented orator, told our side of the story. His summation painted a watercolor version of our night, but no one who wasn't there could hold it up against the original and tell the difference. He revealed the nature of my part-time job in order to explain our interest in the *Cora Ann*. He admitted to tutoring me in order to bridge the gaps left in my education during my imprisonment to explain his current residence. And then he expounded on how the two intersected when we decided to explore the *Cora Ann* after learning about its highly publicized ghost.

I didn't make a conscious decision to vanish through the door in my head to escape the dissection of my character, but I careened into awareness when Linus brushed his icy knuckles against mine.

Someone had asked me a question, and I had been too far away to hear or answer.

"As I said, Grier provided a distraction while I painted containment sigils around the room," Linus reiterated. "Our goal was to protect ourselves from Ambrose. We had no clue as to the identity of his vessel until after he was contained and relinquished his aspect."

The dame was staring a hole through me. "Do you have anything to add?"

Uncertain how much or what Linus had said, I shook my head. "No."

"I will withdraw to my chambers for deliberation," the Grande Dame announced. "I will return within the next half hour to render judgment."

Thirty minutes to decide Amelie's fate. I wondered if I had been given so many.

The Grande Dame and her retinue descended the back stairs and entered her private chambers, leaving those of us trapped on the floor to afford passive entertainment for the rest of the assembly. I mimicked Linus's rigid posture and bored expression as best I could, but each second stretched an eternity.

I worked up the nerve to cut my eyes toward Boaz, but he was staring at his sister like this might be the last time he saw her, and his hands were flexing like he was debating the tensile strength of her chains.

Finally, a low creak announced the opening of a faraway door, and the Grande Dame returned with a click-clack of stilettos upon marble. The silence in the Lyceum was deafening while the trio resumed their seats and settled their gowns around them. With the suspense drawn out to the last possible millisecond, the Grande Dame rested her palms on her armrests and stared down at the Pritchard family.

"Amelie Pritchard murdered nine members of the Undead Coalition while under the influence of the shade, Ambrose. Eight of the nine clans are willing to settle for tithes to be paid in the amount of twelve million dollars. The final clan is calling for a blood tithe instead." Her bored voice droned on. "Matron Pritchard, will you see these debts paid?"

"Twelve million dollars would empty my family's coffers." She wet her lips. "There must be something else."

"There is," the Grande Dame agreed amiably. "A blood tithe will satisfy any and all outstanding debts."

A tremble started in my knees and migrated upward until my teeth chattered. "I'll pay her debt."

Every head in the room whipped toward me while Linus sighed my name through his parted lips.

"No," Matron Pritchard snapped. "We won't be indebted to you."

"What's the alternative, Mom?" Boaz demanded. "Amelie is your daughter."

His mother ignored him. "We can't afford the tithe."

"Shall we arrange for an execution then?" The Grande Dame directed the question to the made vampires huddled in the row a half step below the level where we stood. "We are all in agreement that satisfies the debt, correct?"

"Yes," nine voices chorused.

"I'm inclined to give you what you crave. The girl was foolish, and she won't learn without punishment." The vampires made a fingernails-on-chalkboard sound as they rubbed their upper fangs against their lower teeth that curdled my blood. "Except there's one small problem. Six of the nine vampires Ambrose murdered weren't killed in cold blood."

Whispers raced through the room as we all scrambled to figure out why that could possibly matter now.

"The most curious aspect of this case is not that they were murdered by a dybbuk, but that they were killed within the high wrought iron fences surrounding Woolworth House." Her red lips bled into a smile. "What are the odds that a horde of vampires, each bound to a different clan, would descend upon my niece's house on the same night at the same time?"

The nine salivating vampires ceased their scraping and fell as silent as the dead. Or the undead in this case.

"Where is the proof?" a man I recognized as Clan Master Truong barked. "What evidence do you have?"

"The incontrovertible kind," Linus informed him as he pulled a cell phone from his pocket. "Let the record show the video I am about to share with the assembly was forwarded to the Grande Dame on the night the incident occurred."

The lights dimmed, and a large projector screen unspooled from the ceiling. Linus pushed a button on his phone and, through the magic of Bluetooth, we were all treated to a short film blasted from a projector overhead.

The movie was set in my front yard and starred six unfamiliar vampires. They scuttled over the fence like spiders, weaving through shadows toward Woolly. Ambrose intercepted them on the lawn wearing wrinkled pants spotted with concrete and a bloodthirsty grin, his headful of flames dancing wickedly.

"Who might you be?" his silken voice implored. *"I don't recall seeing your names on the guest list."*

"Step aside, abomination," one snarled. *"We have business here."*

"The lady of the house isn't home." Ambrose rocked back on his heels. *"You'll have to come back later."*

Another vampire unslung the wooden bat from his shoulder and aimed it at Woolly. *"We'll just leave her our calling card then."*

"No need for that." He affected gripping a pen poised over a notebook. *"I'm happy to take your names."*

"We're under orders," a third barked. *"We aren't leaving until we've done as the Master bid us."*

"I'm afraid then that you won't be leaving at all." The comment wasn't made as a threat, or an invitation to brawl. He was simply stating the outcome as he saw it. He stood there while that registered on all their faces, then spread his arms wide. *"I await your decision."*

Their answer was to bare their fangs and rush him with their weapons drawn, and his response was to become a weapon. He thinned the flats of his hands into blades, so that where he sliced, fingers and arms and heads thudded to the dew-misted grass. Within minutes, he stood king atop a mountain of severed limbs, and he winked right into the eye of the camera before bowing to his captive audience.

"Where did you get that footage?" Boaz demanded before I could put voice to the words.

"You placed several motion-activated cameras along the Pritchard/Woolworth property line. They each offer a different vantage point of Grier's home and yard. I discovered them when I did a search of the property after moving into the carriage house." Linus ended the film, and the screen rolled away as the lights brightened.

"Eleven days ago, I encountered the dybbuk using a hose to wash blood off the lawn. I reported the incident, and the assembly allocated resources to secure the footage for their records. That's when the massacre was discovered."

A massacre. On my lawn. That no one had seen fit to mention to me. One sanctioned by the Master.

The past two weeks of quiet had been an illusion. A silent battle had been waging on my property, among my friends, and I'd had no idea. I was being treated as spoils of war instead of as a fellow warrior who might lend aid to the cause that was protecting my own life.

Spitting mad, I whirled on Boaz. "You've been keeping me under surveillance?"

"I was trying to protect you." Muscles fluttered along his jaw. "I worry about you."

"And you?" I blasted Linus next. "What's your excuse for not telling me?"

"I forbade him to mention the incident to you," the Grande Dame interceded on his behalf. "That meant he couldn't share his sources, either." She tapped a garnet fingernail against her ruby lips. "He could have lied, I suppose, and told you he witnessed it first-hand, but my son never lies." The urge to roll my eyes forced me to study the toes of my slippers. Everyone lied. All except the fae, and they were said to be so gifted at misdirection as to be impossible to catch in the act. "Linus discovered new evidence in an ongoing investigation. Discretion was of the utmost importance."

Again, the cool brush of his knuckles chilled me to attention, and I stared up at the Grande Dame.

"What say you to this?" she demanded of the Clan Masters. "Who is this Master whose orders supersede yours within your own clans?"

None of the previously ravenous vampires made a peep.

"We shall continue this discussion in my chambers." She snapped her fingers, and three dozen Elite sentries poured into the room to secure the master vampires. They were marched beneath the box seat down the darkened hallway to the Grande Dame's private domain. "They forfeit their tithes with their treachery."

Boaz's relieved sigh carried across the room to mingle with mine. Six down. Three to go.

"That brings reparations to..." She bent her head together first with the dame on her right and then the matron on her left. "The tithe owed is a paltry three point five million dollars."

A stab of hope left me breathless. Surely Matron Pritchard would pay such a reduced fee.

"We haven't heard from our daughter." Her stare hung where the screen had been. "I want to hear the truth from Amelie's own lips."

"Very well." The Grande Dame gestured to the sentinel standing behind her. "Remove her gag."

He scrubbed the sigil from her forearm with a wet cloth then fell back into position.

"Tell the assembly you're innocent," her mother ordered. "Tell them who is really at fault."

Call me paranoid, but I suspected, to her, the person *really at fault* meant me.

The room held its collective breath in anticipation of what juicy morsels Amelie might hand-feed them.

"I summoned Ambrose," Amelie rasped through a dry throat. "I bound him to me."

Matron Pritchard's face snapped hard toward her daughter as if the words had been a slap. "No."

"Yes," Amelie said, and I don't think I imagined the loathing simmering there.

"I have pressing matters to attend before dawn, Matron Pritchard," the Grande Dame said. "What is your answer?"

"The Pritchard Family will not be held accountable for the actions of Amelie Madison," Matron Pritchard enunciated clearly. One frail tear snaked from each eye before she gathered her composure. "I, Annabeth Pritchard, Matron Pritchard, hereby disown my middle child, my only daughter, and leave her fate to the assembly to decide."

Amelie hit the marble tiles on her knees, her mouth open on a silent scream.

Madison was her middle name, her last name now. She was no longer a Pritchard.

"You made me do this," Matron Pritchard hissed at me. "This is on your head, not mine."

Rushing to his sister, Boaz dragged Amelie into the protective circle of his arms.

"Step away," his mother warned him. "She's no longer a member of this family."

"You disowned her." Ice glazed his voice. "*You*. Not me." He pulled back to stare into Amelie's vacant eyes as he said, "She's my sister, my blood, no matter what you say."

"Don't test me." His mother vibrated with rage. "The Grande Dame has not granted my request yet."

"Macon will make a fine heir" was all he said, but his mother swayed on her feet.

Mr. Pritchard was slow to come to his wife's aid, and he steadied her with as much care as a tornado paid a telephone pole.

She didn't speak again.

"Your petition is granted. Amelie Madison Pritchard will be stricken from your lineage and histories." The Grande Dame made a shooing motion toward the couple. "You may go now. The rest of these proceedings no longer concern you."

Mr. Pritchard opened his mouth to protest, but his wife shook her head, and they left together with enough space between their bodies to fit some small countries.

"You there. Boy." The Grande Dame made an impatient gesture at Boaz. "You're excused as well."

His glare was a loaded weapon in search of a target. "I'm not leaving her to face judgment alone."

"Mother," Linus called her attention to him. "The clan who

called for a blood tithe—" He stepped forward, appearing curious, and used his body to block Boaz from her sight. "You didn't mention if that debt was satisfied."

"Oh. Yes." She smiled warmly at him. "It is the belief of this assembly that the blood tithe was an empty gesture meant to inflict pain upon the intended target as her relationship with the defendant is well-known. That debt is, as you say, satisfied."

"That leaves the total sum of Amelie's debt as three point five million dollars." The numbness was wearing off, and in its place boiled a simmering rage I would have felt for any girl abandoned by her family to face sentencing alone, guilty or not, but it struck me doubly so because it was Amelie. No matter what she had done, we were friends. I couldn't lose her too. I had lost too much already. "Will there be other stipulations or penalties?"

"The punishment for summoning is six months imprisonment," the right-hand dame informed me. "She must pay the tithe and serve her time."

"If she is unable to pay the tithe at the end of six months," the left-hand matron continued, "her bond will be made available for purchase. She will remain a detainee of the Society until her debts are absolved."

"Ms. Madison has been disowned. There's no hope of her paying the tithe. Let's not pretend otherwise." Linus folded his hands behind his back. "She has no priors, her record is spotless, and she has pursued an education tailored to providing valuable services to our community. All things considered, I propose a lucrative compromise that will please us all."

His mother watched him with a sparkle in her eyes. "I'm listening."

"Grier is also a victim," he reminded the room, "and she is owed reparations for the grievous injury she sustained helping me contain Ambrose when the Elite failed in their duties."

A low sound, too fierce to be a mere growl, drew my eye toward Boaz, who still cradled Amelie.

Who had earned that fury? Ambrose for hurting me, Linus for exposing Amelie, or himself for what he saw as a failure to protect both of us?

A tittering debate rippled through the amphitheater before the Grande Dame asked, "What is it you propose?"

"Grier is in the process of rebuilding her household. She has no employees to help her manage her finances or her property." The High Society gawkers each gasped at my wretched living conditions. "I ask the assembly to consider allowing an advance sale of Ms. Madison's bond. Grier has already mentioned her willingness to pay the tithe, and she could use someone with Ms. Madison's skills to advise her. She was just reinstated, after all, and her inheritance requires routine maintenance."

Her nails started *tap-tap-tapping*. "And the mandatory prison sentence?"

"Allow Ms. Madison to serve the time under house arrest at Woolworth House."

"That's quite a large favor to ask," she mused. "What guarantee do we have she won't escape?"

The concern was me allowing her to run. That much didn't have to be spelled out for me.

"I will bind her myself." He cut his eyes toward me, and they belonged to a savvy businessman making a deal, not a friend striving to save another person from hurt. "For an additional fee, of course."

There was no hesitation on my part. "I agree to pay the fee."

"You haven't asked what it is yet." The Grande Dame chuckled. "Be careful you don't go too far in debt."

"I trust Linus to be fair." As I said it, I realized it was true. I did trust him. At least this much.

"The deal is struck," he murmured to me before turning to the Grande Dame. "Mother?"

With a put-upon sigh, she conferred with her advisors. There was much whispering and nodding, a few head shakes and some laughter. But at last the three women straightened in their chairs. "It is the decision of this assembly that Grier Woolworth be allowed to pay the tithe for Amelie Madison. It is also the decision of this assembly that Amelie Madison be allowed to spend her six months of confinement within Woolworth House as penance for the crimes committed against Grier Woolworth."

In the aftermath, I was too afraid to glance at Boaz. He hated the High Society. This added more fuel for the fire. I couldn't check on Amelie without risking his reaction, so I examined Linus instead. His hands were still pinned at the small of his back, his expression bored, but his knuckles were white, and his nails bit into his palms.

"Ms. Madison will be released into my son's custody as soon as we receive confirmation the tithe has been paid." The Grande Dame rose, and her advisors stood in tandem a moment later. "Now if you will all excuse me, there are other pressing matters that require my attention."

Yet another trap clamped shut, this time around the master vampires the Grande Dame had lured into the Lyceum with the promise of justice for their clanmates. Through their greed, she had captured six additional sources of information on the whereabouts and identity of the Master.

The gratitude I ought to have felt never manifested. The cost for this intel had been far too high.

Mr. Hacohen appeared in the vacuum left by their exit like a magician and whisked me away to a private conference room to do the necessary paperwork. A half hour later, I was the proud owner of Amelie's indenture. Except pride wasn't what I was feeling, not at all. The roiling in my gut kept churning over how simple the transaction had been. Until tonight, I hadn't known purchasing bonds was a thing the Society allowed. Naïve of me, I know, considering how it was a means of recouping costs, and they worshipped at the altar of the almighty dollar.

Linus waited for me in the hall, and Mr. Hacohen left me with him while he went to file the paperwork.

"I can't decide if I'm mad at you," I told him. "I want to be, I should be, but you saved her."

"I wanted to tell you. Everything. I didn't agree with the decision to keep you in the dark, but I understand why it was made." He mashed his lips together. "I hope you can forgive me."

"I need to think about who you are, and which Linus is the real one. Growing up the way we did, the way *you* did, I understand you needed to build yourself armor, but it fits you too well." The Linus from the Lyceum snugged him like a second skin, but then again, he wore so many faces and with such ease. "I can't see the real you between the seams when you're suited up, and that worries me."

"I understand." He hesitated a moment. "I told Mother I would bind Amelie to your property."

"Yes, you did." A prickle of irritation worked its way to the surface. "I wish I had been in a position to decline."

He nodded as though he'd expected as much. "I told her I *would* do it, not when."

There was a clicking sound as my jaw opened and then shut. "W-what?"

"I didn't tell her when I would perform the binding. I might wait until we're in our three hundreds." He stuffed his hands in his pockets. "I didn't mention what I would bind her to, either. Property has a broader meaning than land. I might choose to tie her to a toaster on your counter or a pencil she can carry in her pocket."

"I made up my mind." I launched myself at him, trapping his arms against his sides, and squeezed until he grunted. "I'm not mad at you. I might still have to dealphabetize your library to get you back one day, but right now, we're square."

"Your early-warning system is broken," he deadpanned.

"I'm a hugger." More these days than ever now that I was starting to reacclimate. The thing about love is, when you're raised with an excess, the overflow splashes onto those around you. Not even Atramentous had broken that part of me. "You'll get used to it."

His heart beat fast beneath my cheek, and his breaths quickened. "I'll take your word for it."

"Grier."

The sound of my name spoken in Boaz's tired voice sent my eyelids crushing shut on a soundless groan. I hadn't been doing anything wrong, but I could imagine how it looked finding us embracing in a dark hall. What concerned me most wasn't that he would assume it was anything romantic. What had my heart twisting was fear this might read more like collusion than a release of tension.

Boaz's gaze skipped over me and landed on Linus, but no spark of jealous temper ignited. There was no light there at all. This close, I could tell he hadn't thawed from that numb place where he had lingered since finding Amelie.

"The Grande Dame sent me to collect you," he said formally. "They're ready to release Amelie."

"Hey." I freed Linus and trotted over to Boaz. "Do you mind if I walk with you?"

"Mind?" Boaz shook his head, and his eyes cleared a fraction. "Why would you have to ask?"

The list was so long I couldn't see the top to find where to even start. "Let's go get our girl."

I slid my hand into his and guided him down the hall, checking over my shoulder to make sure Linus followed. We entered the amphitheater as the sentinel in charge of Amelie unlocked her manacles. The chains clanked onto the floor, and he kicked them aside before he knelt in front of her to attach a thick metal cuff around her ankle. The whiff of blood and pennies on the air told me the sigils within it had been activated.

"What does it do?" I asked the sentinel. "Will it hurt her?"

"So long as she behaves, she'll forget it's there." He coiled the chains around his arm then stood. "These sigils are like boomerangs. Whatever she tosses out, physically or magically speaking, comes back at her. She can't hurt you or anyone else without feeling that pain tenfold."

Beneath my hand, Boaz's fingers twitched in the promise of a tight fist. I worked out the worst of the tension with my thumbs, silently urging him to let this be over and done, to let us all go home. He must have received the message. His palm relaxed, and he brought my hand to his lips for a long minute.

Amelie was a statue rooted to the marble. Boaz released me then crossed to his sister and slung his arm around her shoulders. He guided her out of the Lyceum while Linus and I kept a respectful distance. They rode the elevator up together, and I waited until Linus and I stood in the booth before asking the next hard question.

"What happens to Ambrose?" I wrapped my arms around myself. "He's still in there, right?"

"He is." His smile was sad, like he'd hoped I might somehow forget that part. "You can't separate the two without performing an exorcism. Ambrose is too fat on his kills to go willingly. It would kill her prying him out right now."

"He won't stop killing." He couldn't if he wanted to live. "How do we control him?"

"I'm going to tattoo a containment ward on Amelie. It won't last forever, but it should subdue Ambrose for a few months. It will buy us time for him to weaken before we take the next steps."

"What is it?" I shivered under his regard. "What aren't you telling me?"

"Lots of things, I imagine." He lightened the comment with a smile that didn't sit right on his mouth. "What happened on the *Cora Ann* wasn't what the ward you copied was designed to do. It should have contained Ambrose, and it did, but it also ripped Amelie out of him. He never would have relinquished his hold on her, not when he was strong enough to fight."

In the silence that followed, I got the feeling he was waiting for an answer to a question I hadn't heard him ask.

"You want me to...what?" I rubbed my arms. "I can't tattoo her. I don't know how."

"All you have to do is draw what I show you," he promised. "I'll copy your design onto transfer paper, apply it, and tattoo her using a special ink blend that helps with suppression."

I nodded reluctant agreement then followed Linus out of the elevator and into the night. I smelled pizza before I spotted our ride. Boaz was eyeing the driver with suspicion, so I went to smooth things over with him. I made it halfway before noticing Linus hadn't followed. "You're not coming?"

"Not this time." He flicked a glance at Boaz. "Here. Take this for the ride home."

"Put it on my tab." I grudgingly accepted the fifty he passed me. "How are you getting home?"

The red Continental glided into sight as he scanned the curb. "I made other arrangements."

On some unspoken signal, Cletus made his presence known, swaying between Linus and me, and I snapped my fingers. "It was you."

Linus raised an eyebrow and waited to hear my latest accusation. "You'll have to be more specific."

"Those nights when Cletus lingered at the *Cora Ann*. It was because you were onboard, hunting."

"Yes." That was all he said, no specifics, and I itched to press him for details. "We'll continue this later."

Later wasn't never, so I was satisfied as he headed for his ride, and me for mine.

After dusting fries off the seat beside Pizza Dude, I sat and passed him his tip. Boaz and Amelie settled on the bench together in the back, her curled against his side, silent tears streaking her cheeks. Only in the aftermath of my whirlwind decisions did I start wondering if I'd made a huge mistake in binding her to me.

Boaz was the type of man who would use a rusty saw to hack off his own foot before wearing a cuff that controlled him. That was what made him a bad bet romantically. He might accept a collar for a little while, but eventually he would gnaw through any leash.

Amelie had already shown me her teeth, and now I had backed her into a corner then clamped on a choke chain.

May the goddess be merciful.

EIGHTEEN

Juicing up the wards and expanding Woolly's consciousness
had seemed like a stellar idea at the time, but I was starting to
regret my urgency in forcing those repairs. Woolly, who had
been told a sanitized version of the events aboard the *Cora
Ann*, had touched my mind during my earlier pit stop home and read
Amelie's guilt for my injuries.

Amelie was officially persona non grata as far as the old house
was concerned.

While I paced the foyer, attempting to convince my house to
grant Amelie sanctuary, Linus prepared his workstation in the
carriage house. Woolly loved Amelie, but Amelie didn't taste much
like Amelie to Woolly's new wards, and she had hurt me.

That was Woolly's line in the sand. Amelie had hurt me. There-
fore, Amelie was bad.

The majority of her overprotectiveness sprung from guilt. Some
of it over Maud. Most of it over Volkov.

I was so very tired of being the weak link.

Amelie was not alone in her ostracism. Woolly had nothing to say
to Boaz, either. She allowed him to enter the house, she permitted

him to plead his sister's case, but she remained unmoved by his argument. Even Keet turned away when Boaz offered to scratch his earholes.

Too bad Odette had slipped away while we were gone. She might have helped me convince Woolly, assuming they had made their peace. Without her calming influence, that left the two of us standing in the living room without many options.

"There are two bedrooms in the carriage house," I said at last. "Amelie could room with Linus."

"Hunger for power got her into this mess," Boaz countered. "If aversion therapy was going to work, it would have by now. She's been your friend for years." He cut me a look. "Amelie won't have much of a reputation after this, but I don't want how she lived with Linus while working off her debt to be one of the things she's remembered for."

The blood rushed from my cheeks, and I nodded. "I don't want that for her, either."

The Society thrived on inventing foibles to tarnish the reputations of its members. Forcing Amelie to live with Linus would give them meat enough to feast on for years. She would never escape the shadow that cast over her viability as a potential match, not that she would have many options outside of human partners thanks to her disownment.

"Woolly, you have to work with me here." I tipped my head back and stared at the ceiling. "We have to keep them both. We don't have a choice."

The old house faked a case of selective hearing while dimming the lights in a muted but firm *no*.

I reached up to worry the button on my necklace when it hit me I had a bargaining chip. "Boaz, can you wait outside a minute?"

"Sure." His fingers trailed down my arm before he joined his sister on the front porch swing.

"I forgot to mention I made a new friend." I rubbed the button like it was a lamp and Oscar a genie. Thanks to my connection with

Woolly, a perception sigil wasn't necessary to see when the boy popped into existence, rubbing his fists in his eyes and yawning. "Oscar, meet Woolly. Woolly, meet Oscar." I removed the necklace and placed it on the mantle beside Maud's remains. "Oscar wants to live with us, at least for a little while. What do you say to that?"

The house reached out its magic to taste him, and Oscar burst into a fit of giggles.

"It tickles." His feet left the floor as laughter buoyed him. "Is she a ghost too?"

"Something like that." It was close enough to pass for the truth. "Well, Woolly?"

The floorboards groaned, indecisive, but her lights kept brightening the higher he flew.

That, more than anything, told me she was sold on the idea. She loved kids. She couldn't help herself. That's why she and I had bonded so deeply. In her own way, she had helped raise me. And Oscar was the same age as I was when Maud took me in. Nostalgia would do a lot of the heavy lifting for me with her.

"I'm glad you've welcomed one of our guests." Time to beat the dead horse. "But you still have to pick one of the other two to live with us."

The floor register sighed a tired acknowledgment.

"Do you want Amelie?" I made it easy on her. "Blink once for yes, twice for no."

The lights winked out then came back and stayed on.

"Thanks, girl." I patted the nearest doorframe. "She's been a good friend to us, and she needs us."

Woolly flipped a curtain to send me on my way while she instigated a game of hide-and-seek with Oscar.

I joined Boaz and Amelie on the porch and gave them the good news. "Woolly has agreed to allow Amelie to stay."

"I knew the old girl wouldn't let us down." Boaz rubbed his hands over his face. "Thank you, Woolly."

Proving she could multitask where Boaz was concerned, even if he wasn't totally forgiven, she flared the porch light in muted confirmation before I felt her attention slide back to Oscar.

Amelie said nothing at all. She stared straight through me, her breaths slow and deep, like she was sleeping with her eyes open. I thought she might have gone into shock, but that didn't change what was about to happen. She had to get tattooed to be made safe. Maybe the distance would help her the way retreating into my head spared me from immediate pain. What a miserable thing to be thankful for.

"Everything is prepared," Linus called from the safety of the yard. "Bring her into the kitchen, please."

Boaz helped her stand, and she walked on autopilot down the steps and through the gate into the garden. I held the door open while he guided her into the kitchen and sat her in the chair Linus indicated with a sweep of his arm. Pots of red ink with a peculiar black glitter sat on the table along with a squirt bottle of clear liquid and a few other supplies.

Linus caught my eye. "Grier, can you step into the office for a moment?"

"Sure." I left Boaz to stand watch over his sister and joined Linus at the desk. "You just want me to draw what I see?"

"Yes." He pushed a worn sketchbook and a cup containing several black markers with tips ranging from extra fine point to bold toward me. "Use my design as a reference, but trust your instincts."

I labored over the design for an hour, incorporating extra flourishes when my gut told me to go for more detail, and I was proud of the final product. Homework still sucked, more some days than others, but I couldn't argue with the end result.

"This reminds me of a Celtic knot." And a story Maud told me forever ago about using knots to confuse troubled spirits who would get lost following a thread and never find the end. Learning the same stories had inspired his work hardly surprised me. "What do you think?" I passed over the drawing, then I sat back and waited. "Too much?"

"It's perfect." He traced the pattern with his finger while shaking his head. "Your mind is beautiful."

I flushed clear to the tips of my toes and escaped while he worked his mojo on the transfer.

For the first time since the *Cora Ann*, I addressed Amelie. "Where do you want the tattoo?"

Her eyes lifted to mine, but she wasn't seeing me. She sat there, unblinking, until I looked away.

"I can't remember her ever wanting a tattoo." I aimed the comment at Boaz. "Did she mention it to you?"

"She talked about getting an infinity symbol for all of about five minutes after I got my first tattoo." He searched his memories. "She was thinking about the inside of her ankle, but I warned her it would hurt like a sonofabitch."

"Do we try to give her what she wanted, or do we choose somewhere less sensitive?"

"I have sigils I can use to lessen the pain," Linus offered from the doorway. "It's your choice."

Boaz ran a hand over his head, leaving hair sticking up in a stripe down the middle. "Can I see it first?"

"Of course." Linus held up the transfer paper. "Not many will guess what it does, but she can hide it with a sock if she's self-conscious about it later."

"A reminder will do her good," Boaz decided. "Let's go for the ankle." He took her hand and held it like she would have wanted him to if she were present. "Just...don't hurt her more than you have to."

"I'll do my best," Linus vowed as he set to work.

The tattoo slowly emerged as a filigree knot, shaded and bold and lovelier than any tattoo I had ever seen. The red ink made it stand out, and the black glimmer when light hit it gave it a shadowy appearance, like the tattoo was alive under her skin. Part of me wondered if that liveliness was Ambrose fighting his new constraints.

Leaning over Linus's shoulder to watch his vision unfold, I lost track of time, and then it was over.

"I'm done." Linus sat back and turned off his tattoo gun. "Let me clean it and wrap it."

Feeling like the other shoe was about to drop, I waited for the tattoo to do...something. But it didn't do anything as dramatic as when Woolly detonated as her wards snapped into place. And the change in Amelie wasn't as dramatic as when she was ripped from Ambrose. Maybe using Linus as a buffer between me and my sigils worked.

After he pronounced her ready for bed, I noticed the spark of awareness trickling into her expression. I couldn't say if it was the tattoo or simply time. She'd had hours to start processing what had happened. Maybe she was coming around on her own.

Boaz helped her to her feet, and she swayed a bit, another sign of waking from her robotic trance.

"Grier." Linus gripped my wrist when I stood to join them. "The design we discussed?" He placed a hand above his hip, as if I needed reminding of his ward against LS and their persuasion. "It's been registered."

"Already?" I sat back down. "Does this mean...?"

"I'm warmed up." He flexed his fingers. "I might as well."

"I need to get her to bed," Boaz said, hooking his arm around Amelie's waist. "Do what you need to do. We'll talk before I leave."

Leave, which was not the same as *go home*. The house next door might not wear that label anymore.

"Okay." I settled in the chair Amelie had vacated. "Make yourself at home while you wait."

The door closed behind them, and Linus lifted another sheet of transfer paper for my inspection. "The design has been refined. The only real difference is the ink I'm going to use. It's created from blood taken from the avowal. Are you all right with that?"

"The idea of having Volkov's blood in me gives me the creeps." A shiver rippled down my arms. "But I can't deny it's effective in warding off Last Seeds." I blasted out a breath. "Let's do this quick before I change my mind."

He smiled a little, probably used to first-time jitters. "Where do you want it?"

"Artist's choice?" I considered and then dismissed the idea of mirroring my tattoo to Amelie's. As much as she resented me for having what she didn't, I didn't want her thinking I had to have what she did too. "I have no preference."

"Your shoulder?" He placed a latex-covered hand across the blade. "Spine?" He moved it toward the center. "Thigh?" He dropped it into his own lap. "Forearm? Upper arm? Wrist?"

This was taking too long. I was starting to second-guess how badly I wanted a talisman inked into my skin. "You're going to make me choose, aren't you?"

"It's your body," he said simply.

"I live in tank tops and shorts. I don't want it visible. I want to keep the element of surprise."

"We could do your hip or ribs," he offered. "Lower back tattoos aren't as popular these days."

I bet they hurt like crap too. "The tramp-stamp label ruined that one, huh?"

While I turned the possibilities over in my mind, he set about sanitizing his workstation and getting ready for his next client. *Me.* After giving me several minutes to consider my options, he settled in to wait on my answer.

"I want it on my spine, positioned between my shoulder blades." That meant saying buh-bye to backless or low-cut dresses, but it's not like I had any intentions of embracing the role of Society darling. "Right in the spot where it prickles when you're being watched."

"All right." He took a paper towel and his squirt bottle. "You'll have to remove your shirt."

"No bra." Though, to be honest, as the dawn approached, I became less and less concerned about nip slips. "Will this work?"

I tugged the hem up my back and pulled it over my head while keeping my arms in the sleeves and my front concealed. I had worn more revealing swimsuits back in the day, but showing this much skin left me feeling vulnerable.

"I can't tattoo through the band, so this is perfect." He traced a line from my nape to the center of my back with his fingertips, as though measuring the distance. "Your bones are so pronounced."

"I'm starting to develop a complex." I twisted around to face him. "I get it. I need to put on weight."

"That's not what I meant." He retraced the same path with a single finger. "This is going to hurt." He stopped at the point where I had requested my tattoo. "Will you let me use the—?"

"No sigils." Dampness swamped my palms. "I want to feel it."

Pain kept you honest. Hurt made you real. Besides, I had a well-worn path to oblivion tread through my head if I needed a time-out.

The first bite of the needle made me gasp. The others, and there were hundreds more, blended into a pleasant warmth that flooded across my shoulders and up my neck. Between the cool pressure of his hand on my back and the pecking sting heating my skin, I couldn't help drifting. Not up the stairs into my mind, but to some deeper place where time ceased to exist and all my troubles fluttered away on butterfly wings.

"THIS IS A FIRST FOR ME." Linus crouched in front of me, his palms cupping my rounded shoulders. He was all that kept me from sliding off onto the floor and curling up there for a nap. "I'm not sure if I should be flattered or concerned you fell asleep in my chair."

"Flattered," I assured him, stifling a yawn. "What time is it?"

"Around seven."

"Are we done here?" I tucked the front of the shirt tighter against my chest. "Can I see it?"

"There's a mirror in the bathroom..." He laughed under his breath. "But you already know that."

My bones creaked from prolonged slumping as I stood and cut a path around the stacked trunks to the downstairs bath and its generous vanity. Linus followed, switched his phone's camera to selfie mode, and passed it to me to use in lieu of a second mirror.

The bold design nestled against my spine, centered at the lowest points of my shoulder blades, right where my bra strap normally sat. The black limbs of the yew tree stretched through a crescent moon. Its tangled roots grew to form a circle that encompassed the topmost portion of the design. The overall effect was one of a paintbrush on skin, lending the design a traditional aspect that spoke to my roots, to all those weekends spent learning the craft at Maud's knee. Shifting from side to side made the dark glitter catch the light, and I marveled at its beauty.

"I would forget all this heir nonsense and tattoo full-time if I were you." I met his eyes in the mirror. "This is amazing work. You're a talented artist."

"I love it," he said simply, leaving me to wonder if he meant the act of tattooing or this particular tattoo.

I allowed myself one last gawking session. "Do you need to wrap me up like you did Amelie?"

"Yes." He waved me back into the kitchen. "Let me wipe it down, and I'll tape a pad over it."

While I got cleaned up, I let my thoughts drift next door to Woolly. "Do you think Amelie will hate me when she realizes what I've done?"

"I don't know her well enough to guess." His icy fingers slid over my skin, smearing ointment. "If she's anything like her brother..." I felt the shrug in the upward jerk of his hand. "I'm sorry I couldn't do more."

He had been hunting her just as hard as Boaz, whether he knew it was her or not in the beginning. "Can I ask you something?"

His exhale skated cool air across my shoulders as he affixed the sterile pad in place. "I thought you might."

"Why were you hunting the dybbuk? You're the Grande Dame's son. Even before her ascension, you were still the Lawson scion. This was a job for the Elite." I glanced back at him. "How did you get involved?"

"I'm a potentate."

I scrunched up my face at him. "A who-what now?"

"The Society can't maintain control throughout the United States with only my mother and the Lyceum to keep them honest. Savannah is a long way from New York or Washington State." He untucked his shirt and peeled up the hem to allow me a glimpse of tattooed skin. "Some days it's a long way from Atlanta." He indicated a city seal inked over his heart. "Atlanta is my city, Georgia is my territory. Savannah has its own security, but it's within my rights to investigate incidents that threaten the Society or its members."

"You do teach at Strophalos, right?" I cocked my head. "That's true? Not a cover story?"

"It's a little of both," he allowed. "I do teach, but I have more responsibilities than that." He lowered his shirt. "It was the price of my freedom." His half-smile drooped. "You had to suspect there was a cost for living the way I do."

"I was surprised your mother let you out of her sight." I stared at his covered chest, remembering the designs beneath, wondering at their meanings. "But I'm just as surprised that she lets you play sheriff like Georgia is the Wild West."

"Bonding with a wraith wasn't a step I took lightly, but all the potentate employ them. They're our only backup in the field." He scratched his chest like the old ink itched when he thought about it. "I am sworn to the office of the Grande Dame, we all are, and that means I am sworn into Mother's service for as long as she holds the title. The arrangement suits her at present."

"I bet."

This revelation complicated things, and yet it didn't. I had expected him to report my movements to his mother, but I hadn't anticipated him to be oath-sworn to do as she commanded. Yet again this made sifting through his layers to the real Linus near-impossible to the point I wondered if there was a real Linus in there at all.

Maybe this was all he was—myriad facets that together formed a cohesive whole, true to themselves if not to their entirety.

"I pay for my autonomy every day. Coming back here..." A frown knit his brow. "Mother used you as bait to lure me home. She knew I wouldn't be able to resist the mystery of you. Everything I've worked so hard to achieve hangs in precarious balance, Grier. Never think I take it for granted, and never believe it was handed to me."

"How many more secrets are you hiding?" I eyed the pockets where his hands most often resided when not drawing. "Where do you keep them all?"

"I am a secret," he said, a wistful smile on his lips, "bound in a thin skin of humanity."

"That's not creepy at all." I laughed, unsure if he was quoting at me or being earnest. With Linus, it was hard to tell. It could be one or the other, or it could be both. "What does it mean?"

"That I may never tell you the whole truth, but I will never lie to you."

Omission was still a lie, but I was too tired to argue semantics. "Am I done yet?"

"You're free to go." He guided my head through the collar of my tee then pulled it down my back. "Get some rest. We'll start a new lesson at dusk."

"No rest for the wicked," I grumbled.

"Nor the weary," he agreed.

I wondered which of us was which.

WOOLLY PAID me zero attention when I hit the back porch. I took that to mean she was too busy playing with her new BFF to remember her old one. At least that meant she was also too preoccupied to focus on Amelie. Or on me.

Despite the clawing need to put my eyes on my best friend, I couldn't screw up the nerve to enter the house. Coward that I was, I decided to circle the wraparound porch and peer through the windows until I spotted signs of life. Or undeath, considering half the house's occupants weren't alive in the traditional sense.

Soft humming distracted me enough I bypassed a few windows to check the front porch swing.

"Odette." I stumbled over my own feet. "I thought you'd left."

"Without saying goodbye? Never." She patted the spot beside her, and I sat. "I smudged the house and invoked Hecate in the upstairs guestroom where our poor Amelie rests."

"You knew," I surmised. "That's why you stayed behind." Probably why she came at all.

"The people you love are shadows to me, but I still snatch bits and pieces from others on their periphery." Her arm snaked around me, and she pulled me down until my cheek mashed against her bony shoulder. "I don't know why you must hurt so." She rested her chin on top of my head. "This world seems determined to make you suffer, and I can't see the whys or hows or whens. Sometimes I hate your mother for binding me. Sometimes I hate Maud too. They left you defenseless."

"I'm working on it," I assured her. "I won't be defenseless forever."

"Ah, *bébé*." Her deep sigh rustled my hair. "I worry for you, but I do not doubt you."

"Odette?" The smell of her skin, ocean and seagrass and sand, burned my nose in a pleasant way. "Will you sing to me?"

"Your ears would bleed." She jostled me then jerked her chin toward the front door. "Better to leave such things to the young men inclined to serenade."

Boaz watched us from the doorway, his expression inscrutable. "Don't let me interrupt."

"It's time for me to return home." She peppered my face with kisses then drifted over to Boaz, where she jerked to a halt, her frame trembling, and the voice that poured from her mouth was multilayered and as foreign as I imagined fae lands would be to human eyes.

"You stand at a crossroads, Boaz Pritchard. Choose well, and you will have your heart's desire. Choose poorly, and you will lose that which matters most to you." A shudder broke the spell, and she rasped, "Choose, child, and do it soon."

"Thank you for your wisdom, ma'am." His tone was solemn. "Do you need a ride home?"

"I think I'll walk." She patted the nearest column. "Take care of our girl, old friend."

Woolly shifted her consciousness in a wave that rippled through me, and the porch creaked agreement.

We watched until Odette vanished from sight, and then Boaz joined me.

"It's a long walk to Tybee." He craned his neck. "Will she be all right?"

"Odette does everything for a reason." That much was for certain. "For all we know, she's going to come across an accident while walking, dial 911 and save a life. Or, maybe she forgot her phone, and she stands there to bear witness to a death that otherwise might have been prevented. Either way, she sets a series of events into motion that mere mortals such as us can only begin to fathom."

That relaxed him enough he assumed Odette's position, draping the comforting weight of his arm across my shoulders. I folded my legs under me and settled more fully into his side while he took up the chore of rocking us. We didn't talk. There was too much to say.

The blare of a ringtone had Boaz lifting his hips to retrieve his phone from his back pocket. "Pritchard." He closed his eyes and listened. "Yes, sir." A heavy exhale punched from his lungs. "Yes, sir." His knuckles whitened around the phone. "I'll be there, sir." He ended the call with a mash of his thumb that could have splintered the glass. "I'm being called in. As far as the Elite are concerned, I did my job, and it's time to get back to my unit."

I rescued his phone before he thought better of it and hurled it in the bushes. "What about Amelie?"

"She doesn't exist anymore, Squirt." His heart was a relentless drumbeat in my ear. "They won't make any allowances for her as far as I'm concerned." His arm resettled against me. "I don't know what we would have done without you. She has nowhere else to go, no one else to protect her."

"I'm happy to do it." Amelie was only the latest of Boaz's treasures to seek asylum in my care.

Twisting on the swing, he slid his hands under my arms and lifted, hauling me across his lap so that my knees braced on the seat to either side of his hips. "Don't make light of something that means everything to me." Sincerity burned in his eyes. "You're a gift that keeps giving, Grier. I open one box, and there's another inside waiting, and another inside that and so on to infinity." His arms linked around me, crushing me against him and forcing me to brace on his shoulders to keep from smooshing my boobs in his face, which, honestly, might have been his intention. "How do you do it? How are you this person? How are you in my arms?"

"I'm not sure who this person is yet," I admitted. "You look at me, and you still see the girl who grew up next door, but she died in a cell in Atramentous. That Grier is a comfortable shirt I wear sometimes so I look like I fit in with you and Amelie, but it's too small. One day I'm going to pull it on, and the buttons are going to pop off, and you're going to see what's really underneath."

"I'm going to stop you there and say I'm a fan of buttons popping off any shirt you're wearing."

"I suspected that metaphor might get away from me." I linked my arms behind his neck, fingernails rasping his nape. "We good?"

With his hands bracketing my hips and my thighs spilling over his, I didn't have to shift my weight to feel his answer. "We could be very good."

"Be serious." I braced my forehead against his. "Just for a minute."

The charming veneer Boaz wore like a second skin peeled away beneath my stare, revealing a passionate man stripped of his pride and arrogance. One who had fought hard to save a sibling he loved and lost her all the same. His heart was a gaping wound that made each bruise and cut easier to see. The puckered scar tissue he exposed had built up over the years we had spent apart, and it made me wonder if I wasn't the only one who wore a familiar-looking shirt to fool people I cared for into believing nothing had changed.

"Time's up." The wicked curve spreading over his lips knit his façade back together before my eyes. "I have to go."

"I know." I stayed right where I was, breathing him in. "I wish you could stay."

"You just want me around for when you work up enough mad to holler at me about the cameras."

"There is that." I wanted those cameras gone yesterday, though I might be persuaded to install my own. "But I also miss you when you're not here sucking up all the oxygen to inflate your ego."

"Hmm." He pressed his lips to mine. "Oxygen deprivation would explain why you haven't wised up and left me."

I scowled at his phone when it started going off in my hand. "Whatever they want, tell them no."

He checked the display then answered in a clipped tone, "Whatever you want, the answer is no."

"*Boaz.*" Hammering his shoulder with my fists, I gaped at him. "What are you doing?"

"Following orders, ma'am," he told me with a wink before returning to his conversation. "Yeah, I'm on my way." He ended the call and exhaled long and slow. "Becky says there's a situation in Athens. Our whole unit is being deployed."

"Is this going to be our new normal?" I leaned back to look at him. "Kisses and goodbyes?"

"I'm a soldier. This is my normal, period." He drank in my features, his brow furrowed. "Is that going to be a problem?"

"No." I climbed out of his lap. "Slow is a good idea for us."

Adding Amelie into the mix would complicate things before all was said and done. Gratitude might come easily to him now, but given time and space, that might change. As much as I wanted to believe he would see things from my perspective, a Pritchard attempting to view the world through High Society glasses was what started this trouble in the first place.

"You still think we're a good idea." He dialed up the charm. "And that *we* are an *us*."

"No, Boaz, I sit on the laps of all the men who visit me." I spun on my heel in a huff. "You didn't think you were special, did you?"

Boaz, being a subtle man, bum-rushed me. I got out a squeak before his arms closed around my newly healed middle from behind, and he hoisted me in the air. He whirled me in a circle until Woolly took notice of the shenanigans on her porch and put her foot down. The board under his foot warped, and he stumbled enough my feet touched planks. That leverage was all I needed to break his hold and skirt his reach.

Woolly kept the porch boiling like an angry sea until he was forced to pinwheel his arms to maintain his balance.

"Fair warning." He pointed at me while stumbling down the steps. "I'll be back to finish this."

I winked saucily at him from behind the safety of the wards. "I'll be counting down the days."

Boaz backed toward the garage where he cranked Willie and set out for Athens after blowing me a kiss I refused to catch on principle. With no other handy distractions available, I entered the living room and went in search of Amelie.

I followed the scent of sage from Odette's smudging up to the second floor and down the hall to Amelie's new bedroom. I cracked open the door to peek in on her, but her back was facing me. I settled for watching her breathe, a habit learned from Maud, one she had developed after Mom died. I don't know how long I leaned there, cast in a slice of sunlight, untangling the messy worries in my head.

"Grier?" Amelie's muzzy voice rose from beneath a mountain of quilts. "Is that you?"

The combination of time, distance, smudging and ink was bringing her around. Sleep would only help.

"I'm here." I straightened. "I didn't mean to wake you."

"S'alright," she mumbled and lifted one edge of the quilt. "Get under here before my buns freeze."

After kicking the door shut with my heel, I crawled under the covers with my clothes still on just like when we were kids. Maud always refused to let us sleep in the same room when she claimed there were plenty to spare. "Amelie…"

Gentle snores announced her descent back into sleep. Unwilling to leave just yet, I turned onto my back and stared at the ceiling until her breathing smoothed into an even rhythm. The temptation to stay snuggled up in bed with her, to pretend everything was okay, that the outside world could wait, kept me breathing in the scent of detergent on the quilt and listening to the comforting sounds of sharing space with another person longer than Maud ever would have allowed.

Fear of getting punished, though there was no one left to catch me, prickled at my skin until I conceded defeat and sneaked into my room. Once there, I found Oscar waiting for me. "Do you need a glass of water before bed?" I was mostly kidding, but the boy kept wringing his hands. "What's the matter?"

"I'm scared of sleeping in new places," he whispered. "Woolly gave me my own room but…"

I saw where this was headed and pulled an Amelie. I was too tired to fool with stripping off my clothes or finding pajamas. I dove between the covers and lifted an edge for him. "Come on if you're coming."

Oscar stopped fiddling and hurled himself at me across the mattress where we snuggled until he faded to ether.

Alone in my bed, I stared at the ceiling, unable to sleep while actions and consequences tumbled through my head in a grind of shame and sadness and guilt. I was about to go in search of Eileen to get in more ward practice, though I couldn't remember the last place I remembered seeing the grimoire, when I heard a muffled voice drifting up from the garden. "What is that?"

ABOUT THE AUTHOR

Hailey Edwards writes about questionable applications of otherwise perfectly good magic, the transformative power of love, the family you choose for yourself, and blowing stuff up. Not necessarily all at once. That could get messy. She lives in Alabama with her husband, their daughter, and a herd of dachshunds.

www.HaileyEdwards.net

Head Above Water #2

Hell or High Water #3

Gemini Series Novellas

Fish Out of Water

Lorimar Pack Series

Promise the Moon #1

Wolf at the Door #2

Over the Moon #3

Black Dog Universe Shorts

Out for Blood

The Bakers Grimm

Thrown to the Wolves

A Stone's Throw Christmas

Araneae Nation

A Heart of Ice #.5

A Hint of Frost #1

A Feast of Souls #2

A Cast of Shadows #2.5

A Time of Dying #3

A Kiss of Venom #3.5

A Breath of Winter #4

A Veil of Secrets #5

Daughters of Askara

Everlong #1

Evermine #2

Eversworn #3

Wicked Kin

Soul Weaver #1

Made in the USA
Las Vegas, NV
29 December 2021

39764460R00166